Books by
DANA WAYNE

Secrets Of The Heart

Mail Order Groom

Whispers On The Wind

Chasing Hope

Book Liftoff
1209 South Main Street
PMB 126
Lindale, Texas 75771

Book design by Champagne Book Design
Cover design by Just Write.Creations

Library of Congress Control Number Data
Wayne, Dana
Chasing Hope / Dana Wayne.
1. Contemporary—Romance—Fiction.
2. General—Romance—Fiction.
BISAC: FIC 027020 FICTION / Romance / Contemporary. | FIC 027000 Fiction / General.
2019901371

ISBN: 978-1-947946-48-4

www.danawayne.com
www.bookliftoff.com

CHASING
Hope

DANA WAYNE

ACKNOWLEDGEMENTS

As always, I am very grateful for the many people who have supported, encouraged, challenged and celebrated my writing efforts. My critique partner and friend, Patty Wiseman deserves a special thank you. Your mentorship means more to me than I can ever say. Thank You is not nearly enough but thank you I do.

I am also deeply thankful for my fellow writers in ETWA, NETWO and ETWG who made me believe I had some talent after all. Thank you, guys! I could not do it without you.

And last, but by no means least, my wonderful, understanding and supportive husband. I would not be here without you. I love you.

CHASING
Hope

Dear Readers,

When I first got the idea of *Chasing Hope*, I wanted to address in some fashion the effects of PTSD (Post Traumatic Stress Disorder) on a soldier. The more I researched the subject, the more I decided that a romance novel wasn't the place to do it, at least not to the extent the subject warranted. Therefore, the hero, Max Logan, has been in treatment for almost a year and a half and has, to a good extent, developed skills to address the effects of PTSD on his life. While we discuss the subject some in the story, that is not the focus; that belongs to Max, Sky and Maddie.

The way in which I chose to address PTSD in no way diminishes how devastating this disease can be on a person. Anyone who has lived through a traumatic event can suddenly find themselves experiencing emotional challenges long after the event has taken place. Although it's common for people to experience some emotional effects after the event, these symptoms can lessen over time as they go through the healing process. Those who suffer from PTSD, however, find themselves experiencing symptoms that continue to inflict significant distress and can range from minor to severe and affect every facet of their life and relationships.

I was surprised to learn that around eight million people in the US are living with some form of PTSD, and it's estimated that about seventy percent of adults have experienced some sort of traumatic event in their lives. However, it's also important to note that most people who experience such events will not develop PTSD.

I found several websites that provide information on PTSD. This one from the VA, while designed for veterans and their families, has some great information that anyone can use. www.ptsd.va.gov/public/index.asp.

All that being said, I do hope you enjoy Max's story.

Thanks for reading!
Dana

CHAPTER
One

T he first bullet grazed his cheek, followed by searing pain and the acrid smell of singed flesh and gunpowder. *"Sniper! Three o-clock!"* He shouted to the small band of Marines clustered behind the disabled Humvee. *"Stay down."*

Jenkins, a kid from Idaho so green his boots weren't even scuffed, looked at him with worried eyes. "What'll we do, Gunny?"

Before he could reply, all hell broke loose. One sniper became six. Pinned down, they waited. And prayed. The whistle of a mortar pierced the roar of a shitload of automatic rifles a split second before Jenkins disappeared in a haze of blood and mangled flesh.

Max Logan jolted awake from the nightmare, a scream lodged in his throat. Heart racing, gasping for air, he threw off the sheet and sat on the side of the bed. The last nightmare happened nearly a year ago. He thought he was over it.

Evidently not.

Control your breathing, lower your heart rate. The shrink's instructions ran through his mind as he struggled to escape the hellhole that nearly destroyed him.

Recurrent pain in his left leg, compliments of shrapnel

1

from the IED, was another reminder of his brush with death. He pushed off the bed and limped to the window.

Must have been my conversation with Big John today. That's what stirred up the memories. He pressed his head against the cold glass. Not for the first time, he asked himself why. "Why am I alive, and they're all dead?"

A sudden light from the kitchen next door ended his introspection and drew his gaze to the woman who paused in the middle of the room, arms straight at her side.

Her name was Skylar Ward, though everyone called her Sky. She worked at the local diner where he took a lot of his meals. Their conversations rarely went beyond did he want the daily special or his usual burger and fries, but something about her piqued his interest. Gut instinct said the awareness was mutual, yet he hesitated to test the waters. He'd come a long way in the last sixteen months but couldn't bring himself to take the next step. Not yet.

A single mom, she had the cutest and smartest little girl who never missed an opportunity to engage Max in conversation at the diner or when they were outside at the same time. Truth be told, the child did most of the talking, usually in the form of a gazillion questions, but he didn't mind. Especially if it meant an opportunity to chat with the mother as well.

He straightened when Sky swiped her cheeks with one hand and dropped into a chair at the small table near the window.

He glanced at the bedside clock, 0430. There were no curtains on the window and the narrow driveway between their houses in this older neighborhood allowed him to see her in sharp detail. She sat drill-sergeant straight, hands clasped together in her lap, auburn hair disheveled, loose-fitting pajamas boasting an animal, maybe a cat, on the front.

It wasn't the first time he'd observed her in the wee hours of the morning. Not that he was a wacked-out Peeping Tom, either. He wasn't. He just had trouble sleeping at times and prone to be up at all hours of the night. Lately, so was she.

Sometimes, she just sat there. Sometimes, she made coffee or did paperwork.

Tonight, though, something was different. She was different.

Rigid as a poplar, she ran slender fingers through shoulder-length hair, then gripped the sides of her head, face contorted as though in agony. She tilted her head back and rolled it side to side. Her chest rose and fell with deep, measured breaths. She crossed her wrists on the table and sat frozen for the space of a heartbeat before her shoulders slumped, and she lowered her head. Her slender body shook with the force of her sobs.

"I know how you feel, ma'am," he whispered to the darkness, "I know just how you feel."

Skylar Ward hated crying. It never solved anything and left her with red, puffy eyes that no amount of makeup would hide. So what if the rent was due, her car hovered one crank away from the scrap heap, and Christmas loomed a month away? That wasn't reason enough to host a pity party for one. Yet here she sat in the predawn hours blubbering like the world just came to an end. Who knew? Maybe it had, and she didn't know it yet.

Never one to feel sorry for herself, at least not for long, Sky wondered what sparked this infrequent event. The upcoming holidays? Maybe. But in her heart, she knew it went beyond that, beyond monitoring her young daughter's health or pinching pennies.

She loved Maddie more than life itself and did not regret the steps she took to ensure her health and happiness. But more and more lately, she missed not having someone to share her life with, to snuggle on the couch and talk about anything or nothing. She was so tired of watching life from the sidelines, doing everything, facing everything alone, with no one to watch her back or hold her close in the darkness.

"Suck it up, buttercup," she mumbled when the waterworks ceased. "It's not like you have a lot of options." She got up from the table and splashed her face with cold water. A quick glance at the wall clock produced another groan. No point in going back to bed now. She started the coffee maker, then leaned against the counter, arms braced on either side. Surrounded by a sense of imminent doom and a loneliness so profound it bordered on physical pain, she sucked in a ragged breath.

I've been alone practically my whole life, why is it bothering me now?

Her father died when she was young. Her mother was a physical therapist, and they lived in a modest yet comfortable home. A drunk driver turned her once vibrant, happy mother into an invalid a week after Sky turned sixteen. The only relative was a grandmother whom she hadn't seen since her father died, so Sky left her carefree life behind and became her mother's caretaker, working after school and on weekends at a local pharmacy to make ends meet. Despite the burdens she shouldered, she managed to graduate from high school and then enroll in nursing school.

Memories of those dark days threatened to initiate another round of self-pity, and she gave herself a mental shake.

Deal with the problem at hand—how to pay the rent this month—and save the rest for another day. Mr. Jenkins was a kind-hearted older gentleman, but kindness only went so far when money was involved.

A tingling on the back of her neck pulled her to the window where only darkness and the house next door loomed. The occupant, Max Logan, had moved in about six months ago and was a frequent customer at the diner where she worked. Maddie had more conversations with him than Sky, and when they did talk, it rarely went beyond casual conversation. His demeanor, heightened by tips that exceeded the norm and covert looks cast her way, indicated more than casual interest. Sadly, as a single mother barely making ends meet, she focused on getting through the next crisis, which left no room for a personal life, no matter how badly she wanted one.

Max was the only man she'd met in Bakersville to even halfway draw her attention, and she briefly considered encouraging him. The few men who had expressed interest up to now quickly cooled when they discovered she had a child. Max, however, didn't seem to mind. He would patiently answer Maddie's multitude of questions and occasionally encouraged more. He appeared to enjoy their interactions, which provided Sky an opportunity to get to know him better.

Her friend and neighbor, Gail Brown, said Max was a former soldier. She didn't need that last piece of information since everything about his bearing screamed military.

She guessed him to be a little older than her thirty-three

years. Tall, maybe six-three or four, his well-muscled body moved with an easy grace, despite a slight limp. He wore his dark chestnut hair in the traditional buzz cut favored by soldiers, and heavy brows rested above unsmiling, coffee-colored eyes. His features were hard, chiseled like an unfinished sculpture, and he possessed an air of authority that commanded attention.

The beep of the coffee pot brought her back to the counter, where she filled a mug and, with only a brief hesitation, scooted a chair near the window and sat down, calling herself a pathetic fool for pretending she wasn't alone.

CHAPTER
Two

"**H**urry with your breakfast, Maddie," urged Sky as she gathered her purse and jacket, "we're going to be late."

"Almost through." Seven-year-old Maddie shoveled another bite of scrambled eggs into her mouth. "You told me not to eat fast, or I'd get sick."

"I also told you not to lollygag around."

The impish smile made Sky's heart lurch. *She'll be a beautiful woman one day.*

"Yes, you said that, too." A last bite of eggs, a gulp of juice, and she slid from the chair. "I gotta brush my teeth and get my backpack. After I put my dishes in the sink."

"Make it quick. We need to get going."

A few minutes later, Maddie followed Sky out the door. "Think Ole Blue will start today?"

Her daughter's question mirrored the one making Sky's anxiety soar. The old Taurus teetered on the edge of done-for, and there was no money to fix it. "Keep your fingers crossed."

The brisk November air cut through her lightweight jacket as they hurried to the car. It wasn't locked since no one in their right mind would want the beat-up old clunker. Once behind the wheel, she said a silent prayer and turned the key.

Nothing. Not even a click.

She gnawed her lower lip. *No, no, no. Please…not this.*

She tried again.

Silence.

"What's wrong, Mama?"

She stifled a groan. "I'm not sure—battery maybe."

"Do we have another one of those?"

"No. We don't." Consumed with dread, she unbuckled the seat belt. "Stay put. Let me take a look." *Like I have a bloody clue what to look for or could fix the damn thing if I did.*

Her stomach threatened to purge its meager contents of toast and coffee. *Please, God, please. Give me a break. Just one small break. That's all I ask.*

She propped open the hood and peered inside. *Yep. There's the motor and the little oil thingy. There's the doo-hickey I put window washer fluid in before it sprung a leak. Yep. It's all there. Now what?*

"Something wrong, ma'am?"

Startled, she squealed and jumped back into the rock-solid wall of a man. Strong hands clamped around her waist kept her upright.

"Sorry, ma'am. Didn't mean to startle you."

His warm breath washed over her cheek. She twisted around and found herself face to chest with Max Logan. She jerked her gaze upward, chilled body sucking the heat radiating from him like a sponge.

"Ma'am? Are you okay?"

The intensely male voice penetrated the stupor robbing her of speech, and she stepped back. "Y-yes. I'm fine. You just surprised me."

He nodded toward the car. "Won't start?"

"No, and I have no idea why."

"Mind if I try?" He folded his huge frame in the front seat without waiting for a reply, only to exit a moment later. "Battery's dead." He walked toward his shiny new F-150 crew cab parked a little farther up the narrow drive.

It took a moment to process what had just happened. *Okay. He tried to crank the car, it wouldn't start, and he just walked off. What the heck?* "Well, um, okay. Thanks for trying."

Before she finished the sentence, the huge engine roared to life, and he backed up. Once even with her car, he got out with the motor still running and pulled long, thick wires from behind his seat.

Jumper cables? Maybe. I think.

Once he had them connected to each vehicle, he looked at her. Didn't say a word. Just stared.

She stared back.

One bushy brow kicked up.

Duh. Crank the car, you idiot.

Slow to respond, Blue did, finally, thankfully, start.

He waited a moment, then unhooked the cables and moved to the driver's side. "Where are you going?"

His question was gruff, and she bristled, about to tell him none of his business, but her mother's ancient speech about manners stifled the impulse. And he did crank her car. And was a good tipper. "I have to take Maddie to school."

"How long will that take?"

She gritted her teeth. "Twenty minutes."

"Don't kill it, or it won't start again."

You could've started with that statement. "Oh. Okay. Thank you, um, Mr. Logan, I—"

"Max. No mister." Hands braced on his hips, the inquest continued. "Are you working today?"

"No. I'm off every other Friday."

"Honk when you get back, and I'll hook up a battery charger. But you'll probably need to replace it soon. It's old, and cold weather is hard on them."

Lips pressed together, she swallowed hard. She could barely pay her bills now. A new battery was out of the question. "How much do they cost?"

"Depends on the battery."

She counted to ten. "Ball park?"

One shoulder rose then fell. "A hundred give or take."

"Dollars?"

His jaw muscles moved, whether to smile or grimace, she couldn't tell.

"No. Pickles."

Maddie's musical laughter floated from the back seat. "You can't buy a battery with pickles, Max."

He glanced at her daughter, and a ghost of a smile appeared then vanished. "No, you can't." He looked back at Sky. "Honk when you get back."

Before she could reply, he got in his truck and left.

Sky watched his exit in her rearview mirror. Despite his brusqueness, she still found herself attracted to him. Just like the first time he came in the diner. There was just something about him…

"Max is really nice, ain't he, Mama?"

"What? Oh. Yes. He is."

"I heard Miss Gail say he got hurt being a soldier. Is that why he limps?"

Thoughts scattered, Sky backed out the drive. "What?"

"Did Max get hurt being a soldier?"

"I don't know." Aware of the child's boundless curiosity, she added, "And don't ask him, either. That would be rude."

Maddie nodded, but Sky could almost hear those inquisitive wheels turning in the little scamp's head and made a mental note to talk about boundaries. Again.

Half an hour later, she pulled into the drive.

Max leaned against his truck, arms folded across an impressive chest. Heat burned her cheeks when he glanced at his watch and then back at her.

She jumped from the car and hurriedly explained. "I'm so sorry if I kept you waiting. Everyone was just so slow today."

He raised the hood without comment. "Go ahead and kill it, then see if it will start again."

"You said it wouldn't if I killed it."

He inhaled and spoke slowly as though she were a child. "When it runs, the battery charges. I want to see if it held anything."

"Oh." Chagrined, she followed his instructions. Blue barely groaned and made no effort to start.

He hooked up this contraption to the battery, presumably the charger he spoke of, without saying a word.

A burst of cold air swirled around her, and she pulled the edges of the thin jacket tighter. Winter was blowing in quicker and colder than usual this year. The weatherman warned of a hard freeze this weekend, with sleet and snow possible. As what usually happened with East Texas weather this time of year, temps would go back up to the forties next week. Still, she needed a warmer coat, but that, too, would have to wait. Something else she couldn't afford.

"I don't think it will hold."

The terse announcement took a moment to process. "And that means?"

"You need a new battery." He wiped his hands on a rag, then threw it back behind the seat of his truck. "But we'll see how it goes. When will you need to go out again?"

"I have to pick Maddie up at three-thirty. I have a couple of errands to run, but they can wait."

"Leave it on the charger. I'll take it off when I get back."

"I don't know how to thank you." Flooded with feelings of inadequacy, she hugged herself a little tighter. "I don't know any of this stuff."

He grunted, then stepped into his truck. "I'll be back in time to unhook it. Don't mess with it."

Before she could reply, provided of course something got past the lump in her throat, he left.

Sky spent the day on housework, crunched a few numbers—such as they were—and tried in vain to figure out how to add a battery to her must-have list. Max came and left a couple of times but didn't speak.

Worse-case scenario, she might ask her boss, Ruby Sloan, to advance her some money, but then she would have to pay it back.

Tips represented the bulk of her income, but with the holidays approaching, folks didn't eat out as much, and tips dropped off.

She had a little money earmarked for the few items on layaway for Maddie's Christmas and vowed not to touch it. If she had to spend that on a new battery…

"Nothing I can do about that right now," she muttered and strived to come up with a way to repay Max's kindness. The list of options was practically nil, and she eventually settled on cookies. Who didn't like cookies? And, thankfully, they wouldn't use up too much of her precious resources.

Around two, she pulled the last tray of peanut butter cookies from the oven and placed them on a cooling rack, when a sharp knock sounded on the kitchen door.

A blast of cold air came through when she opened it to find Max on the steps, hands stuffed in his front pockets. "The battery was shot. I put another one in and fixed the window washer. And you were a quart low on oil. You're good to go now."

Before she worked through his brief statement, he turned toward his house.

"Wait!" She wrapped her arms around herself to ward off some of the chill. She moved to the top step and pulled the door shut behind her.

Max stopped but said nothing.

"What do you mean you put another one in?"

"I thought I was pretty clear."

"I can't—I don't…"

He sighed and stepped toward her. "Look, I work at the auto parts store. I get stuff at a discount. It's no big deal."

"It is to me!" She shivered from the cold and growing anger at his presumptuousness. "I can't pay for it. Take it back."

"And how will you get to work and your daughter to school?"

"I'll—I'll think of something. Take it back."

"No." He headed toward his house.

"What do you mean *no*?"

He ran long, slender fingers through non-existent hair. "Look. You're making a big deal out of this. I don't want anything, *anything* from you. Got that? Call it a neighborly act or whatever. I ain't taking it back." He looked at her a moment, tight features relaxing a miniscule amount. "Your teeth are chattering. Go inside where it's warm."

"Do you like peanut butter cookies?"

The warmth inside the kitchen blindsided Max and it wasn't just heat from the stove or the mouth-watering aroma of fresh-baked cookies. Everything shouted *home* to him, or at least what he thought home would be like, though he had no personal experience with it. Growing up in a broken foster care system, *home* was an unfamiliar concept.

He pulled his thoughts away from that dark corner. Ancient history. He survived. Just like he survived the ambush. Over and done. End of story. Move forward.

A sudden cramp in his leg reminded him he'd skipped the daily stretches, and he swallowed a groan.

"Please, sit down. I'll get you some coffee."

His hostess motioned to the table, and he sat in the chair she had used earlier this morning. He stretched his leg out to loosen the cramp. If she noticed his discomfort, she didn't comment, which suited him fine.

She placed a mug of coffee in front of him, along with a plate of cookies. One whiff of those peanut buttery morsels, and his stomach growled loud enough to be heard, which brought an embarrassed flush to his cheeks.

Once again, if she noticed, she didn't comment.

"I'm afraid I don't have any cream for the coffee since I drink mine black. I do have some milk, though. And sugar."

"Black is fine. Thanks." Suddenly nervous about what to say or do next, he sat there with his hands on either side of the cup.

The chance I wanted is right here, and I'm a tongue-tied imbecile. Just fricking great.

"I hope the coffee is all right. It might be a little strong."

He took the hint. The rich, aromatic brew assailed his nostrils. "If it tastes as good as it smells, I'm sure it will be fine." More than fine. It was perfect. "Great coffee, ma'am."

Her cheeks took on a rosy hue, and her face brightened with a smile that lit up the room. "Thank you."

Not for the first time, he noticed her delicate beauty and extraordinary eyes. A rich, hazel color lit from within with a golden glow, they darted around the kitchen, not focusing on any one thing.

Those auburn curls were trussed up with this weird hair clip do-dad. An insane urge to remove it engulfed him. He reached for a cookie instead.

"About the battery—"

"I love peanut butter cookies." He downed one whole and chased it with coffee.

"How much—"

"They're my favorite." He picked up another. "Especially ones like this with peanut chunks inside."

"I need to—"

"Everyone raves about chocolate chip." He studied the morsel in his hand. "But I bet it's because they never tasted a peanut butter cookie like this."

Her shoulders sagged, and her head drooped a little. "How can I ever repay your kindness?"

Uncomfortable with such sincere gratitude, he finished off the last of the treats on his plate. "Cookies are fine with me."

When their eyes finally met, his breath caught. She was beyond beautiful. She was stunning. He had no idea what prompted the sleepless nights or lonely tears, but in that instant, he desperately wanted to make it all better, and for a split second, he thought it worth the gamble. Hope sparked by the idea shriveled and died when reality set in. *I have nothing to offer her but more problems.*

He placed the empty cup in the sink. "Thanks for the cookies."

"I made some for you to take home." She hurried to the counter and grabbed a paper plate wrapped with foil. "It's not much, but…"

"Thank you, ma'am. I appreciate it very much."

"Please. Call me Sky." She chewed her bottom lip and lowered thick, dark lashes before she straightened and met his steady gaze.

The bottom fell out of his stomach.

"Thank you…Max."

His name never sounded so good before.

CHAPTER
Three

Sky watched Max limp out the door and close it softly behind him. The small kitchen seemed even smaller with him inside and surprisingly empty when he left.

She sighed and looked at the chair he'd vacated, easily recalling his features in sharp detail.

His eyes were not just dark brown. They had these gold rings around the edges and were framed by long, lush lashes she couldn't mimic with a full tube of mascara. His lips were bow-shaped and full, their natural pink highlighted by a dark, scruffy beard, except where a narrow scar crossed his left cheek. Crow's feet at the corners of his eyes suggested a lifetime of squinting at the sun, as did his tanned, weathered complexion.

A quick glance at the clock on the wall, and she jumped from the chair. Time to pick up Maddie.

She smiled when Blue started right away and said a quick prayer of thanks for Max's generosity. Cookies weren't enough. Someday, somehow, she *would* repay him.

Maddie was unusually silent when she climbed into the back seat a short time later.

"Hey, Munchkin. How was your day?"

"…Fine."

Sky watched her daughter in the rearview mirror. "That didn't sound very fine."

Maddie looked out the window. "I hate Bobby Franklin."

"Hate is a pretty strong word." Sky eased into the flow of traffic. "What happened?"

When her daughter didn't answer right away, Sky probed again. "What happened, Maddie?"

"He's a jerk with oatmeal for brains."

"Maddie…"

She caught her mother's gaze in the mirror and asked softly, "Where's my dad?"

Sky's heart dropped to her stomach. She wasn't prepared for this conversation, though she knew the day would come.

Born premature and barely weighing two pounds, Maddie spent the first five months of her life in a neonatal ICU. So many things had to be dealt with. As a nurse, Sky understood the medical piece of it, but the emotional one was altogether different. That particular roller coaster didn't stop when Maddie came home, either. Her resistance was so low, any infection was potentially life threatening and required constant monitoring, so Sky placed her nursing career on hold to care for her.

Brett, her ex, honestly tried but couldn't deal with the day-to-day life of a sickly, premature infant. With Sky's attention so focused on their daughter, they soon drifted apart. The divorce came two months before Maddie's third birthday. Within a year, he remarried and moved to Austin.

By that time, Maddie's health had improved, and Sky was ready to go back to work. But then Maddie contracted pneumonia and nearly died. Sky endured those agonizing weeks alone. Brett called once but never came to the hospital. His reason didn't matter; the fact that he didn't come did.

She pushed the past away and focused on an answer to the question. "I know this is hard for you to understand, baby, but his job took him away for long periods of time. And people change." Even now, the hurt and anger lingered. She could count on one hand the number of birthday cards and Christmas presents he'd sent over the last four years. His picture she had made for Maddie had long since been relegated to the bottom drawer of the child's dresser.

"Did he love us at all?"

A sob lodged in her throat, and she struggled for control. Maddie meant did he love *her*. "He did—does—love you, sweetheart, but sometimes, well, people just aren't meant to be together." Eyes focused on the road ahead, she eased through the school zone. "But it doesn't mean he didn't love us. In his own way."

"But he didn't stay with us."

"No. He didn't." What else could she say?

Maddie didn't speak again until they were almost home. "Why didn't you find another one?"

"Another what?"

"Male companion."

Sky almost hit the trash can on the corner when she turned into the drive. "A what?"

"A male companion, you know, a boyfriend. Maybe someone who wanted a kid like me."

She twisted in the seat to look at her daughter. "Where did you get that idea?"

Maddie ducked her head.

"Madeline Adele?"

"I heard Miss Gail say so one day. Wasn't sure what it meant, so I Googled it at school." She squared her small shoulders and looked Sky in the eye. "You need one, you know. Like for when Blue don't work and stuff. And you need a male companion to talk grown-up stuff to, stead of just me all the time."

Shocked at her young daughter's intuitiveness, Sky couldn't think of a single thing to say.

"You're really pretty when we go to church and stuff, and I bet a male companion would be easy to find." Her face suddenly went from gloomy to happy. "I bet Max would do it."

CHAPTER
Four

"What a piece of crap."

Max peeked around the corner of his house where he had just finished wrapping an outside faucet in anticipation of the early freeze.

Maddie sat on the cold ground in front of her mother's car, a faded pink bicycle beside her, a broken chain in her hands.

"What's a piece of crap?"

She jumped at his question, then ducked her head. "Don't tell Mama I said that, please."

"Why not?" He bit back a grin. Her mother probably wouldn't approve of such language from a kid.

She squirmed on the ground, then stood and faced him. "She works really hard and wanted me to have a bike like the other kids." The wind whipped her hair around, and she stepped toward him, voice lowered. "We got this one at the Goodwill 'cause it was cheap."

Long, dark curls swirled around a cherubic face, highlighted by eyes of the deepest blue. *I bet this is what Elizabeth Taylor looked like as a kid.*

"She'd get her feelings hurt if she knew I called it crap."

For a moment, her earnestness stunned him into silence. "Let me see. Maybe I can fix it."

"I doubt it. Mr. Brown fixed it three times already. I think it's broke for good this time."

Max inspected the bike and saw the seat needed a new pad, the handle bars were loose, and a couple of spokes were missing from the crooked front wheel, which needed to be replaced. "This may take me a few minutes. Why don't you go inside? It's cold out here."

"Can't I watch what you do? I might have to do it by myself next time."

He started to argue, but one look at her determined face, and he changed his mind. "Well, fixing the chain is pretty involved since we don't have the right kind of tool."

Delicate brows puckered, and she sighed. "Well, that's that then. Thanks for trying, Max. And for fixing Blue. It sure made Mama happy yesterday."

"I didn't say I couldn't fix it. I said it would be involved."

Immediately, those blue eyes sparkled, and a smile lit up her face. "You can fix it? Really?"

"I can."

"What do we do first?"

The chain proved to be a pain in the butt, and the fix would only be temporary. He made a mental note to replace it with a new one as soon as possible. Without telling Sky, of course. He didn't want her to be embarrassed again or feel obligated in any way. Even if it meant he missed out on more cookies.

Maddie wanted to help, so he let her hand him tools and hold things, but mainly she delayed the process, though he didn't really mind. She was extremely bright with an inquisitive mind and talkative nature. She always spoke when she saw him outside or at the diner. Their conversations were interspersed with a multitude of questions on a wide range of topics. *Why* seemed to be her favorite word. No one was more surprised than him to discover he didn't mind in the least.

"Max? Can I ask you something?"

She continued before he had a chance to reply.

"Are you married?"

Of all the questions he anticipated, that didn't even make the top one hundred. Eyes focused on the bike, he shook his head. "No."

"Do you have a girlfriend?"

He cut his eyes toward her and frowned. "No."

She nibbled on her bottom lip and dropped her gaze. Low voice soft and gentle, she asked, "Do you like kids?"

"Only ones like you." He spoke without thought or hesitation. Her face brightened with a huge smile, and he was glad he did so.

"You really need a girlfriend."

Okay, so that was certainly not something he would expect from a kid, but damned if he wasn't totally captivated. "You got someone in mind?"

"Uh-huh. My mom needs a male companion."

The wrench used to tighten the handle bars slipped from his hand. His eyes widened, and he stared a full ten seconds before he could form a reply. "She what?"

"I overheard Miss Gail tell her that the other day." She handed him the dropped tool.

"I see." *Like hell I do.*

"I didn't know what it meant, so I Googled it."

"You Googled it?"

She inspected the handle bars. "Uh-huh, I mean yes, sir. We don't have a computer, so I used one in the library." She slipped him a curious glance, eyes focused on the scar on his cheek. "Some of it I didn't really understand."

Yah think?

"But I got the gist of it, and I think you'll do fine."

The little pixie left him speechless. "How old *are* you?"

Blue eyes sparkled with glee. "I'll be eight on Christmas Eve."

Eight going on thirty.

"I'm pretty smart. They wanted me to skip some grades at school, but Mama didn't like that idea, so they put me in some special classes for smart kids." She looked at his scar again. "Did you get that being a soldier?"

Off balance, he gave a quick nod of his head and tried to focus on the handlebars.

Undeterred, she fidgeted on the step beside him. "I have scars, too. I fell off the monkey bars in first grade and broke my collar bone real bad. And I had my 'pendix took out when I was five." She concentrated on his hands as he worked. "Mine don't hurt, though. Do yours?"

Suddenly, images of the ambush, screams and bullets flying, swamped him out of nowhere. He couldn't get enough air, and his hands trembled. His heart rate soared, and he froze. *Don't let it in. Concentrate on the now…what you're doing. Don't let it in.*

He had no idea how much time had passed as he sat there, fingers frozen around the rusted handlebars. When he finally regained a measure of control, he looked up and saw those all-too-seeing eyes focused on him.

She placed a hand on his arm and squeezed. "It does hurt,

doesn't it?" When he offered no reply, she raised up and placed a soft kiss on the wound that went so much deeper than the surface.

"Mama always does that when I have an ouchy." She rubbed a tiny finger over the puckered scar and sat back down. "I know it doesn't actually help, but it always makes me feel better inside."

Max couldn't move, couldn't speak as his heart rate slowly returned to normal, and his labored breathing calmed. He looked at the wide-eyed, innocent child beside him, wise beyond her years, and a shard of light pierced through the darkness eating away at his soul. "Thank you," he whispered.

"You're welcome. I'm sure Mama would kiss it, too, if you asked her."

The wrench hit the ground again.

Half an hour later, he watched as Maddie, now bundled up in a scarf and mittens, rode her wobbly bike down the driveway.

"Maddie!" Sky called from the kitchen door. "Time for lunch."

"But Mama, Max fixed my bike, and I wanted to ride down to Bonnie's house."

"Now, Maddie. I have to get you to Miss Gail's before I go to work."

The child stopped in front of Max. "Can Max eat, too? He fixed my bike for me. See?"

Instinct told Max an extra mouth to feed might be a burden. "Thanks kiddo, but I need to finish wrapping pipes." A little white lie to save them all from a potentially embarrassing situation.

"It seems I am in your debt again, Max." Sky's cheeks held bright spots of pink, and she didn't quite meet his gaze.

"No, problem, ma'am. Glad I could help." He turned to leave, and Maddie spoke up.

"We're having chicken spaghetti, Max, with garlic bread. Mama makes the best you ever tasted. You have to try it."

"Maybe another time," said Max.

"Mama make him stay. He fixed my bike. And he made Blue work."

"Max?"

His name on her lips was music to his ears, and he looked back.

"You're more than welcome to join us. That is, if your pipes can wait."

He started to decline again when Maddie grabbed his hand.

"Good. Come on. You can sit next to me."

CHAPTER
Five

Max had never eaten chicken spaghetti before, but after to-day, he decided it was one of his favorite dishes. Especially when he added something Sky called Hot Stuff to it. The zesty, sweet-hot mixture resembled pickle relish. She claimed it was like a spicy chow-chow, whatever the hell that was, and went well with the spaghetti dish. Pungent garlic bread, sweet tea, and a simple tossed salad completed the meal.

Maddie chattered away about school and some kid named Bobby Franklin, who apparently had oatmeal for brains.

Sky appeared more relaxed, though she kept an eye on the wall clock.

When the little magpie finally ran out of things to say, Max looked at Sky. "Do you have any outside faucets?"

Brows bunched together, she stared. "One, I think. Back of the house. Why?"

"Have you wrapped it?"

The frown deepened. "Wrapped it?"

He wiped his mouth on the paper towel that served as a napkin. "It's gonna freeze this weekend. Maybe not a hard one, but outside pipes can freeze pretty quick and burst." He pushed back from the table. "I'll take a look at it. Thanks for lunch."

Her cheeks glowed a rosy color, and her stubborn chin jutted out. "I can do it myself if you can just tell me what I need."

He shook his head. "I have enough left over." He walked toward the door. "Thanks for lunch. That hot stuff was really good."

Maddie jumped from her chair. "Can I help, Max?"

"No," said Sky, "you can't. I'm sure he's got other stuff to do. I'll take care of the pipes myself."

Max figured pride prompted such an assertion and doubted she had a clue what needed to be done. "When?"

"When what?"

"When will you do it? You have to work today, and the freeze should happen tomorrow night."

"In the morning," she replied a little too quickly, "before I go to work."

"Do you have the stuff you need? Do you know how?"

"He's got a point, Mama," interjected Maddie. "Might as well let us fix it."

"You have to go to Gail's."

"I can walk across Max's yard to her house when we're done." She reached up and took his big hand in her tiny one. "Max doesn't mind me helping, do you?"

Max knew he was in deep trouble when he couldn't stop the smile edging up one corner of his mouth as he gazed into trusting orbs, blue as a summer sky. He tapped her upturned nose with his finger. "Mind your mother, Tink." The nickname rolled naturally off his tongue as he looked back at Sky, whose face held a strange expression. "I'll have it done shortly."

Before either of them could protest further, he left.

When he saw them drive away a few minutes later, he

grabbed up the supplies he'd placed by the door and went in search of the faucet. Turns out she had two, and he was working on the second one when he heard soft footsteps behind him.

"Shoot. I wanted to help."

Maddie's exasperated voice brought another infrequent smile.

"Mrs. Brown know where you are, Tink?"

She nodded. "You called me that before. What does it mean?"

"Short for Tinkerbell." He glanced at her when she squatted down beside him. "Do you mind the nickname?"

Ebony curls bounced when she shook her head. "No, sir. I like it." She craned her neck to watch him wrap the roll of foam around the pipe. "Mama calls me Munchkin sometimes."

The next few minutes passed quickly as his companion bombarded him with questions, peppered with comments about her mother.

He discovered Sky liked to sing and, according to Maddie, had a nice voice and at one time was a nurse. He wondered why she would give that up to work in a diner but decided it was none of his business. The child never mentioned her father, and his curiosity grew on that point.

His experience with kids was limited to waiting rooms at the VA clinic or when they accompanied parents to the auto parts store where he worked. Most of those fell into the noisy-bothersome-kids category. Maddie, however, was different. She was so intelligent, he sometimes had to remind himself she was a child.

When both faucets were wrapped and a loose board on the back steps repaired, he placed the unused supplies in a small portable shed behind his house. "Come on. I'll walk you back to Mrs. Brown's."

She reached for his hand. "I'm sorry if I ask too many questions, Max. Mama says I do that sometimes."

"Your hands are cold. Where are your gloves?"

She ducked her head. "Well, I left 'em on the playground when..."

"When what?"

Thin shoulders sagged, and she shook her head. "Bobby Franklin."

"The kid with oatmeal for brains?"

She stopped and looked up at him. "Can you keep a secret?"

Uh-oh. Danger ahead. "Depends on the secret."

She cocked her head to one side. "I don't understand. If it's a secret, then it's a secret."

He squatted down so she wouldn't have to crane her neck to look up to him. "I think it's very important to always be honest. It saves a lot of unhappiness down the road."

She gave a light nod, and he continued.

"And some secrets are okay to keep."

"Like when?"

"Like when someone tells you something really special. Something only the two of you know."

She looked off in the distance, then back at him. "Like how your scar sometimes hurts?"

He swallowed hard. "Yeah. Like that."

"So, when do you not keep a secret?"

Happy to talk about something besides his scars, Max nonetheless chose his words with care. "Let's say someone I cared about asked me to keep a secret. A secret that might mean the other person could get hurt or maybe get in trouble." He paused, maintained eye contact. "Then, I couldn't keep that secret." He waited a beat. "Do you understand?"

"Yes, sir. I think so." She tugged on one corkscrew curl next to her cheek. "It might not be a bad secret. I'm not sure."

When they reached Gail's back steps, she plopped down on the middle one and pulled the zipper of her jacket a little higher. "He's always teasing me about stuff."

It took a moment to pick up the thread. "Bobby?"

"Yes, sir. He's in third grade and lives next door to my friend Bonnie down the street."

He nodded and joined her on the steps, allowing her to proceed at her own pace.

"He's always around at recess and lunch. He pulls my hair and stuff and calls me a nerd." She glanced his way. "I'm in second grade, but I get to take special classes because I'm smart."

No brag. Just facts. "And he teases you about that?"

She nodded. "He did before."

"…Before?"

She sat up straighter and angled her body to face him. "He said I'm a bastard because I don't have a daddy."

Ouch…didn't see that one coming.

"I know that's a bad word, but I wasn't really cussing, Max, I was just telling you what he said."

"Roger that."

She tilted her head to the side. "Is that soldier talk?"

"Yes. It means I understand." He folded his hands over his knees. "Is that the secret? He called you a—bad word?"

She nodded, curls bobbing around like pogo sticks. "I'm not really sure what it means, but I don't think it's good. I could ask Mama, but if it ain't good, it might make her sad, and I don't want that." Earnest eyes searched his. "Can you tell me what it means, Max?"

Holy crap. Walking through a minefield wasn't half as scary as trying to find an answer to her question.

When he didn't answer right away, she asked softly, "It is bad, isn't it?"

He inhaled and started. "Just because your dad isn't around doesn't mean you're a—that word he said."

"But what *does* it mean?"

He focused on a faded plastic watering can on a table beside the steps, praying he'd say the right thing. "In my experience, when someone picks on someone else, it's because they want their attention or because they're bigger than the other person, and it makes them feel even bigger when they pick on someone smaller." He cut his eyes toward her. "Understand so far?"

"Roger that. Like a bully."

He nodded. "Sometimes a boy wants to let a girl know he likes her but doesn't really know how. In Bobby's case, my guess is he probably likes you but feels intimidated because he thinks you're smarter than him."

"I am."

He covered his snicker with a cough. "Calling people names is never cool, Tink. It can be really hurtful and usually makes things worse." He paused. "But my guess is when Bobby pulled your hair and stuff, he just wanted to get your attention. When that didn't work, he tried something else."

"Like calling me a bad name?"

"Did you talk to him?"

"Uh-huh, I mean, yes, sir."

"Then he achieved the objective."

Eyes wide, she sat up straight. "He called me that just so I'd talk to him?"

"I can't be certain since I wasn't there, but that's my guess."

Her mouth moved from side to side as she digested the conversation, then she gave a light huff. "Men."

He laughed. Out loud. For the first time in a very long time, he laughed out loud.

She stood and faced him, hands planted on her tiny hips. "Well, if you're gonna be Mama's male companion, Max, talk nice to her. Don't call her bad names and stuff. Women don't like it."

"Yes, ma'am."

Just then, the door opened, and Gail Brown stood there smiling down at them.

"Hello, Max. I hope Maddie wasn't a bother to you."

He stood and shook his head. "No problem, ma'am."

"Didn't talk your ear off, did she?" she asked with a smile.

He glanced at Maddie. "No, ma'am. She was fine."

"I haven't thanked you for wrapping those pipes for us. Or for fixing the leaky faucet in the kitchen. Frank's back is much better, but he still can't stand for very long." Her expression softened with a heartfelt smile. "You're a good man, Max. I wish you'd let me pay you for your trouble."

He shrugged off her gratitude. "No problem, ma'am. If I can do anything else for you, let me know." He looked at Maddie. "Next time Bobby tries to get your attention, Tink, talk to him. See what he has to say."

Her smile melted his heart.

"Roger that."

CHAPTER
Six

Sky couldn't stop thinking about how Max looked when he smiled at Maddie and softly called her Tink. Everything about him changed. The rock-hard soldier became soft and approachable. Dark, perpetually hooded eyes were open and warm. His deep, masculine voice softened and hinted at a hidden, gentler part of him.

A part that suddenly intrigued her.

"I think Max will do just fine for your male companion." Maddie's parting statement as she dropped her off at Gail's house kept playing through her mind.

The more she tried to ignore it, the harder it persisted. Maybe she did need a male companion. Maybe it *was* time she put some emphasis on her own needs. She declined each time anyone asked her out, mainly because she worried about how Maddie would react, but also because the ones doing the asking didn't interest her.

Max, on the other hand, interested her on a totally unexpected level.

Now that the seed was planted, she struggled with what to do about it. "Nothing. That's what I'll do," she chastised herself. "Nothing. I have too much to deal with as it is."

She parked behind the diner and hurried inside. Saturday afternoons were typically slow, but, hopefully, things would pick up later.

She donned her apron and walked out front.

"Hey, Sky," said Ruby Sloan, the owner. "Everything all right? You look a little down in the dumps."

"I'm good. A little distracted today." *By dark brown eyes and a haunting smile.*

"Blue's not acting up again is he?"

"No. He's fine." She saw no reason to elaborate. "Where do you want me?"

"You got it alone till four. Bethany called in sick, and Louise can't come till then."

"No problem. Things are usually slow this time of day."

"I'll be in the back making pies if you need me."

The next hour flew by as a few locals came in for afternoon pie and coffee. A couple of travelers wandered in as well, which meant slow tips.

The tinkle of the bell over the door announced another customer. Without looking around from her task of making coffee, she called out over her shoulder, "Sit wherever you like. I'll be right with you."

Coffee started, she turned to find Max sitting at one of the stools at the counter. Every rapid beat of her heart sounded in her ears as she moistened suddenly dry lips. "Hey." *Really? That's the best you got?*

In his usual way, he simply nodded and didn't answer.

"What can I get for you?"

"Just coffee."

She placed the cup in front of him and started to ask about the pipes when another customer walked in.

Cade Jackson, a local businessman, headed for the counter.

Oh, just great. Why him? Why now? The man had been asking her out for weeks, not the least bit put off by her refusals.

"Afternoon, Skylar," he said as he sat a stool away from Max, placing his black Stetson on the seat beside him.

"What can I get for you, Cade?"

"Usual."

"Coffee and apple pie coming up."

She placed the order in front of him. "Anything else?"

Hazel eyes gleamed with interest as he picked up his fork. "Not unless you changed your mind about the dance next Saturday."

She forced herself not to look at Max, even as she felt those penetrating eyes focusing on her. Cade was attractive enough, with thick, tawny-gold hair that tapered neatly to his collar and fair skin that magnified the rich hazel color of his eyes. A dimple in his left cheek drew attention away from a thin, cynical mouth. But he was a player looking for his next mark. It would not be her. "I have to work."

"Get someone to swap with you."

"I can't."

The arrival of her landlord, Tom Jenkins, who took the table behind and to the left of where the two men sat, ended the discussion. All thoughts of dates or male companions vanished in a cloud of anxiety-ridden mental dust. *Please don't mention the rent right now. Not where they might hear.*

"Afternoon, Ms. Ward," said the older man. "How are you today?"

She clutched the menu tightly to her chest. "I'm fine, sir. And you?"

"Cold weather is hard on these old bones, but otherwise doing good."

"Do you need a menu?"

"No, just some coffee and a piece of pecan pie." He looked toward the two men at the counter. "Howdy, Max, Cade."

Cade looked at the newcomer. "How's the world of real estate today, Tom?"

The two men entered into a casual discussion of the ins and outs of real estate, and Sky breathed a sigh of relief. For now.

"I got the pipes wrapped," said Max as she refilled his coffee. "And fixed a loose step on the back."

From the corner of her eye, she noted Cade's head jerk back toward her. "Thank you, Max, but you didn't have to do the step, too."

He shrugged. "No big deal. Maddie helped." He sipped his coffee and added, "Gail said it was okay for her come over." One corner of his mouth turned up in what sufficed as a smile. "Besides, I needed to earn my next batch of cookies."

"I hope she didn't pester you too much. She can be a bit… inquisitive."

Dark, haunted eyes met hers, and for a moment, time stopped. Something flashed between them, an almost imperceptible moment of connection. Emotions, tangled and fleeting, bombarded her. Pain, fear, hope, resignation. And in the blink of an eye, it was gone.

He rose and placed some money on the counter. "No problem. She's a good kid. I'll see you later."

Before she could recover enough to breathe again, he was out the door.

"How do you know Max?"

Cade's curt question drew her back from the edge. "He's my neighbor."

"Evidently a good one."

The tone of his voice perturbed her, and she turned toward him

He pushed the coffee cup forward to refill. "Just be careful around him."

Immediately, her ire ignited. "Excuse me?"

He held both hands up in a take-it-easy gesture. "I just know he's had a hard time since he got back. Guys like him…"

"Guys like him?" She planted one hand on her hip. "What's that supposed to mean?"

Pale cheeks showing a tinge of red, Cade continued. "Look, I'm not trying to get in your kitchen—"

"You could have fooled me."

"I'm just saying you should be careful around him. Especially with the kid. He's a loose cannon."

"How do you know that?"

He picked up his cup and blew across the top. "Went to high school with him. Always had a chip on his shoulder, begging someone to knock it off."

And I bet you were in line to try.

"He's bad news. Stay away from him."

She bristled and was saved from embarrassing herself when Mr. Jenkins rose and headed for the register. Jaw clamped tight, she plopped the coffee pot on the burner and went to take his money.

"I do believe Ruby makes the best pecan pie in the county." The older man's eyes were sincere and kind. "But don't tell my Ethel I said so."

Forcing a calmness she didn't really feel, she smiled. "Your secret is safe with me."

He placed money on the counter, and she handed him his change.

She glanced around, then lowered her voice. "I'll have the rent money next week, Mr. Jenkins."

He nodded, then stopped in the process of turning toward the door. "Max is one of the good ones," he said softly, then walked out before she could reply.

Max cursed himself for seven kinds of a fool as he drove back to the auto parts store. He'd had a delivery to make and, on a whim, stopped by the diner. Sky appeared glad to see him, and when she smiled, he all but lost the ability to speak. Maddie's assertion that he would be a suitable male companion for her mother weighed on his mind. He struggled with the desire to get to know her better, hashing out the pros and cons but unable to take that next step. What if it turned out to be a disastrous mistake for all of them? After a lot of soul searching, what-ifs, and maybes, he talked himself into exploring the possibility.

And then Cade Jackson showed up.

He owned the local hardware store and looked every inch the Texas cowboy. From his dark Stetson hat and starched white shirt to his faded jeans and snakeskin boots, he commanded attention. Tough, lean, and sinewy, he certainly looked the part, though Max doubted he'd ever been on the back of a horse in his life. Three inches shorter than Max, he was still an imposing figure.

And he'd been a thorn in Max's side since high school.

Some folks, Cade more so than anyone, considered him a ladies' man, and Max knew he was attractive and unscrupulous enough to go after any woman he wanted.

Apparently, he'd set his cap for Skylar.

"Not this time, asshole," he muttered as he went back to work. "Not this time."

CHAPTER
Seven

Sky pulled into the drive after picking up Maddie, refusing to admit how disheartened she found the absence of Max's truck. It was Saturday night. Unlike her, he probably had a life.

"Miss Gail let me help her make some cookies today." Despite being close to her bedtime, Maddie was full of chatter. "I told her you made some for Max when he fixed Blue, so we made him some for helping her."

"He helped her?"

"Yes, ma'am. He wrapped her pipes and fixed a faucet." She opened her door and got out. "I bet he could fix that leaky one in the bathroom."

Headlights and the familiar rumble of the Ford's powerful engine announced Max's arrival, quelling any retort.

Maddie ran to the front of Blue and waited for him. "Hi, Max."

He slowly rolled forward and killed the engine, abruptly filling the air with silence and opened the door. "Hey, Tink."

Maddie looked at her mother. "That's short for Tinkerbell."

Silhouetted by the interior light, Max grabbed something

from the other seat and slid to the ground, a sack from a local fast food restaurant clutched in his hand.

So much for him having a life.

"Evening, ma'am." The cold air formed a vaporous fog around his mouth when he spoke.

"If you don't mind," said Sky as she dug in her purse for the house key. "I prefer Sky to ma'am."

He moved the sack to his other hand. "Yes, ma'am. I mean Sky."

Her hands were so cold, she had trouble getting the key in the lock, and then the stupid thing wouldn't turn. Again. She needed to ask Mr. Jenkins about it.

Maddie immediately turned to Max. "I bet you can un-stick it, can't you?"

He stepped up beside Sky, jiggled the key once and handed the bag he held to Maddie. "Hang on to this for me, Tink." He went back to his truck and pulled a tool box from behind the seat. He removed a can of something that he sprayed inside the lock. He reinserted the key and rotated it smoothly.

He twisted the knob a couple of times, sprayed the little piece that stuck inside the notch in the door, then rotated the knob again. All without saying a word.

By the time he handed her the key, Sky was chilled to the bone.

"Go on inside, ma—uh, Sky, before you freeze."

"I need to get some stuff from the car." She turned, and he touched her elbow. A tingle, like an electrical shock, raced up her arm, and she flinched.

Immediately, he removed his hand. "I'll get it. Go inside."

"In the front seat," she managed through chattering teeth. "Two sacks."

She went inside and flipped on the light. Next, she lit a small gas heater against the back wall, and she and Maddie stretched their hands toward its warmth.

Max entered and placed the sacks on the counter. He walked to where Maddie stood in front of the heater, still holding his supper. He reached for the sack. "Thanks, Tink. See ya later."

"Can you fix this leak in our bathroom, Max?"

Blood pounded in Sky's temples as unwelcomed heat raced up her cheeks. "Maddie!"

Dark eyes, gleaming like volcanic rock and filled with a strange, faintly eager look before being quickly hooded, locked with hers. "It's all right…Sky. I'll check it out tomorrow and see if I can fix it."

She couldn't meet his gaze. "I hate to impose on you again." Her voice dropped to an embarrassed whisper. "I can't, I don't…"

Max rolled the top of the sack tighter. "Do you work tomorrow?"

She nodded. "Eleven till two."

"I'll come over tomorrow afternoon and look at it. Probably just needs a gasket replaced."

She couldn't think of anything to say. "Okay. Thanks."

"Are you going to eat all by yourself, Max?"

Maddie's innocent question brought a fresh onslaught of heat to Sky's face. Her daughter had more manners than she did.

"Why don't you stay and eat with Mama. I already ate at Miss Gail's. That way y'all won't have to eat by yourselves."

Max opened his mouth, but Maddie continued. "And you can look at that leak while Mama cooks her supper." Without waiting for a reply, she took the sack from his hand and placed it on the table before leading him down the hall.

Sky stared at the empty space where Max had stood a moment before. *What the hell just happened?*

Max looked at the back of the child's head as she towed him toward what he assumed was the leaky faucet. *How the hell can one four-foot-tall kid completely overpower one well-trained Marine?*

"Mama was going to ask Mr. Jenkins about it, but she hasn't yet 'cause the rent is due."

Once again, the child's innocent statement made him think things were strained for them, and he vowed to do what he could to help without causing Sky any more embarrassment.

"Here it is," said Maddie, and they entered a bathroom much like his own, except this one had a pink flamingo shower curtain around the tub. "That one."

She pointed to the fixture on the right, then stood back out of the way.

After a quick inspection and a twist of the handle, Max decided the cold-water faucet needed a new gasket. "I'll have it fixed in a jiffy."

His stomach rumbled when he followed the heady aroma of frying bacon to the kitchen. "I think it just needs a new gasket. Had to replace mine last week. Have what I need in the truck." He continued toward the door, and his stomach growled again.

"I like to have breakfast for supper," said Sky as she turned the bacon. "If your fast food will keep, I'd be happy to fix you an omelet."

The statement came out rushed, almost in a single breath. Her low voice, soft and clear, held a slight quiver. *I wonder if she knows how sexy she sounds*? Max's heart skipped a beat, and he had to clear his throat to speak. "You don't have to go to any trouble on my account, ma'am."

"It's no trouble. Really." She finally met his steady gaze, bright spots of pink on each cheek. "And it's the least I can do for all you have done for me—us."

"You forgot to call her Sky," said Maddie as she motioned to a chair at the table. "You can sit here."

"In a minute, Tink. I need to fix that leak."

Fifteen minutes later, he reentered the kitchen. "Just as I thought. Needed a gasket replaced."

Sky spoke over her shoulder. "Almost ready. Have a seat. Help yourself to whatever you want to drink."

Max placed the toolbox on the floor and shifted his feet, unsure what to do. He didn't want to impose, but damn, that bacon smelled good. And the chance to spend some time with Sky was too good to pass up.

Maddie bounced in wearing pink pajamas with *I'm a Princess* emblazoned on the front. "I'm going to bed now, Mama, so you and Max can talk grown-up stuff."

He didn't miss the quick intake of air as she bent and kissed her daughter. "Night, Munchkin. I love you." She straightened and spun Maddie toward the door. "I'll be in shortly to tuck you in."

"I'm nearly eight," she sniffed. "I can tuck myself in."

Maddie stood in front of Max, head craned back to look at him. One index finger curled inward, beckoning him lower.

He bent down, and Maddie placed a soft kiss on his cheek. "Night, Max. Thanks for fixing the faucet. And my bike. And Blue, too."

Before he formulated a reply, she skipped off down the hall.

He raised up and noted Sky watched closely, captivating eyes filled with a soft, inner glow, one hand pressed over her heart.

"I'm sorry if she embarrassed you, Max. Maddie is… very caring."

Touched by the child's unconditional acceptance, and more self-conscious than ever, he shoved his hands into his front pockets. "She's a good kid."

Sky didn't appear to notice his discomfort. "Please. Sit. It's almost ready." She pointed to the coffee pot on the counter. "Help yourself. Milk and juice in the fridge."

"Coffee's good."

"Cups are in the cabinet above the pot."

He pulled a mug down and looked at her. "You?"

"Yes, please." An engaging smile graced her face. "I probably drink too much of the stuff but got used to it when I worked nights."

"Maddie said you used to be a nurse."

One shoulder rose and fell slightly as she focused on the omelet. "Maddie was born early and had…issues when she was younger," she said softly. "It was hard to work, keep up my CEUs, and care for her, too. Rather than let my license lapse, I went inactive when we moved here." She filled two plates with food and carried them to the table. "I've been thinking about getting it reinstated."

He filled both mugs and joined her at the table. "What does that entail?"

"I'm not sure. I know there are time limits and other stuff involved." She sat down and picked up her coffee. "On my to-do list."

He took that to mean off limits and changed the subject. "How long have you lived in Bakersville?"

"We moved here when Maddie was four."

"Why here?"

She spooned more homemade hot relish onto her eggs. "A social worker at the hospital where I worked at the time recommended it. I didn't want Maddie to grow up in Dallas. Too big. Too noisy." Clear, observant eyes assessed him. "What about you?"

A sudden tightness in his chest made him freeze for a moment. Face devoid of emotion, he gave an inconsequential shrug. "Foster kid. Moved around a lot. Ended up here when I was fifteen." He kept his eyes on the food, not wanting to see the pity he knew he would find in her face.

"My dad was adopted."

Okay. That he did not expect, and he glanced up.

Eyes, a vibrant combination of green, gold, and brown, radiating life, pain, and unquenchable warmth, locked with his. "Someone literally left him on the door step of a half-way house when he was three. Luckily, he ended up with a great family who simply wanted a child to love." She toyed with the food on her plate. "He died when I was ten. Heart attack. It was just Mom and me for most of my life."

"Does she live around here?"

The happiness of a moment ago vanished in a heartbeat. "She died when I was nineteen."

The thought that he caused her pain filled him with regret. "I'm sorry. I didn't mean to bring up bad memories."

She straightened and met his gaze. "There are no bad memories, Max. Not really. I mean there were hard times of course, especially after the accident, but even those memories are special to me." She paused. "I wish Maddie could have known her." A genuine smile banished all trace of gloom. "Talk about a spoiled rotten child."

"I can't see you letting that happen."

"I probably let her get away with more than I should."

"She's smart as a whip," said Max. "I sometimes have to remind myself she's still a kid."

Sky nodded, pride evident by the gleam in her eye. "The first thing she told me when we moved here was that it was time she learned to read." She forked a bite of omelet, then held it close to her mouth. "I found some books and taught her."

"She has an inquisitive nature," said Max. "I can see her wanting to read."

Joy bubbled in her voice. "That's a nice way of saying she asks a lot of questions."

"Maybe. But they're good questions." A cozy glow, like a subdued flame fanned to life by a breeze, grew inside him, and he relished the shared moment. "You've done a great job with her. I know it couldn't have been easy." *At least you tried. Didn't drop her off at school one day and never looked back.*

Golden lashes that shadowed her cheeks jerked upward, accompanied by a timid smile. "Thank you."

"You're welcome."

Thankfully, she didn't ask about his parents, though he intuitively knew she waited for him to talk. He wasn't ready. Not yet.

Lost in their own thoughts, neither spoke for several

moments. Max reached for the jar of hot stuff. "You really should market this, Sky. It's awesome. Hot as hell but awesome."

She managed a choking laugh. "Thanks. I'm glad you like it. It's my mother's recipe."

The next hour passed quickly as they finished their meal and talked of trivial things. He insisted on helping with the dishes. Afterwards, they sat back at the table with the last of the coffee in their cups.

"Um, do you, um, have plans for Thanksgiving, Max?"

"Thanksgiving? Already?"

She nodded. "Next week."

Sky's simple question gave him pause. Holidays were just another day for him. He'd known people who went all out, but he never had that pleasure. Suddenly, the idea appealed to him. A lot. "No. No plans."

"Would you, um, like to join us for dinner?"

His mind raced with a myriad of objections. *I'm no good for you. I have nothing to offer. I'll only bring you down.* But when he opened his mouth, something entirely different came out. "I've never had a real sit-down Thanksgiving dinner. Well, they did stuff for us in the service, but it wasn't the same."

Tight features softened, and she visibly relaxed. "I love the holidays. I want Maddie to always have fond memories to look back on."

An idea formed, and the words came out before he could censor them. "How would you feel about cooking dinner at my house? I mean, you'd have to tell me what I need to buy and all."

"Well, I—"

"I'll have to make sure the oven works, though. I've never used it."

"You've never used your oven?"

He shrugged. "No point for one person."

He looked up to find her watching him as she fingered the tiny starfish dangling from a silver chain around her neck. "I haven't cooked a meal like that in a while."

"I'm guessing it will take a lot of time and effort on your part. I can't cook, but I can shop." His self-deprecating laugh was barely audible. "There is virtually nothing in my kitchen that isn't fast food related. Other than coffee, of course, so, if you could just make me a list of things I need, I'll get them."

Her lips twitched, and a smile threatened. "So, you know how to choose the right turkey? The difference between corn meal and corn bread mix? Jellied cranberry or whole?"

Chagrined, he conceded defeat. "Okay. You have a point. What do you suggest?"

Slender fingers drummed on the table. "Do you have a roasting pan, pots, dishes?"

"To be honest, I don't know."

Her eyes widened in surprise. "You don't know if you have dishes?"

"I have stuff. My shr—uh, a friend of mine stocked the place before I moved in. About the only thing I've ever cooked though is coffee and bacon and eggs. Yours are better."

Eyes brimming with excitement met his. "Okay. If you don't have what I need, we can use mine. No point in buying something you may never use again." The tap, tap, tap of her fingers on the tabletop sped up as her face scrunched in thought. "The list will be pretty long."

"I'm okay with that. Whatever you need to make it special. I mean, like you want it."

She spun her cup on the table and lifted it to her mouth.

"To buy everything I'd need for a...a traditional meal will be expensive."

"More than a thousand dollars?"

She coughed and sputtered. "Heavens, no!"

"Then we are good to go."

Uncertainty mixed with a quickly suppressed spark of excitement flashed in her eyes.

"If you're sure."

"I'm sure." He forced his hand to remain steady as he drained his cup. "Just tell me what you think you'll need...or however you want to handle it."

She pushed an errant curl behind her left ear. "Maybe I need to see what you have on hand first, so we don't end up with extra stuff."

He snorted. "I have salt and pepper. And some pots and pans. I have no idea what a roasting pan is and seriously doubt I have one."

"Okay. We start at square one." Brows creased, she nibbled her bottom lip. "What if...maybe we could go together. That way, you'll know exactly how much everything costs and can stop me if I suggest something you don't like."

He ignored the sudden jump in his heart rate. *It's not a date or anything. We're going to the grocery store. No big deal.* "When do you want to go?"

She hesitated, then met his steady gaze. "Tomorrow afternoon maybe? I'll be working Monday and Tuesday of next week, and I'm off Wednesday and Thursday. But I'd rather not wait till the last minute to shop."

The restrained excitement in her voice made his heart stammer. "I get off at three. How about I pick you up a little after?"

"Okay." She blew out a long breath. "I'm taking advantage of your kindness again, aren't I?"

"No, you're not." He stood and placed his cup in the sink, then picked up the tool box. "I buy. You cook. I clean. We're even."

She stopped near the back door, arms folded across her middle. "Thank you, Max. For everything."

"I'll see you tomorrow." He needed to leave before he could act on the raging impulse to crush her to him. An impulse that skyrocketed when her gaze locked on his mouth, and she lightly licked her lips.

"Tomorrow."

How could one whispered word hold so much promise?

CHAPTER
Eight

"When's Max gonna get here?" Maddie's anxious question was followed by yet another trip to the kitchen window. "It's already after three."

"Any minute now." Sky sat at the kitchen table reviewing her extensive shopping list. Even with just the basics, it would cost a small fortune to outfit his kitchen. For one meal. Okay, so there would be leftovers, and some ingredients he could use later, but essentially, one meal. She couldn't remember the last time she was able to cook anything she liked without worrying about where the money would come from. They weren't destitute, of course, but things were tight, making it necessary to watch every penny.

Just the thought of being able to shop unimpeded made her smile. Even Cade's appearance right before she got off work didn't quash her good mood.

He said he had good news for her, but she was busy and didn't have time to chat. When the doors were locked a little later, he'd already gone. She had no idea what his good news was and, frankly, didn't care. He was so not her type. Max, on the other hand, appealed to her on many different levels. True, they were essentially strangers, but at the same time, she sensed a connection with him from the beginning. An innate goodness that shone through his sometimes-gruff demeanor stood out, along with the patience and kindness he exhibited with Maddie. As did his masculinity. And sex appeal.

"Finally," said Maddie as she hurried outside.

Sky rose and made it to the door in time to see Maddie tug him back toward the house. "Come on. Mama's got her list all ready. I helped."

She closed the door behind them and suddenly found herself nervous and unsure. Should she go through with this, trust her intuition? What if she was wrong? What if, what if, what if?

Maddie, on the other hand, was happy as a clam. "Mama's a really good cook, Max. You'll be happy you're her male companion."

Sky's heart lurched. "Maddie!"

"Ma'am?"

She couldn't look at Max. "Don't say…male companion."

"Why not?"

"Because not everyone is as smart as you," offered Max, "and some people might not understand what it means."

Pixie brows scrunched together. "Hmmm. Okay. Then what do we call you?"

"Just Max is fine."

"But you will be Mama's ma—friend, right?"

Hooded dark eyes revealed nothing of his thoughts. "If she's okay with it."

Sky blushed like a school girl on her first date and nodded.

"Good," said Maddie as she zipped up her coat. "Can we go to the store now?"

Two hours later, Sky put away the final sack with an envious sigh. Her pantry would never be this well stocked. If her list said one of something, Max added extra, *just in case*. He stipulated she replenish the coffee, bacon, and eggs he'd eaten the night before, along with some snack items Maddie liked. She returned the favor by insisting he stock items other than canned chili and crackers for quick meals.

When the final tally appeared, she struggled for air, suddenly embarrassed and inundated by guilt as Max paid the checker.

Once out the door, he touched her arm lightly, switching her focus to him. "This was my idea, Sky. If anyone should feel like they're taking advantage of someone, it's me."

His comprehension of her unease should have bothered her. Should have. "Why do you say that?"

"You can cook. I can't. You know how to shop for real food. I don't. The way I see it, I'm the winner here."

And just like that, her good mood resurfaced.

Sky roused herself and looked around the kitchen, noted the empty plastic bags scattered over the counter as well as the table, and gathered them up. "Did you put the turkey in the fridge?"

Max gave her an of-course-I-did look and didn't reply.

"I forgot to ask about your schedule," said Sky. "Will you be home Thursday morning? I'll need to start cooking early. Some stuff I can do at home and just bring it over later if you'd rather."

He pulled a key ring from his pocket and removed a key. "I work Wednesday and need to do a couple of things for Gail on Thursday." He held the key out to her. "Here's my extra key. Just do what you need to whenever you need to."

She hesitated. A key to his house? That was a little too—something.

"It's just a key, Sky," he said softly. "With no strings attached."

Once again, his perception of her feelings should have been disquieting but weren't. She reached for the key. "Will it be okay if I come over Wednesday while you're at work to do some of the prep stuff? Maybe bake that peach cobbler you wanted?"

When he smiled, her stomach did a somersault, and awareness raced through her like lightning.

"You're going to leave me here alone with a fresh peach cobbler?"

Maddie's gleeful laugh broke the spell. "You'll get in big trouble, Max, if you nibble on stuff before Mama says you can."

A flash of humor softened the hard lines on his face. "Then I guess I'll have to wait."

"Come on, young lady, we need to get home." She gathered up her items. "You still have homework to do."

The child pulled her coat from the back of the chair. "Can we have chili dogs for supper, please?"

Sky saw movement out the kitchen window and leaned over for a better view of who walked toward her back door. She couldn't stifle a groan as Cade's lean form came into view.

Max saw the sudden change in Sky's posture and followed her gaze. *Dammit.*

Cade chose that moment to glance toward them. Even at this distance, Max saw his expression darken and his jaw tighten before long strides brought him to Max's back door.

He looked at Sky for some indication of how she wanted this to go down. All he saw was apprehension and resignation. Max opened the door before Cade knocked.

"Hello, Cade." Max worked hard to keep his animosity hidden. "What can I do for you?"

"I wanna to talk to Skylar."

His sharp, clipped tone swung Max into protective mode in a heartbeat. He glanced to where she leaned against the sink, hands braced on either side. "Sky?"

She looked from one man to the other, then folded her arms across her chest. "About what, Cade?"

"I'm freezing my ass off out here."

Max hesitated, dark eyes focused on the man who had made his high school years a living hell. "Watch your mouth," he barked as he stepped aside for him to enter. "Maddie's here."

Cade didn't glance at Max as he entered the small kitchen and addressed Sky. "Can we talk in private?"

Sky glanced at Maddie, who watched with nervous eyes. "Maddie, honey, why don't you go start your homework. I'll be there in a minute."

The child looked from her mother to Max, who gave her a slight nod of encouragement.

"You may have one cookie and some milk before you do your homework," said Sky.

Maddie wavered, then smiled at Max, completely ignoring Cade. "I had a good time today, Max."

"Me too, Tink." He tapped her nose with his index finger. "Run along like your mother said."

Sky watched through the kitchen window as Maddie entered the house, then turned back to the two men. "What do you want, Cade?"

Max didn't miss the strain in her voice or the tenseness in her stance, which heightened his protective instincts.

"To talk to you in private," he snapped. "This is the third time I've been by since you got off. Where have you been?"

She ignored his question. "Anything you have to say to me can be said here."

Cade stepped forward, and like flipping a switch, a charming man replaced the irritated one. He smiled and reached toward her. "I've got it set up for us to go to the dance next Saturday night."

What the hell?

"I told you I have to work."

"I got Louise to work for you."

His self-satisfied grin made Max grind his teeth.

"You what? I have to work."

The sharp edge in her normally soft speech surprised Max. Apparently, Cade, too, because he flinched.

"You said you couldn't go because you had to work. I got her to work for you, so now we can go."

Max watched Sky's transformation with a heady mixture of delight and desire. Face awash with color, eyes shooting daggers at Cade, her chest rose and fell rapidly as she struggled for control.

It was hot. And entertaining as hell.

"How dare you." Sky took a step forward, hands fisted at her side. "You had no right to do that."

Cade flashed his trademark smirk. "You need some fun in your life, babe, instead of being tied down with the kid and work all the time."

Max almost felt sorry for the self-centered imbecile as he dug the hole deeper. Almost.

Cade reached for her hand, his timbre low and seductive. "Come on, babe. Stop with the games. You know you want to go out with me."

She jerked back. "I am not your babe," she hissed, "and my daughter is not a burden." She took a breath. "And do not EVER interfere in my life again."

"I was—"

"This is the last time we're having this conversation, Cade. I'm not going to that dance or anywhere else with you. I told you before. I don't date."

Cade's furious scowl settled on Max. "What about him?"

"None of your business."

Max moved closer. *Time for this asshole to hit the road.* "I think the lady's made her wishes clear. You can leave now."

Cade focused on Sky, his face an unhealthy red, one purple vein pulsing at his temple. "I told you before. Getting involved with him is a mistake."

"Good night, Cade."

Sky's voice trembled, whether with anger or fear, Max couldn't tell.

"You heard her, Jackson. Leave. Now."

Cade stiffened, hands fisted at his side, as he turned cold, dead eyes on Max. "Loser Logan," he sneered. "You still don't get it, do you? You're not good enough for her or anyone else. You never were." He jerked open the door. "And you never will be."

It took a great deal of willpower not to follow through on the urge to plant his fist in Cade's face as the man stormed outside.

"I've never encouraged him." Sky grabbed up one of the plastic sacks and roughly stuffed it inside another. "I don't know why he persists in asking me out."

"You turned him down. That's encouragement enough."

Her back to him, Sky stopped and hung her head. "He sees Maddie as a burden."

"He's an asshole." The knife-sharp words were out before he could stop them.

Her light laugh eased some of the tension in the room. "He is that." She finished with the empty sacks and turned around. "These make handy liners for bathroom trash cans and trash bags for the car."

Who puts liners in a bathroom trash can? "Good to know. Thanks."

Those intoxicating, soul-searching eyes locked on his. "He's wrong you know."

Jaws clamped so tightly they hurt, he finally ground out a reply. "You don't know that. You don't know me."

"I know all I need to."

She placed her hand on his chest, and he feared he would combust on the spot.

"You're a good man, Max, with a kind heart."

He swallowed hard, unable to break eye contact. He couldn't say who took the first step forward. Maybe they took it together. One minute they were three feet apart, the next his nose was filled with the citrusy aroma of her shampoo.

For her sake, he tried to be reasonable. "I'm no good for you," he whispered as he drank in her beauty. "Cade was right about that."

She ran her hands up his chest. "He's an asshole. What does he know?"

Of their own volition, his hands slid around her waist, the dreaded words wrenched from his soul. "Afghanistan messed me up. I'm still not over it."

"One day," she whispered, "one thing at a time."

Standing on her tip toes, her lips lightly brushed his.

And he was lost.

Her touch was a command, and he obeyed.

He slowly pulled her against him, lightly tracing the silky fullness of her lips with his tongue before delving inside to explore the softness hidden there. He pressed his mouth to hers, caressing more than kissing it, savoring the taste, the feel, the smell of her. A kiss for his wounded spirit to melt into.

She responded with a soft moan as her hands gripped his shoulders.

He deepened the kiss, and she countered, matching his fire with fervor of her own.

From…somewhere, willpower he didn't know he possessed emerged, and he ended the kiss, resting his forehead on hers.

She shivered and gulped in air.

Old doubts and fears assaulted him. Cade was right; he wasn't good enough. She was too good for the likes of him. He needed to stop now before things went any further.

"Please don't do that," whispered Sky. "Don't shut me out."

"I'm a mess."

"Who isn't?"

"You deserve better."

"So do you." She slid her arms around his waist and rested her head on his chest.

He hesitated a moment, then folded her in his arms and kissed the top of her head, pulling the goodness she radiated into his shattered soul. How long they stayed that way, he didn't know. He only knew how right it felt to hold her in his arms. At long last, he whispered, "Maddie's going to be worried."

She nodded against his chest. "Yeah. I should get home."

He ran his hands up her back, enjoying the feel of her body against his, terrified his past would destroy her. Them.

She pushed back enough to look up at him. "It's been a long time since I met someone I wanted to be with. Someone who didn't mind a woman with a child." She brought her hands around and rubbed them on his chest. "I don't know what's going to happen with us, but I want the chance to see if it can be as good as I think it will." She stretched up and lightly kissed him again. "Good night, Max."

She picked up her things and walked out, Cade's words echoing through his mind. *You aren't good enough. You never will be.*

CHAPTER
Nine

S ky went through the motions of work, but her mind kept returning to last night's events. The warm atmosphere in Max's kitchen as she put things away while he and Maddie chatted just seemed…right.

And then Cade ruined it. Even now, his presumptuousness spiked her temper.

"Morning, Sky."

The greeting from the local doctor, Samantha Delaney, Sam or Doc to most folks, broke into her musings. "Morning, Doc. What can I get you?"

"Just coffee for now. Waiting on Coop to join me for lunch." She settled into a booth. "How's Maddie? Any new issues with her breathing?"

"No, she's fine. The inhaler worked great, and she hasn't had any other episodes. But we keep it handy just in case." Asthma, another side effect of Maddie's premature birth, had not been an issue in some time. Recent episodes of shortness of breath dictated action. Doc thought the colder-than-normal weather was the cause, and the inhaler she prescribed worked well thus far.

"I know it's difficult to keep her inside," said Doc, "but when it's this cold and damp, it's probably best."

"Yeah, she's not much for being cooped up."

Sam sipped her coffee. "I know this isn't really the time or place to ask, but have you given any more thought to my proposition?"

Once Sam discovered Sky was a registered nurse whose license was inactive, she offered to help her get reinstated. In return, Sky would work for her at the clinic. Sky understood there would be hoops to jump through, but Sam was confident they could make it happen.

"I would love to get back into nursing, Doc. I really would."

"But?"

"I don't know what all will be involved or if I could even do it."

"I've taken the liberty of looking into the process. As for any cost involved, including any classes you may have to take, that's on me till you get on your feet. Then we'll work something out." Sam's eyes sparkled with sincerity. "And, to be perfectly honest, I asked some people I know who still work at your old hospital about you. They had nothing but high praise for you. You can do this, Sky. I know you can. And I'll help make it happen."

To be a nurse again would be a dream come true, but having to depend on someone else to help her, well, that had never worked to her advantage. "I'll think about it and let you know after Thanksgiving. Will that be all right?"

"Of course. Ah, here comes Coop, and he has that I-need-coffee-now look."

The lunch crowd filtered in, then it was the afternoon coffee and pie group. The constant activity kept her busy, but Sam's offer remained foremost in her mind. Common sense said take it; lack of confidence made her hesitate. What if she had to go back to school? Was she up to that? Plus, the closest one was over an hour away. And she was thirty-three years old now; would she be competing with twenty-somethings? What about Maddie? How could she work it all out?

By the time her shift ended, she was no closer to a decision than before.

Head bent against the cold wind, she didn't see Cade until he touched her arm, making her jump. "What is it, Cade?"

"Sorry. Didn't mean to startle you. I just wanted to apologize for last night. I was out of line."

"Yes. You were."

He took a breath and ducked his head. "I'm sorry. I should not have talked to Louise without asking you first. I'll tell her never mind."

"Don't bother. I already did."

He shuffled his feet and extended his hands out, palm up in a pleading manner. "Look, I just want us to get to know each other better. I'm sorry if I overstepped my bounds. It won't happen again."

His contrite manner probably worked on most women.

Sky wasn't most women.

"Good. Now, if you'll excuse me, I have to pick my daughter up at school."

He tried to put his hand over hers as she gripped the door handle, but she jerked it away in time.

Unruffled, he continued as though nothing happened. "How about we all go out for pizza tonight? You, me, and the kid."

It wasn't the first time he referred to her daughter as *the kid,* and it ticked her off. "The kid's name is Maddie."

"Fine. Okay. You, me, and Maddie. How about it? I'll pick you up at six."

His smile said he thought he'd won.

He hadn't. Not by a long shot.

"Maddie has something at school tonight." She yanked on the door handle.

"Great. I'll take you, then we can go for pizza afterwards."

She took a deep breath. "My answer hasn't changed, Cade. No."

His jovial expression turned sour. "You going with Logan? Is that it?"

The instant change in his attitude caught her off guard for a moment. Relying on her combative patient training, she straightened and faced him. "As I said before, none of your business. Now, please remove your hand."

"Everything all right, Miss Sky?"

The question came from Big John Andrews, a local handyman, who stood at the back door holding a narrow piece of wood trim. At least six five with a huge barrel chest and tree-trunk arms, he dwarfed the door's narrow opening. Snow-white hair hung below a worn toboggan, his weathered face covered by a peppery beard that reached mid-chest. His age could have been fifty or seventy, the lines and scars on his face attesting to a life lived hard. Rumor had it the only thing he liked better than a good fight was Ruby's pecan pie.

To Sky, though, he was a gentle giant of a man who looked out for those he cared for. Happily, she and Maddie fit that category.

John inclined his head toward Cade. "He bothering you?"

"No. He's just leaving."

Big John dropped the trim and took a step forward. "He need some help?"

Cade's jaw clinched and relaxed. "Logan's nothing but trouble, Skylar." He tipped the brim of his western hat. "I'll be around when you come to your senses."

John watched until Cade was out of sight. "He gives you any more sass, Miss Sky, just let me know. I'd love to have a chat with him."

She released the breath she held and jerked on the door handle again. "Thanks, John, but I don't think that will be necessary."

"Guys like him don't like being told no." His battle-scarred face was grim as he picked up the discarded piece of wood. "My offer stands."

"You've made great progress, Max, so I was a little surprised at your call today. What's going on?"

From their first session over a year ago, Dr. Oscar Bellamy's smooth cadence, coupled with a deep southern accent and calm demeanor, put Max at ease. Pale blue eyes radiated compassion and understanding, seeing past a multitude of hurts and anger that made it easy to talk.

The faux leather on his chair squeaked as Max sat up straighter. "I had it again…the nightmare—a few days ago. Not as bad as before, but…"

"But…?"

He pulled in a ragged breath. "I thought I was past that."

"Even though you may no longer experience the nightmares, Max, the memories of the event are still there. Consequently, certain situations or people or even thoughts can cause them to resurface." He leaned forward, hands clasped in front of him. "We can't eliminate the memory itself, but we can reduce its effect on your life by continuing to practice the coping skills we've developed for you."

Max nodded. "I had a conversation with another vet. Afghanistan was a walk in the park compared to what he went through in 'Nam." He paused and rubbed his hands on his thighs. "You think maybe that dredged up the other?"

"It's possible. Did you experience any discomfort when you were talking with this man?"

"Surprisingly no, I didn't. I listened to Big John talk about being over there and what he went through when he got home, and all I felt was anger that he had to go through that alone."

Over the next half hour, Max was relieved to discover that what he faced was part and parcel of his new normal. He had not regressed in his treatment.

Dr. Bellamy removed his glasses and wiped them with a tissue from the box on his desk. "I get the impression there's something else on your mind, son. What is it?"

Max rubbed his hands together, not sure how to begin. He wanted to talk about Sky and Maddie but didn't know what to say.

"Is it the upcoming holiday? Just talk, Max. The right words will find their way out."

He took a deep breath. "I met someone. A woman." He met the man's attentive gaze. "She has a child. A little girl named Maddie."

"And?"

Consumed with nervous energy, Max stood and paced the area behind his chair. "They're awesome. Sky is kind and compassionate with a beautiful smile. And Maddie." He shook his head lightly and grinned. "She's a terrific kid." He braced his arms on the back of the chair, head downcast. "I'm better, I know that, but…I'm still a mess." Thoughts of Cade's parting insult warred with Maddie's unconditional acceptance. And Sky. She wanted to be with him. "I'm no good for them. Or anyone else."

Dr. Bellamy waited until Max looked at him to reply. "So, you don't think you're worthy to have them in your life?"

"Yes. No. I mean…hell I don't know what I mean."

"Have you told her about your PTSD?"

He shook his head and shoved his hands in his back pockets. "Just that Afghanistan screwed me up."

"What did she say to that?"

He sighed. "She wants a chance to see if we can make it."

"What do you want to do?"

Max's short laugh held no mirth. "Hell, Doc, you know what a mess I was. Just because the nightmares have all but stopped, and I'm able to hold down a job, doesn't mean I'm cured."

"No, it doesn't. That takes time. And support. But you're a strong young man, Max. You *want* to get better and work hard to do so. I know you'll succeed." Dr. Bellamy placed his glasses on the desk and folded his hands together. "What's her name?"

"Sky. Skylar. She's a waitress at Ruby's Diner." He smiled as the memory of their recent dinner and shopping together washed over him. "She used to be a nurse but had to give it up when Maddie was younger." He gazed at the array of awards and certificates on the wall along with photos of what appeared to be his family. "I bet she'd be a good nurse."

"How do you feel about the child?"

"Maddie? She's a pistol." He laughed. A genuine laugh that

made Bellamy smile. "She wants me to be her mother's male companion."

By the time Max finished the story, the psychiatrist had joined in the laughter.

"What if I mess up, Doc? What if something happens, and I go off the deep end or, God forbid, hurt one of them?"

"You can't live your life worrying about what-ifs, son. You take it one day, one thing at a time."

"That's what Sky said."

"Sounds like a smart woman."

Max dropped into his chair. "I won't lie, Doc. I like her. A lot. Since the first time I ever saw her. Maybe too much. And Maddie, too. We…we all…fit, you know?" He scrubbed his face with both hands. "They've been through a lot. Sky has had to struggle to get by. It would kill me if I did something to hurt them."

Bellamy walked around the desk and sat in the chair beside him. "Look at me, Max."

When he complied, the psychiatrist continued. "Be honest with her. Tell her the truth. All of it. From what you told me, I don't see her backing away. But if she does, it wasn't meant to be, and the sooner you know that, the better for all of you." He placed one hand on Max's shoulder. "I think you need her, Max. She could be good for you."

He stiffened. "I won't use her just to get well."

"That's not what I meant, son. You need someone in your life who cares about you. Someone you care about in return, to be beside you on this rough path you have to walk."

Max struggled to keep the tears stinging his eyes from spilling out. *Marines don't cry.* "I want it to be her, Doc," he whispered. "And Maddie. I want it so damn bad."

"Then you have to work for it. Talk to her. My guess is, her answer will make you smile again."

He pulled in a lungful of air and blew it out through pursed lips. "She's cooking Thanksgiving dinner at my house."

Bellamy patted his shoulder and smiled. "Something tells me this will be a new beginning for you, Max. You have my cell number. Call me. I want to know how it goes."

By the time Max exited the building, not even the cold north wind could douse the fire inside.

For the first time in his life, he allowed himself to hope for a brighter future.

CHAPTER
Ten

Max turned into the drive, noting Sky's Taurus in its usual spot, but the house was dark. Disappointment turned to delight when he saw her through his kitchen window. He didn't really think she would use the key. A rare smile tugged up one corner of his mouth, and his heart rate escalated. He couldn't remember the last time he was happy to be home.

The aromas assailing his nostrils stopped him cold when he entered the kitchen. "I don't know what you've been cooking, but it smells wonderful in here."

She whirled around at his entrance. "I'm sorry. I thought I'd be done before you got home." She glanced at the clock and then back at him.

Her voice held a note of unease he hadn't heard before. She stood in front of his seldom-used stove, an apron tied around her waist and a small towel tossed over one shoulder, hands encased in what looked like oversized mittens. Her face glistened with a light sheen of perspiration, and several curls escaped a lop-sided ponytail and clung to her neck. Her cheeks boasted a bright shade of pink, whether from the heat or something else, he couldn't say.

She was a beautiful sight to behold.

He cleared his throat. "Yeah, well, they closed early. The holiday and all."

She jumped when something dinged behind her, then twisted around and opened the oven door.

He watched in fascination as those mitten-clad hands reached inside and pulled out a rectangle dish and placed it on top of the stove.

His mouth watered as the enticing smell of cinnamon and sugar wafted toward him. "Is that what I think it is?"

A tentative smile greeted his question. "Peach cobbler. You said it was your favorite, so I made a big one. Thought you might be able to eat on it for a couple of days."

With two long strides, he stood in front of the stove, head bent, inhaling deeply. "If it tastes half as good as it smells, it may not last that long."

She chuckled as she removed the mittens and placed them on the counter. "Well, I hope you like it."

"I'm sure I will." He glanced around the kitchen. "Where's Tink?"

The smile vanished and worry knitted her brow. "She's watching TV in the living room." She folded her arms around her middle. "She's not been herself today. I thought she might be getting sick again, but she's not running a fever. I hope you don't mind. About the TV, I mean."

"Of course not. Is there anything I can do?" He didn't know much about Maddie's history beyond that she had some medical issues. The thought of her being ill made his mouth go dry.

Sky straightened and shook her head. "No. We're fine. Sometimes cold weather causes her asthma to act up. I'm sure that's all it is." She looked around the kitchen as though cataloging what she saw, then turned back to Max. "I think I have everything ready for tomorrow. I'll put the turkey on at my house, and we'll get it when it's time."

"Is there anything you need me to do?" He kept his expression neutral as he added, "besides test that peach cobbler?"

The smile froze on her face as their eyes met.

The connection was so strong, the pull so magnetic, he had to force himself not to close the distance between them.

When her gaze dropped to his lips and jerked up again, he reminded himself to breathe.

Do I have the right to do this? What if Dr. Bellamy is wrong? "…Sky…"

Before he could force the words out, Maddie entered the kitchen. One look at her usually cheerful face, and Max understood Sky's concern. He took a step toward the table. "Hey, Tink. You okay?"

Red-rimmed sapphire eyes darted from Sky and then to him. She drew in a jerky breath and paused. "Is PTSD like cancer, Max? Are you gonna die?"

"Maddie!"

Even Sky's sharp tone didn't penetrate the roar in his ears.

Maddie ran to him and wrapped her arms around his waist. "I don't want you to die!"

"Madeline Adele—"

Maddie squeezed tighter, the words pouring out as her tiny body trembled with sobs. "Miss Gail said it was like cancer and sucked the life out of you."

Max couldn't move. Didn't know what to say. He wasn't prepared for this conversation. Especially not with a kid. His heart pounded, and he forced himself to focus on controlling the encroaching panic.

Several moments passed before he could speak. He pulled her arms away and took a step back.

Her lips trembled, and another sob escaped as she watched him with the saddest eyes he'd ever seen.

"Let's sit down." He whispered and didn't wait for a reply as he dropped into a chair at the table, nor did he look up as Maddie and Sky joined him.

"Max…" Sky's stricken voice found its way through the fog. "I'm so sorry. Maddie—"

"No." The single word sounded harsh even to him, and he tried to soften it. "It's okay." He looked at Maddie, whose shuddering breaths continued. "I'm okay, Tink. I'm not going to die." He looked at Sky and took a deep breath. "But I do have PTSD."

Sky heard what he said but didn't really process it at first. She knew about PTSD of course but had never actually known anyone who had it. Max seemed perfectly normal to her. Try as she might, she couldn't dredge up anything on the subject.

"I've been undergoing treatment since I got home."

He sat ramrod straight, one tightly fisted hand rested on the table. The misery in his voice was so acute, her heart ached for him.

"It's not like cancer?"

Maddie's childlike lilt drew his attention. "No, Tink," he said softly, "It's not like that."

"You're not gonna die?" Her voice broke, and she inhaled deeply.

"No."

She jumped from the chair and ran to him, throwing her arms around his neck. "Oh, I'm so glad. I knew Miss Gail didn't know what she was talking about."

Stiff at first, Max didn't react to Maddie's enthusiastic response. Then, slowly, his head bowed and rested on hers.

Sky didn't miss the tear that slid down his cheek.

Maddie pulled away and looked at Sky. "When will supper be ready?"

"Not until you tell me what brought all this on." She waved her hand in a circle for emphasis.

Maddie ducked her head. "I overheard Miss Gail talking to Mr. Frank this morning when you went back to the store."

"We'll talk about your eavesdropping later. What did you hear?"

She cut her eyes toward Max, who watched intently. "Well, I didn't actually hear much, just the part about PTSD being like cancer, and then later she said something about Max, and I thought she was saying he was sick."

She struggled to find a way to explain something she didn't really understand herself when Max spoke up.

He folded his hands in his lap and took a deep breath. "PTSD is…something that people…soldiers who have been in combat, sometimes have."

"Does it hurt?"

He blew out a long breath. "Not in the way you mean, but yes, it can hurt."

"That's how you got that cut on your face, isn't it?"

"Maddie!"

If they heard her rebuke, neither gave any indication as their conversation continued.

"Yeah."

"I'm sorry you got hurt, Max."

"Thanks, Tink."

"Are you well now?"

Sky didn't bother to interrupt again since they acted like she wasn't in the room. Besides, she wanted to know the answer, too.

"I'm much better than I was a year ago, but, no, I'm not totally well."

Maddie nodded, eyes clear and bright. "But it's not cancer, so you'll *get* well, right?"

He nodded. "I hope so."

"Can we help you get better?"

Sky heard the quick intake of breath, could see he held it for several heartbeats before he let it go and looked at her.

"I'd like that, but it's a lot to ask."

"Why?" Maddie's voice was firm. "We'd like to help you, wouldn't we, Mama?"

"I'm sure your mom needs some questions answered before she decides." He unfolded his hands, placed one on the table. "How about you go watch some TV while we talk?"

"Oh. I see. You need grown-up time." She turned toward the living room.

"No eavesdropping, young lady." Sky knew her daughter too well.

"Yes, ma'am." As was her habit when scolded, Maddie drew out the last word on a deep sigh.

The silence following her exit became uncomfortable, but Sky didn't know what to say.

Finally, Max sat up and faced her. "I was going to have this conversation later, but now is as good a time as any."

He clenched his fist so tightly, the knuckles turned white, yet his voice never betrayed distress. "I've been in the Marines since I was eighteen. I've lost count of the hellholes I've been to. And most of them don't matter anyway."

She listened in silence as he talked about the last mission. The one that killed his squad and nearly killed him. She had never heard anyone speak so dispassionately about something so horrific and wondered how long he could keep such a tight rein on his emotions.

And what might happen when that tenuous connection broke.

Even as doubts raced through her mind, pain squeezed her heart. He'd been through so much, witnessed so much grief… and faced it all alone. It was a miracle he had made it this far.

When he was done, the only way she knew he suffered was the white knuckles in front of her and the pain-ravaged eyes that waited for a response.

Intuitively, she knew it wasn't sympathy he wanted or needed, but understanding and compassion. Was she strong enough to do that for him? Would it be more than she could handle? What about Maddie? What would happen to her if things went south?

She pulled in a breath and let it out slowly. "Is that all?"

His guttural laugh held no humor. "That's not enough?"

She didn't react to his sharpness. "I know nothing about PTSD, Max. Nothing that's useful anyway. But I'm willing to learn." She hesitated briefly before placing both her hands over his fist. "You've been to hell and back. I can't imagine what it's been like for you."

She felt the tremble in his hand, heard the hitch in his breathing, and tightened her grip.

"It'd kill me if I hurt you," he whispered through clenched lips, "or Maddie."

"You're a good man, Max. That much I know." She paused. "I've never been through the kind of trauma you have, but I know what it's like to face adversity alone."

"I may not be as messed up as I was a year ago, Sky, but I'm not over it. They don't happen often anymore, but the nightmares still come around, the panic attacks…"

"I know. But my heart tells me you're someone worth taking a chance on." She squeezed his hand again. "One day, one thing at a time, Max."

His throat moved with each rapid swallow as his gaze remained locked with hers. "Maddie?"

"I'll talk to her tonight." She gave a rueful shake of her head. "If I know her, she'll Google it the first chance she gets."

"I don't want her…or you to be afraid of me. But…something could happen. If something should trigger an episode…" He inhaled deeply. "Dr. Bellamy's number—my shrink at the VA—is on speed dial on my phone. The first one."

She considered his statement. How violent was he? She didn't really know anything about him. Once again, her gut countered. She trusted him. He was a good man. Deciding information was power, she picked her questions.

"Are the episodes…violent?"

He shook his head. "Usually just anxiety, panic attacks." Twin lines of worry formed on his forehead, and his gaze bored into hers. "Doesn't mean that won't happen, though." He shifted in his chair, pulled his hand from under hers. "I've had a couple of minor episodes lately that I was able to control."

His jaw clenched and released. "Had the damn nightmare the other day, too. Hadn't had one in almost a year."

"Medication?"

"No. I hate drugs. And Dr. Bellamy said I seem to do better on my own." Sadness clouded his features. "Cade was right about one thing, though." He drew in a shaky breath. "I'm no good for you."

She went to him and knelt on the floor, resting her hands on his knees. "Well, Cade's an asshole, and we don't care what he thinks."

He gave a low, raspy moan. "I don't deserve someone like you."

She rose and clasped his head in her hands. "You deserve better than me."

He froze, hands fisted on his thighs. "There is no one better than you," he whispered. Slowly, as though afraid movement might break the spell that bound them, he slid his hands up around her waist and pulled her forward.

He rested his head against her chest as she rubbed the tight muscles in his back. Silent sobs racked his body as they clung to each other. Two lost and lonely souls overwhelmed by the knowledge that they were no longer alone.

CHAPTER
Eleven

Sky pulled the thrift-store quilt up around Maddie's chest and tucked it in. "So, do you have any questions?"

The child shook her head. "No, ma'am. I understand. He got hurt being a soldier and sometimes has bad dreams. Like when I watched that scary dinosaur movie." She placed her stuffed bunny in the crook of her arm. "And sometimes he remembers when he doesn't want to, and it makes him sad."

Leave it to a child to reduce a complex subject to its simplest form. "That's right."

"He's really nice, isn't he?"

Sky smiled. "Yes. He is."

"Can we help him not be sad?"

"We can try." Sky chewed her lower lip, unsure of just how much more to say. "But something might happen that we can't help him with. Or he might say or do something that's, well, a little scary."

Bow-shaped lips pursed. "Miss Gail said he got a purple medal for being a soldier. That makes him a hero, right?"

"Well, yes, I suppose so."

"Heroes don't hurt people."

Sky had no rebuttal for her child's determined statement.

"One more thing." She smoothed the covers on Maddie's bed. "You have an inquisitive nature and ask a lot of questions. But this isn't something you can ask about."

"Max doesn't mind my questions. He said so."

"I know. But this is different. This is…very personal and not something you should ask about."

"You told me when I had my bad dream that talking about it made it go away."

Okay, you got me there. "I know this is hard for you to understand, but you can't ask him about it."

Maddie's eyes narrowed, and she opened her mouth.

Sky held up one finger, silencing the argument brewing in those baby blues. "I mean it, Maddie. Off limits."

"But what if *he* says something about it?"

"If, and only if, Max brings it up, you may talk about it. But only if *he* brings it up. Got that?"

"Yes, ma'am." A prolonged yawn followed her agreement. "'Night, Mama. I love you."

Her heart swelled with love for her precocious child as she kissed her forehead. "Night, Maddie. I love you, too."

Sleep eluded Sky for the greater part of the night, and when it came, it was filled with a troubling mixture of images that left her restless and anxious, filled with questions for which she had no ready answers.

And Max occupied center stage.

Could she deal with his PTSD? How bad was it really? Was Maddie too attached to him? The questions compounded and rolled on top of each other until she abandoned all thought of rest.

Dawn found her sipping a second cup of coffee as the tantalizing smell of roasting meat filled the air. She looked at the detailed to-do list on the table. "Oh shoot," she mumbled to herself. "I forgot to tell Max I invited Big John to lunch." She looked out the window to the darkened house next door. "Maybe I can catch him later."

The invitation was an impulsive act spurred by the knowledge that John had no family and would spend the holiday alone. His ready acceptance of the offer convinced her it was the right thing to do.

She drained the last of her coffee and went about gathering up things she would take to Max's house later. Her mother's hand embroidered linen tablecloth and matching napkins topped the list, followed by a crystal vase to hold the mixed bouquet she had picked up yesterday.

It saddened her to realize how few tangible items remained of her parents and their life together. After her father's death, it was just Sky and her mother, and they were very close until the horrible accident that changed everything. One minute Sky was a typical sixteen-year-old with teenaged woes, the next she was forced to be an adult caring for an invalid mother.

To this day, those three years were a blur. Thankfully, there was some insurance money to deal with the medical bills, but nothing else. Somehow, Sky managed to work and go to school and care for them both.

The last year of her mother's life was awful, and Sky found herself thankful when death took her away. Losing her was bad enough, but the fire that destroyed their home a year later was the final, crippling blow. A few trinkets, her parents' wedding rings, her mother's starfish necklace, and the table linens were all that survived.

Alone and heartbroken, she threw herself into her

studies. Perhaps that was why she fell so hard and fast for Brett Ward, a young businessman she met through a patient. Their fairy-tale courtship ended with a sunset wedding on a beach in Jamaica. When she discovered she was pregnant a year later, they were over the moon with happiness. Their perfect family was complete.

The exact cause of Sky's early labor was never determined. One day everything was fine, the next she was in the hospital as the doctor tried to delay the inevitable. In the end, the cord became wrapped around the baby's neck, necessitating an emergency C-Section.

The first few weeks were agonizing as Maddie's fate hung in the balance. At first, Brett came to the hospital often, but had a great deal of difficulty handling their daughter's delicate condition. And then his job changed, and he had to travel more, leaving Sky alone to deal with whatever happened.

"Enough," Sky scolded herself. "The past is gone. Get over it and move on."

She pushed up from the chair and went about the business of putting together the first real Thanksgiving dinner she'd had since before her mother's accident.

A short time later, a light knock on the back door found her humming along with a song on the radio.

Max greeted her with a tentative smile. "I just wanted to let you know I left the back door unlocked. I need to do some stuff for Gail, and I'll be in and out."

She pushed open the screen door. "Come in. It's cold out there. I have fresh coffee."

He stepped inside and shut the door. "I don't want to trouble you. You already have enough to do today."

She passed him a mug of coffee and turned back to the

stove. "It's no trouble." She tilted her head toward the table. "Have you had breakfast?"

"Does a Pop-Tart count?"

She snorted and shook her head. "No. It doesn't." She pulled a skillet from the cabinet and placed it on the stove. "Won't take but a minute to scramble some eggs to go with the sausage and biscuits I already made."

In record time, she placed food in front of him, along with butter and grape jelly. "I haven't made homemade biscuits in a while. I hope you like them."

He split the biscuit and slathered butter on both sides. "I'm sure they're fine." He added a dollop of jelly to one side and used it to help slide a bite of egg onto his fork, then stopped. "You're not eating?"

"I ate already." She added more coffee to her cup and sat down. "Eat before the eggs get cold." Unsure of how he might react to adding Big John to the guest list, she proceeded with caution. "I, um, hope you don't mind but I invited someone else to join us for lunch."

She pulled the kitchen towel from her shoulder and rolled it in her hands. "It's John Andrews. I should have asked you first since it's your house, but it was an impulsive act when I found out he had no family and would be alone."

Max stopped mid-chew and stared. A heartbeat passed before he swallowed and smiled softly, dark eyes filled with gratitude. "I'm glad you did."

She released the breath she held and smiled. "I'm sorry I did it without asking, but, well, it just happened."

He reached across the table and placed his hand over hers. At his light touch, heat raced up her arm and exploded through her body. It took massive control not to react.

"No need to apologize. It was nice of you to think of him."

Several seconds passed before Max ducked his head and released her hand. "Whatever you're cooking sure smells good."

Shaken by his effect on her, she mumbled. "I thought we'd eat around twelve-thirty if that's all right with you."

"That's fine."

Maddie walked in then, Bunny cradled in her arm. When she spotted Max, she rushed forward. "Hi, Max. I didn't know you were here." She turned to Sky. "May I eat with Max?"

"Of course." Sky got up and went to the stove. "Scrambled eggs or biscuits and jelly?"

Maddie sat down and plunked Bunny on the table.

"Bunny goes in your lap, not on the table."

"Sorry. I forgot." She looked at Max's plate. "Eggs, please."

While Sky cooked, Maddie chatted about everything, from her good report card to her bike to Max being right about Bobby, whatever that meant. The poor man listened patiently as the child rambled on and never once seemed to be irritated or vexed by the barrage of prattle.

It wasn't until Sky placed food in front of her that Maddie stopped to take a breath.

Max picked up his plate and turned toward the sink. "I need to get moving so I can finish Gail's to-do list before lunch."

Sky took his dishes and placed them on the counter. "She told me Frank hopes to go back to work soon." A fireman, Frank Brown was injured when a roof collapsed under him a month ago. "I know he hates not being able to do much."

"Can I help you with Miss Gail's to-do list, Max?" asked Maddie.

"Another time, kiddo. Weatherman said we may get sleet soon, and it's near freezing outside."

Sky noted her daughter's crestfallen look. "You can help me get things ready and take stuff over to Max's."

"Okaaaay."

Her drawn-out reply made Sky smother a grin. On the heels of that thought came another. Maddie was so taken with Max, what would happened if their relationship fell through?

Max put away the tools and wiped his hands with a shop rag. The list of chores Gail had wasn't long but required time to finish. She had invited him to have dinner with her family and appeared delighted when he told her Sky was cooking at his house.

The thought of a real Thanksgiving dinner, prepared by someone other than military cooks and shared by close friends instead of a battalion of strangers, made him anxious. Eyes closed, he took a deep breath and counted to ten. *Please don't let anything happen today to ruin this.* Another deep breath brought with it the smell of wood smoke from someone's chimney and the faint aroma of a spice he couldn't name. And just like that, the encroaching anxiety disappeared, replaced by the desire to see Sky and listen to Maddie prattle on about whatever she wanted to prattle on about.

He tried not to read too much into the whole affair; it was just a meal after all. But, at the same time, he wanted it to be the kind of holiday meal he had only dreamed about. He took in the grey and gloomy clouds overhead. *God…I know we haven't talked much…okay, never, but since I've never asked for anything, maybe you could see fit to give me today.*

He glanced at his watch. Eleven-thirty. He had time to freshen up.

A gust of frigid air had him looking upward as the first pellets of sleet hit the ground. Jaw clamped tight, he frowned.

Guess I got my answer.

CHAPTER
Twelve

Sky stood in the middle of Max's kitchen and mentally checked off the items yet to be completed. More than anything, she wanted this dinner to be perfect. Not just for Max, who she suspected needed it the most, but for all of them. Each one had a history of holidays and special occasions that went by with hardly a flicker. But not today.

Today they would celebrate.

Max opened the door, and a gust of cold air entered with him. "Sleet started."

His deep baritone held a note of sadness she hadn't heard before. Had something happened? He didn't look upset, only sad.

Maddie skipped in from the living room. "Hi Max, wanna watch the parade with me?"

He ruffled her hair as he walked by without looking at Sky. "Later. Need to clean up."

Maddie watched him walk out and turned to Sky. "Is Max all right?"

"I'm sure he's fine. How about we start setting the table?"

Before they got the tablecloth down, a heavy knock said their other guest had arrived.

Sky opened the back door and stood back as Big John walked in, a gift bag in one hand and a coloring book and box of crayons in the other.

He handed the bag to Sky. "I thought a nice Merlot might go well with dinner."

"How sweet. Thank you, John." She placed the bag on the counter. "Let me take your coat."

He handed Maddie the coloring book and crayons. "A little something for you, too, Miss Maddie."

"Thank you, Mr. John, I love to color."

He pulled off his gloves and stuffed them in the pockets of his heavy coat. "I really appreciate the invite, Miss Sky."

"My pleasure. Please, just Sky. And make yourself at home while I finish things up."

"Is there anything I can do?"

"No, I'm good, thank you. Rolls need maybe another fifteen minutes to rise and twenty to cook, and we're ready."

"Mr. John," interjected Maddie, "Wanna watch the parade with me and Max when he's done cleaning up?"

He looked at Sky again. "Sure there's nothing I can do to help?"

"I'm sure. Y'all go watch the parade for about twenty minutes, then you can help me set the table."

"Hey, Max," said John, "hope you don't mind a freeloader today."

Max's smile was genuine as he shook John's hand, slightly alleviating Sky's fear that something was wrong.

"You know you're welcome here anytime."

Maddie grabbed each man's hand and pulled them toward the living room. "Mama said we can watch the parade till it's time to set the table."

Sky's heart did a little flip as she watched Maddie pull them from the kitchen, though neither man resisted.

She had just put the rolls in the oven when John and Max reappeared with Maddie in tow.

"We're ready to set the table, Mama."

She pointed to the items stacked on the far counter. "Everything is there."

"I'll show y'all how to do it," said Maddie. "It's not hard at all."

An unexpected ache jolted Sky's heart as she watched them set the table. Maddie pointed out what had to go where and made sure each man carried out his assigned task. For so long, it was just the two of them. There were so many things to handle, like bills and Maddie's health, so there was no time for anything else.

Maybe I should have remarried or dated or something.

It never occurred to Sky until today what a void her decisions had left for Maddie. She had no male influences in her life. No grandfather to dote on her, no father to fix her bike or shower her with fatherly praise.

Sky barely remembered her own grandfather, who died when she was twelve, and never knew her mother's parents. After her father died when she was ten, her grandfather filled that male role for only a couple of years before he, too, passed away. Then, it was just Sky and her mother.

"No, Max," Maddie admonished, "the knife goes on the outside."

He smiled and placed the utensil in its proper place. "How's that, Tink?"

"Good."

Sky turned away before anyone saw the tears that threatened to fall. She refused to let anything spoil today.

"Table's done."

Immersed in thought, Max's voice coming from behind her left shoulder made her jump. The sudden movement caused her balance to shift, sending her stumbling backwards. "Oh!"

"Sorry," said Max as his hands circled her waist. "Didn't mean to scare you."

"Mama scares real easy, Max," laughed Maddie. "I sneak up on her all the time."

Sky turned and met his amused gaze. "It is never a good idea to scare the cook."

His hands remained on her waist a beat longer, then dropped away. "Sorry," he repeated, though the smile in his eyes said he wasn't.

"What else can we do, Miss Sky?"

Big John's question sent her scrambling away from Max. "I think we're about ready."

The table was too small to hold all the food, so Sky had borrowed a table from Gail to serve as a buffet. The next few minutes were spent arranging bowls and plates on it.

"You will notice that there is not a single bite missing from that peach cobbler," said Max.

Sky laughed. "You showed amazing restraint, Mr. Logan." She removed the rolls from the oven and brushed the tops with melted butter.

"But I can't resist this," he whispered and grabbed one, eating half of it in one bite. "John, you gotta try these." He plucked another out of the pan and tossed it to his friend.

Both men were silent as they practically inhaled the yeasty concoction.

"If the rest of the meal is as good as this roll," muttered John, "I'll be a happy camper."

Finally, everything was ready, and it was time to sit down at the table. Max pulled out her chair, and she sat, mumbling a shy, "Thank you."

John reached around and pulled out a chair for Maddie. "Miss Maddie."

"Thank you."

Once all were seated, Maddie looked at Max, then John. "Who wants to say grace?"

Caught off guard, Sky was momentarily speechless.

"I think it needs to be Mr. John since he is the oldest," said Maddie.

Without missing a beat, John beamed, "I'd be honored."

"We have to hold hands," instructed Maddie, "and bow our heads."

As the four of them held hands around the small table, John gave a short yet heartfelt blessing about friendship, love, and family that brought the sting of tears back.

Max's grip on her hand tightened, and she returned the pressure.

With the final 'amen,' she looked around the table, and her heart swelled with happiness. The moment was so poignant, so special, it would remain embedded in her memory for a long time.

CHAPTER
Thirteen

The sense of foreboding that had followed Max inside the house earlier was gone, replaced by something he never thought he would experience. A holiday meal that felt like home.

Until Sky and Maddie came along, John was the closest thing to family he had. They spent many an hour talking about things in general and nothing in particular. Perhaps because of their similar military service, or the fact they shared some bad experiences, explained why Max felt a closeness with him he hadn't felt for anyone else.

Until Sky and her daughter wormed their way into his heart.

He didn't understand how it happened. Didn't try to. He would simply cherish it, every moment of it, for as long as it lasted.

Because he knew that somehow, someway, it would stop. Happy endings weren't meant for guys like him.

But until that time came, he would cherish every normal, sappy, and joy-filled minute of it. Even if it meant being instructed on the proper way to set a table by a precocious seven-year-old. He bit his lip more than once when John would do something contrary to her instructions, only to act appropriately contrite when corrected. Max loved every minute of it.

When Sky placed the perfectly roasted turkey in front of him with a flourish and handed him what he later learned were carving tools, he suffered a moment of panic. He had no idea what to do.

"There is no right or wrong way to carve a turkey," she said. "Just pick a spot and start."

"I like the white meat," said Maddie. "You just slice it off right there."

Following her finger, he carefully sliced off a piece of meat and placed it on her plate.

"Thank you, Max."

"You're welcome, Tink."

The next few minutes were lost as plates were passed and food distributed.

Max appreciated all the extras Sky had added. Flowers for the table and a decorative cloth with matching napkins. There weren't any fancy glasses for the wine, but no one cared. Carefree conversation flowed through the room, along with the heady fragrance of spices, cooked meat, and other smells he didn't try to categorize. For the first time in his life, Max enjoyed an honest-to-goodness Thanksgiving dinner with, if not family, good friends who were just as important.

"I have to tell you, Miss Sky," said John as he patted his rotund belly with one hand, "I have not had a meal this good in I can't remember when."

"Thank you, John. I'm glad you enjoyed it."

"Enjoyed it? Darlin', if I died this day, I'd already know what Heaven would be like."

Max liked the way she ducked her head at the extravagant

compliment and the bright shade of pink that crept up her neck.

"He's right," added Max. "You really outdid yourself on the meal."

Her smile made him feel like a superhero.

"I'm so glad you enjoyed it. Both of you."

"I told you Mama was a good cook."

"Good is an understatement," said Max. "I'm not sure I know of a word to adequately describe it."

Sky fanned her face with both hands. "Stop! You're making me blush."

"I think I'm going to have to save dessert for later," said John. "I don't think I could eat another bite."

"Same here," said Max. "Much as I want that cobbler, I'm too full to enjoy it right now."

"I have coffee ready to go," said Sky. "We'll have dessert at halftime."

John got up and began gathering up dishes.

"No, I got this," said Sky, "It's almost kick-off time."

"You cooked. We'll clean up." He looked at the ravaged table, the mass of leftovers. "Just tell me what to do with stuff."

"How about this?" offered Sky. "We all clean up. That way you can tell me what you want to take home with you for later."

John's booming laugh made his stomach shake. "I like that idea."

"You look like Santa Claus," said Maddie. "You just need a solid white beard instead of a black and white one."

Everyone snickered as John did a pretty good imitation of the fat man's signature ho-ho-ho.

In record time, leftovers were stored, John had his to-go box, and the kitchen was once again set to rights.

"I reckon I best be getting on home," said John. "The sleet has let up for now, and I don't want to get caught out if it starts up again."

"What about dessert?" asked Sky, "and the game?"

"I'd appreciate some of that cobbler for later if you don't mind."

Max helped Sky fix the dessert and add it to John's haul as the loveable giant put on his coat, then with only a brief hesitation, his normally reticent friend bent down and grabbed Sky in a gentle hug.

"You don't know how much today meant to me," he whispered. "Thank you for including me."

"Can I have a hug to, Santa? I mean, Mr. John?"

Maddie's gleeful question brought a smile to the big man's face. "Absolutely."

The goodbye process took longer than Max expected. To his way of thinking, you say goodbye, and you leave. Evidently, that wasn't the case here. He counted no less than six goodbyes before John actually walked out the door.

A huge yawn from Maddie got Max's attention. "Sleepy, Tink?"

"Yes, sir. But I don't wanna go home yet. Do I have to, Mama? Can't we stay and watch the game with Max?"

"You want to stay and watch a football game?"

"Yes, ma'am."

The look on Sky's face said she didn't believe her daughter's assertion.

"How about I make a pallet on the floor for you," offered Max. "You can watch the game till you get sleepy, then take a nap."

Immediately, Maddie's face lit up with a huge smile.

"Thanks." She grabbed his hand and headed toward the living room.

Sky's laugh followed him to the door. "I'll bring us some coffee."

A short time later, Max sat with Sky curled up beside him, the game all but forgotten as Maddie lay curled up on her pallet, fast asleep. "Today was wonderful," he said. "And having John here, well, that made it even more special."

"He's a good man. I like him."

"He likes you, too. And Maddie. Not many folks are on that list."

"I know."

No time like the present. He placed his cup on the coffee table, paused, then placed his arm on the back of the couch, bringing Sky closer.

His heart rate spiked when she put her cup next to his and snuggled against him.

"This is nice," she murmured.

"It is."

She looked away, then back to him, those mesmerizing eyes full of something he couldn't name.

"How is it that I feel as if I've known you forever when it's only been a short while?"

Surprised to hear her speak his own thoughts, he nodded. "I know. I feel the same way."

Her smile was timid as she nestled against him, and a comfortable silence ensued.

Afraid to allow the hope blooming inside to grow unchecked, Max mentally ticked off all the reasons a relationship with Sky was a bad idea. But each and every item on his very long list withered like grass in the desert when she looked at him.

"I probably should go before it starts sleeting again."

"You'll have to wake Maddie."

"I wouldn't want to do that."

"Me neither."

"...Max."

His name, whispered so softly as to be almost inaudible, was an entreaty he couldn't refuse. He glanced down at Maddie, then leaned over and brushed his lips against hers, once, twice.

She sighed and leaned into the kiss, opening her mouth to his exploration.

It wasn't a sexual kiss so much as a deep, soul-melding one that went on forever.

When at last she pulled away and rested her head in the bend of his shoulder, Max knew real happiness and contentment. A lifetime of emotions held in check came rushing out, making his breath catch and his heart flutter. He looked at the sleeping child and the woman in his arms and closed his eyes.

Thank you. For today. For this.

Max wasn't brave enough or naïve enough to believe it would last. But he found something he wasn't accustomed to.

Hope.

CHAPTER
Fourteen

Max glanced around the empty store and quickly decided to place a call to Dr. Bellamy. He wasn't surprised when the man answered on the first ring. "I just wanted to let you know things went great yesterday."

Max couldn't keep from grinning as he talked. There was so little in his past to smile about, but perhaps there would be in the future.

"Since I didn't hear from you, I hoped that was a good sign."

"I didn't want to bother you on the holiday since it was all good."

"I'm happy for you, Max."

"Thanks. I appreciate all that you've done for me, Doc. If not for you…" Choked with emotion, he couldn't finish the statement.

"You're a strong man, Max. Stronger than you think. You would have found a way to work it out on your own, if necessary."

Thoughts of the hell John went through alone made Max cringe inside, and he silently vowed to always be there for his friend. "Maybe. I'm just glad I didn't have to."

"So, do you want to come in next week and catch up?"

Max almost refused. Things were going well right now, and confidence in his ability to handle events grew. But another session couldn't hurt. "Sure. I'm off on Wednesday."

They set the appointment, and Max ended the call as a customer walked in. He didn't bother to hide his dislike as Cade Jackson strolled toward him.

"Well, well, well, if isn't Loser Logan in the flesh."

Max gripped the counter with both hands, refusing to allow his high school antagonist the pleasure of getting to him. Again. "You need something, Cade? Besides a personality?"

Cade's jaw clenched as he looked around the store. "I'm surprised Jason allows a loose cannon like you to be alone in here."

When Max remained silent, he continued.

"I hope you enjoyed your cozy little dinner yesterday."

Max grit his teeth.

"It won't happen again." Cade lowered his voice and leaned toward the counter when another customer walked in. "What I want, I get." He tapped the surface with his index finger. "You should know that by now." He winked. "But you can have her when I'm done." He turned to the newcomer, charm meter pegging out. "Morning, Rodney. How's the family?"

"Fine, Cade. Just fine." The man looked at Max. "Morning, Max. Glad y'all are open today. I need a new battery for Louise's car."

It took Max a moment and a mental ten-count to regroup. *Focus on the task. Focus.* "Sure thing, Rod. This way."

By the time eleven o'clock rolled around, Max was pacing like a caged tiger. He needed air. He needed space. When the store owner, Jason Sparks, walked in, Max was ready to bolt.

"Sorry I'm late, Max. Wife had extra things on the honey-do—." He stopped mid-sentence. An Army veteran himself, Jason knew Max struggled with PTSD. But then, so did half the town of Bakersville, thanks to Cade. "You okay, Max?"

"I just need some air." He rounded the counter, rubbing his hands on the front of his thighs. "Okay if I split for a few minutes?"

"Sure, go ahead and take your lunch break. Things are bound to be slow today anyway."

"Yeah. Only a couple of folks so far."

"Max?" Jason stepped toward him and placed a hand on his shoulder. "You got this."

Not trusting himself to speak, Max nodded and headed for the door. Outside, he took several deep breaths. The icy air helped clear his head and banish the caged-in feeling. He pulled out his cell phone and called Sky.

She answered on the second ring.

"Hey. It's Max."

"Morning."

The smile in her voice chased away remnants of his anxiety. "The roads are still nasty today. How about I come by and take you to work? It's not going to get any better with temps close to freezing."

"I hate to bother you."

"It's no bother. On my way."

"Hang on. Someone's at the door."

Muffled words could be heard in the background, but he couldn't distinguish what was said.

"Hey. I'm back. That was Cade. Wanted to drive me to work so you wouldn't have to take off."

Before he could express an objection, she continued.

"I told him you were already on your way."

"Be there in ten."

Cade's audacity infuriated Max, though it shouldn't come as any surprise.

From their first meeting as sophomores in high school, they'd been at odds. Cade was the rich kid with the fine ride, quarterback of the football team, and president of the Student Council. Max was the new kid in town. He was taller, faster, and smarter, and Cade took an immediate dislike to him. Once word circulated that Max was in foster care, Cade never missed an opportunity to embarrass, humiliate, or demean him.

To this day, Max couldn't remember those years without anger.

The final crippling blow came in the form of Anna Sue Watkins.

A pretty girl from the wrong side of the tracks, she and Max became friends right away. Two outcasts seeking companionship, they were never a couple, just good friends.

Until Cade noticed them together.

He didn't act right away. He was too smooth for that. The seduction was slow and steady, and she was easy prey. Nothing Max said convinced her he wasn't the good guy he seemed.

In the end, all Max could do was sit back and watch as Cade slowly turned her against him and ultimately destroyed her world.

The week before graduation, she came to Max in hysterics. She was pregnant with Cade's child. When she broke the news to him, Cade laughed and said, "Good luck with that."

Her parents would be heartbroken. She had no one to turn to for help except Max. She begged him to talk with Cade.

Against his better judgement, he agreed to try. That conversation quickly escalated into a fist fight that took three people to end and kept Max from participating in graduation exercises.

To his credit, Max offered twice to marry her, but she refused.

Thoughts of Anna elevated his anxiety level. *Can't change the past. Let it go.*

He forced himself to remain calm and stopped behind the Taurus.

Sky hurried out before he came to a full stop and ran to the passenger side door. "Goodness it's cold." She pulled her jacket tighter and fastened the seat belt. "I really appreciate this, Max. I'm no good on icy roads."

He cranked up the heat but didn't reply until he maneuvered the big truck out of the drive. "Maddie already at Gail's?"

"Yeah. She picked her up a little while ago." The truck fish-tailed on the ice-coated road, and she grabbed the door handle.

"What time do you get off today?" Even to him, the question sounded terse. *Damn Cade anyway.*

Sky turned her head toward him, brows pinched together. "Seven. What's wrong?"

"I'll be by to take you home."

She waited a beat. "Are you mad at me about something?"

He glanced at her, saw the hurt and confusion on her face and tried to relax. "No. I'm sorry. It's not you."

"Did something happen at work?"

A jumble of thoughts raced pell-mell through his head as he considered how to answer. *She'll find out sooner or later anyway.* He kept his eyes on the road. "Cade."

She sat up straighter and turned toward him, voice edged with resentment. "I didn't ask him to come over today if that's what you're thinking."

He stopped for a red light and exhaled a noisy breath. "That's not it."

"Then what?"

The light changed, and he eased through the intersection, wheels slipping a little before they gained traction. "We went to school together."

"I gathered that."

"And he hates my guts."

"Why?"

Max pulled up behind the diner but didn't kill the engine. "I moved here with my foster parents at the end of my sophomore year. Fred, my foster father, lost his job, so we lived with his parents till he went to work for the county." He kept his tone flat and unemotional. "For whatever reason, Cade hated me on sight and did all he could to make my life a living hell." He looked at Sky, jaw clenched so tight it hurt. "I was smarter and a little taller than him but skinny as a rail. He was the quarterback and worked out all the time."

"And you were an easy target."

"Basically." He shifted in his seat, the painful memories surrounding him. "He had to be the best. King of the hill." He shrugged. "He saw me as a threat to that status."

"I'm guessing it all came to a head at some point?"

"Senior year."

"What happened?"

He leaned back, head against the neck rest, eyes closed.

"Max?" She touched his arm. "We don't have to talk about this now. I can see that whatever it was, it's still painful for you."

He turned his head toward her. "I'm not trying to tend to your business, Sky, but don't let Cade's Mr. Nice Guy façade fool you. He doesn't like being told no, so be careful around him."

"I will." She gathered up her purse and unfastened the seat belt. "Thanks for playing taxi. I don't think things will be very busy tonight, so I should be able to leave right at seven if not before."

"Hold on." He exited the truck and came around to help her out. "I'll walk you in. The ground is slippery."

She stood beside him and linked her arm with his, her breath forming a misty cloud around her mouth. "Ever the gentleman," she said with a smile, then squealed lightly when her foot slipped on the ice. "Whoa!"

He steadied her as they walked to the shelter of the diner's rusted awning. "I'll see you about seven."

She shivered and reached for the door handle. "Thanks again. I'll see you tonight."

Before he could say anything, she rushed inside.

He drove to the other side of the square and stopped in front of *The Sassy Sash.*

That coat in the window should fit Sky perfectly.

CHAPTER
Fifteen

Sky pushed the register drawer closed, eyes drifting to the window. The earlier sleet had changed to light snow, which fell sporadically through the morning, coating the ground in small, white patches. The temperature hovered around the freezing mark, but a frigid north wind made it feel much colder. Only four customers braved the inclement weather since lunch. Things would worsen overnight with the passage of a second fast-moving arctic blast. Come Monday, temps would be back in the forties. *Gotta love East Texas weather…two days of winter followed by three days of fall.*

She rejoined her boss at the long lunch counter, where they enjoyed a cup of coffee. "Where were we?"

Ruby winked over the rim of her cup. "You were telling me about your date with Max yesterday."

"It was really nice. I haven't had a real Thanksgiving dinner in years. And John seemed to enjoy it as well."

"John? Big John?"

"Uh-huh. It was a spur of the moment idea to invite him."

"That was so nice of you to include him. I wish I had thought of that. Some friend I am."

A shrug dismissed the gesture. "It was one of those things

that just happened. I asked, and he accepted. Besides, he and Max seem to be good friends, and Maddie adores him." She resisted the urge to bounce up and down with happiness. "She thinks he looks like Santa Claus."

"Actually, they talked him into playing Santa in the Christmas festival at the community center this year. Our go-to guy had knee surgery and is down for a while."

Sky laughed. "Don't know that I've ever seen a six-five Santa."

"I know. But he'll be great," said Ruby. "He loves helping people." She used a napkin to rub at some unseen spot on the counter, features softened by a smile. "I'm glad you and Max are seeing each other."

She started to say they weren't exactly a couple but changed her mind. After all, he was her male companion. That thought produced a smile. "Me, too. He's a good guy. Have you known him long?"

She shook her head. "He was a few years behind me in school. Didn't have much contact with him back in the day. Heard he went into the Marines right after graduation. Didn't see him again until he moved back earlier this year." She paused, eyes focused on her cup. "You know he was injured in combat, right?"

"Yeah. He told me."

"And has this PTSD stuff?"

"He told me that as well."

Ruby sighed and sat up straighter. "Good. Cade tries to make a big deal out of it, but I haven't seen or heard of him doing anything out of the ordinary."

"What's with them, anyway?"

"You mean besides Cade being a narcissistic jerk?"

Sky snorted.

"Like I said, they were behind me in school, so I didn't have much contact with either of them. After I graduated, I hit the road for a while."

Sky watched her expression shift from happy to sad and wondered what she held inside.

"Anyway, by the time I came back, Max was long gone, and Cade was busy trying to see how many notches he could add to his bedpost." She emptied her cup and stood. "Rumor had it there was a fight. A bad one. Cade got the worst of it. I never asked, so I don't know the details."

Sky picked up both mugs and placed them in the bus tub behind the counter. "Well, whatever happened, there is still bad blood between them."

Ruby placed her hand on Sky's arm. "I'm glad you have someone decent in your life, Sky. You deserve some happiness." She let her hand drop and turned toward the back. "Don't waste time on Cade. I know a good man when I see one. And Max is a good one."

Before Sky could reply, Ruby slipped through the swinging door to the kitchen, leaving Sky more curious than ever.

Max sat at the kitchen table, rewiring a lamp for Gail, when his phone rang.

"Hey. It's me."

The unusual tenseness in Sky's voice immediately sent Max on full alert. "Is everything all right?"

"Yeah. Ruby just said she's closing early because of the weather, so you can pick me up at any time."

He glanced at the clock on the wall. Five-fifteen. "I can come now. Mason closed early as well."

"Great. I'll see you shortly."

The unwrapped box mocked him as he started his truck. *How am I going to give this to her without pissing her off or embarrassing her?*

Instead of pulling around back, he parked out front and went inside. The place was empty save one guy at the counter, who turned at his entrance.

"Hey, Max," said the man, "how's it going?"

"Good, Billy Ray. You?"

"Bout to freeze my tail off. Haven't had this cold a winter in a while."

Sky came out of the kitchen carrying a plate of food, which she placed in front of the man at the counter. "Here you go, Bill. Anything else?"

"I'm good. Thanks."

Sky turned to Max, and his heart did that funny somersault thing it tended to do when she was around.

"Almost done. Just give me a minute."

A short time later, they exited the building into a blast of frigid air.

"Oh, my goodness, it's cold," said Sky as she dashed toward his truck, clutching her thin jacket against her body.

"Wind chill is in the teens." Max started the engine and cranked the heat up to high. "That better?"

Sky nodded, arms still folded across her middle.

"Do we need to pick up Maddie?"

"If you don't mind." Sky looked at the package between them but offered no comment.

Twenty minutes later, he sat at Sky's kitchen table while

she put on a pot of coffee. "We have plenty of leftovers from yesterday," she said. "Won't take long to pull them out if you'd like to stay for supper."

"Don't go to any trouble. I'll have whatever you're having."

He fingered the box at his feet and Maddie reacted.

"What's in the box, Max?"

"A surprise." He swallowed hard. "For your mom."

Sky turned toward him, face registering disbelief. "For me?"

"Oh goodie!" Maddie clapped her hands together and bobbed up and down. "Mama hasn't had a surprise before."

"It's not a big deal. A little thank-you for yesterday. Just something I thought you could use." He cleared his throat and placed the box on the table. Now that it was time to give it to her, he second guessed his impulsive action. Would she be offended? Would she get mad? Would she even like it?

"Hurry, Mama! Open it."

"Um, maybe you should open it before supper. You might decide you don't want me to hang around after all."

Sky stared a beat then smiled. "I don't see that happening." She wiped her hands on a towel and sat down. "You didn't need to do anything for me, Max. You bought all the food, I just put it together."

As she talked, Max noted she carefully opened the box, almost like she wanted to extend the feeling of anticipation about what lay hidden inside.

"And it took you two days to do it, so yeah, I owe you one."

Finally, she eased the pink tissue aside and gasped at the contents.

"I hope you don't mind. I thought …"

She pulled the faux suede trench coat from the box and

stood. "Oh Max, you shouldn't have. This is too much." She held the coat in front of her, running her hand over the smooth dove-grey fabric, slipping her fingers inside to stroke the soft lining.

"Wow, Mama. That will look really pretty on you."

"The lining comes out for when it's not so cold. And the hood comes off, too." Her obvious joy brought a lump to his throat. "There's a neck scarf in there, too."

"I saw this in the window at *The Sassy Sash*," Sky said softly.

She met his gaze, and the pleasure he read in her face made him feel ten feet tall.

"I hope I haven't offended you or embarrassed you, I just…"

"It's perfect. Thank you."

Max stood and helped her slip the coat on. "The lady in the store said this would fit."

"Jeannie comes in the diner all the time." She ran her hands over the coat again. "It's so soft. And warm, too."

"I'm glad you like it."

"I love it, Max. Thank you." She hesitated. "But it's too much. I know what it cost."

It was his turn to be embarrassed. "It's no big deal."

"It is to me."

"Max gave you a really good surprise, didn't he, Mama?"

"Yes. He did."

Maddie faced him, azure eyes sparkling with happiness. "That's the best surprise, ever, Max. Mama really needed a new coat, but we haven't been to the Goodwill yet. Now she doesn't have to go."

Max saw the red flush on Sky's face and changed the

subject. "How about we get out of the way and let your mom finish getting supper ready?"

"Do you like puzzles, Max? I love puzzles. I have one in the living room I'm working on." She grabbed his hand. "Come on. I'll show you."

Half an hour later, Sky called them back to the kitchen.

Leftovers from the scrumptious meal yesterday were on the table. She could have served him cardboard covered in ketchup, and he would have happily consumed every bite. "I didn't mean for you to cook for me. Again."

Her light laugh lifted his spirits.

"Warming up leftovers is hardly cooking."

"Max is really good at puzzles, Mom." Maddie slurped her milk. "He got all the end pieces on the new one Miss Gail gave me."

Dinner was an amiable affair, filled with laughter and Maddie's usual chatter. Afterwards, the three of them worked on the puzzle again, racing to see who could find the most pieces.

Maddie protested, of course, when Sky said it was bedtime but obeyed her mother's directive.

Sky returned from tucking her daughter in and resumed her seat beside Max on the couch. "Would you like more coffee?"

"I'm good, thanks." Suddenly nervous, he dug for something to talk about. "Um, I heard you were thinking about getting back into nursing."

Her surprised expression suggested maybe that was not a good topic to start on.

"I'm sorry. It's none of my business."

She visibly relaxed and leaned back. "Doc wants me to go

to work for her at the clinic while we work at getting my license reinstated."

"You don't seem too excited about the prospect."

"It's not that. I'd love to get back into nursing."

"Then what's the problem?"

She rested her head on the back of the couch, eyes focused upward. "I don't know what all's involved in the process. I'm sure I'll probably have to take some CEUs, maybe even some kind of refresher classes. The closest place is Tyler or maybe Texarkana. Will have to check and see. Both are well over an hour away."

"What about online classes?"

She shrugged. "I don't know. Doc said she'd look into it and let me know what she finds." Voice lowered, she turned her head toward him. "What if I can't do it?"

"You can do anything you set your mind to," Max said firmly. "Just look at what you've done up to now."

She nibbled on her lower lip. "I really want to do this, Max. But what if I can't? What if I've waited too long?"

One finger under her chin, he tilted her face up. "I repeat. You can do whatever you put your mind to."

"How can you be so sure? You hardly know me."

He caressed her chin with his finger. "I know the stuff that matters. You're smart. Beautiful. A wonderful mom. And a great human being." He paused, his thumb caressing her lower lip. "And I'd like very much to kiss you right now."

Her throat moved as she swallowed, followed by a light shiver. "I'd like that."

His lips feather-touched hers with tantalizing persuasion, once, twice, then he gently covered her mouth.

Shock waves of desire coursed through his body. Urgent

and exploratory, he deepened the kiss, smothering her lips with commanding mastery. She tasted of coffee and pumpkin pie, and he couldn't get enough.

Her arms slid up his chest and around his neck, pulling him closer and returning his kiss with reckless abandon.

When her tongue slid into his mouth and touched his, he couldn't stop the explosion of need it elicited. Raising his mouth from hers, he gazed into her eyes. "You're very special to me, Sky. I don't want to do something to mess that up."

"You're special to me, too." Her hands slid down his chest, one resting over his pounding heart. "I…haven't been with anyone since, well, a long time. Haven't wanted to."

He waited, sensing there was more she wanted to say.

"Until you."

His heart stuttered as blood pounded through his veins, the implications of her statement reaching his soul. "I feel the same way," he whispered. "I think we have something special going on here."

"Me, too."

Neither spoke as they gazed into each other's eyes, the connection almost tangible.

Max finally broke the spell when he gently pulled away. "I better go. Maddie might…"

She tugged on his shirt, her gaze soft as a caress. Her eyes fluttered shut, then opened. "Could you…we …just sit a while?"

He eased back on the couch, the meaning in her words crystal clear.

She needed *him*. Wanted *him*.

He gathered her into his arms. Her head fit perfectly into the hollow between his shoulder and neck, and her warm breath floated out on a sigh of pleasure as slender fingers lightly stroked his chest.

His heart rate eased into a steady rhythm as it swelled with a sense of fulfilment and completeness that astonished him.

He'd found it. The thing missing from his meager existence. The thing he desperately wanted but never expected to find.

Love.

At last.

Did she…could she…love him in return?

He pulled her tighter against him and buried his face in her hair.

I love this woman.

Her arm slid across his chest, feet curled up beside her. "Max…"

Her soft entreaty branded him forever. He was hers. Heart and soul.

He lifted her chin with one finger, memorizing every nuance of the moment, composing an image he would take to his grave. "Sky…"

He kissed the tip of her nose, then her eyes, and, finally, satisfyingly, those tempting lips.

A shudder passed through her as she melted against him, a dreamy intimacy encasing them while the kiss went on forever.

At last, he pulled back, his gaze searching hers.

Something intense flared between them.

No words were needed as their hearts spoke to each other.

Regardless of what happened tomorrow or next week or

next year, he had this one moment in time. A moment where hope and love and promise flourished, and he would cherish it as long as he lived.

They drifted off to sleep, her head on his shoulder—his heart in her hands.

CHAPTER
Sixteen

The next week passed in a blur. Remnants of the icy week-end faded more each day as the sun rose in a cloudless sky, though the nights remained frosty. Shaded areas still harbored patches of white, but the roads were clear.

Though she missed being chauffeured around by Max, Sky was thankful for the better weather. Diner customers came and went in a steady flow, making the time fly by.

Since her shift didn't start until eleven, Max joined her for coffee each morning before he left for work and even offered to take Maddie to school a couple of times, which the child loved. Most evenings, she got off by six-thirty, and the three of them enjoyed a late supper.

The ease with which they fell into this new routine made her long for something more. Each time she saw him, her heart mushroomed with emotions she thought long dead, the sense of rightness staggering in its intensity. The night they fell asleep cuddled on the couch, the ecstasy of being held against his strong body remained a cherished memory. When he kissed her goodbye the next morning, an immense void fol-lowed his absence.

There was something special about him, something she

sensed from the beginning. The thought barely crossed her mind before another followed that rocked her to the core.

She loved him.

The acknowledgement both thrilled and terrified her and made for a sleepless night last night as she worried about what happens next. Did he feel the same way? Instinct said yes, but he'd never spoken the words. Maybe she should go first, let him know how she felt.

Lost in a world of possibility, she licked parched lips, unable to stifle a timid smile of hope. *Does he love me, too?*

"Hey, Sky?" The call came from a customer at the other end of the counter. "Can I get a refill on my coffee, please?"

Embarrassed to be caught in her daydream, she hurriedly filled Billy Ray's cup. "I'm so sorry, Bill. Don't know where my mind is today."

"Judging by that smile on your face, I bet I know."

His suggestive wink brought a rush of heat to her face.

"Sorry. Didn't mean to embarrass you." His smile said otherwise. A jailer at the sheriff's office, he was known about town as a notorious flirt and loved to tease.

"Of course not, Bill."

He grinned and sipped his coffee. "You and Max going to the parade tonight?"

In the way of small towns, everyone quickly accepted them as a couple, so she wasn't surprised by his question. "Can't miss the Christmas Parade." She returned the pot to the burner. "He and Maddie will be here about five-thirty."

"Well." That good-ole-boy smile had charmed many a lady. "I tried. Guess I'll just be all alone tonight."

"Yeah. Right." She removed his empty plate and placed it in the bus tub. "We both know that's a crock."

A full-hearted, throaty laugh echoed around the room. "You wound me, Sky." He finished his coffee and placed some bills on the counter. "Gotta get back to work. Keep the change. Merry Christmas."

Before she could argue about the amount of change, he was gone.

The bell above the door announced another customer, and Sky turned to see Cooper Delaney, the local sheriff, headed toward her. "Afternoon, Sky," he drawled as he passed her a large, brown envelope. "Doc asked me to drop this by for you." He touched the brim of his dark Stetson hat. "Said to ask that you give her a call once you've had a chance to look it over."

She took the package and smiled. "Thanks, Sheriff."

He glanced around the half-empty room. "I hope you decide to take Doc up on the offer, Sky. She could really use someone like you."

Unsure how to respond, she simply nodded and stuck to business. "Can I get you anything?"

"Large coffee to go, please. Time for rounds."

Coffee in hand, he headed out as Cade Jackson walked in.

She suppressed a groan as she took the envelope to the back and placed it with her stuff. She'd look at it later when she got home.

Cade occupied his usual spot at the counter when she returned. "Need a menu, Cade?"

"You mean you don't know what I want by now?"

His lewd wink had her clenching one fist for control. "Do you need a menu?" she repeated.

His lips thinned, and he sighed. "Give me the chicken fried steak dinner and coffee. Please."

She turned the order in and placed his drink in front of him, all in silence.

"Aw come on, Skylar," he grumbled, "how much longer are you gonna give me the cold shoulder?"

Until you get the message and leave me alone.

"I said I was sorry."

She was saved from answering when Ruby came out from the kitchen with a pie in each hand. "Sky? Can you put these in the pie case, please?"

"Hey, Ruby?" called a man from the back booth, "Is one of those a pecan pie?"

"It is for a fact, Jerry."

He got up and came to the counter. "Can I buy the whole thing? My Julie loves it."

"Of course. I'll box it up for you."

Cade, thank goodness, busied himself chatting with other customers.

The bell above the door signaled another customer, and Sky turned to see who entered. A young man, maybe late teens, wearing a leather jacket and dark toboggan, glanced around as though looking for someone. It was the third time he'd been in today. The two previous times, he had simply looked around and left.

"Afternoon," she called, "Just sit wherever you like."

He scanned the room, then slumped into a booth near the back facing the door.

Sky didn't recognize him as a local, though something about him looked familiar. She carried the requisite water and menu and smiled. "What can I get for you to drink?"

He didn't take his eyes off the front door. "Just coffee."

"Anything to go with it?"

"I said just coffee," he snapped.

His eyes darted to her then back to the door as the tops of his ears turned bright red. "Please," he added, his tone apologetic.

"You need cream with it?"

He took a deep breath as though calming himself. "Yes, please."

He didn't look up when she placed his drink on the table. Again, something about him looked familiar, and she hesitated. "Can I get you anything else?"

"No. Um, thanks."

"You expecting someone?" she asked.

He stiffened, and hooded, insolent eyes glanced her way then back to the door.

"I saw you earlier, and it seemed like you were looking for someone."

His shoulders slumped slightly, and he shook his head.

For reasons she could not discern, the young man pulled at her. "Well, I know pretty much everyone in town, so if I can help, just ask."

Coffee splashed from his cup when he set it down a little too hard. "Um, well, I'm...looking for someone. A man. His name is Max Logan." His low-pitched voice cracked, then edged higher, and a bright flush covered his face when he glanced up. "Do you know him?"

"As a matter of fact, I do." She smiled, hoping to put him at ease since he was obviously very nervous. She glanced at the big clock on the back wall. "He should be here shortly."

He sat up straighter, pulled the cap from his head and placed it on the seat beside him. He ran one hand over his disheveled hair, the other gripped the handle of his mug. "Thanks."

Sky started to say something else, but his attention was totally focused on the front as Max and Maddie strode in.

"It's almost time for the parade," squealed Maddie as she ran up to Sky. "Aren't you excited?"

Sky laughed and guided her toward the counter. "I think you're excited enough for all of us." She helped her to a stool on the end and removed her coat. "Would you like some hot chocolate?"

"Yes, please."

She turned to Max. "The young man in the back booth is waiting for you."

He looked toward the boy. "What does he want with me?"

"He didn't say. He's been in a couple of times today."

"Okay. I'll talk to him." He looked at his watch. "Parade starts at eighteen thirty. We need to find our spot pretty soon."

"That means six-thirty," chirped Maddie, "in soldier talk."

"I'll bring your coffee over there."

He nodded and started toward the stranger.

Sky got Max's coffee and headed back toward the booth where they sat. She could only see Max's expression from this angle, and it was dark. *Oh dear. Something's wrong.* She was about to place Max's cup on the table when the young man's voice stopped her.

"Answer me. Are you my dad?"

CHAPTER
Seventeen

Max heard Sky's gasp but didn't take his eyes off the boy. He had no idea who the kid was but didn't for a moment believe he was his father.

"Answer me, dammit," snapped the young man.

Sky placed the mug on the table, splashing hot liquid on her hand as she hurriedly took a step back.

Max looked up and met her shocked expression. Eyes wide, she swallowed hard, one hand pressing against her throat.

"No," he snapped, not looking at the boy, "I am not."

Sky turned and rushed back to the kitchen.

Dammit!

He took a deep breath and refocused on the boy. "Who are you, and what makes you think I'm your father?"

The kid's hands shook as he pushed his cup toward the center of the table. "Logan Watkins. My mother is Anna Watkins. I found your name in some of her stuff."

In a matter of seconds, things crystallized in his mind. "How old are you?"

"I'll be eighteen next week."

Shit. He'd be the right age.

The boy looked toward the counter where Maddie sat talking with Sky. "I guess she's your wife, and the kid is your daughter."

The coldness in his voice didn't disguise the hurt. Max kept a neutral tone. "I'll ask again…what makes you think I'm your father?"

Logan shifted in his seat, eyes not quite meeting Max's steady gaze. "We were moving crap from the attic, and I found a box of stuff I'd never seen." He paused, then pulled a wrinkled photo from his shirt pocket and placed it on the table. "This was in there."

Max clenched his jaw when he saw the young couple all dressed up for the prom. On the back, in neat block letters she had written, "*Max Logan and me at the prom. I'll always love my knight in shining armor.*"

Suddenly, Max was transported back to that night so many years ago. Anna Sue, devastated by Cade's sudden indifference, didn't know at the time she carried his child. Max had no plans for the prom but because she was so unhappy, insisted they go together.

In true Cade fashion, he went out of his way to hurt and embarrass them both. It was all Max could do to remain calm.

"You're my knight in shining armor, Max," she'd told him at one point. "And I'll always love you for that. But let it go. Cade's not worth it."

Things went to hell shortly thereafter when she discovered she was pregnant, and Cade blew her off.

"Well?"

Logan's sharp question brought Max back to the present. "Well what?"

He nodded toward the photo Max held. "Explain that."

"It's pretty obvious. We went to prom together."

"And?"

"And nothing."

Logan's quick intake of breath and narrowed eyes warned of a rising temper.

"What did she tell you?"

Body tense, his words were clipped and hard. "That you were dead."

He couldn't imagine why she would say such a thing. "She told you I was dead? That makes no sense."

The tips of his ears turned bright red. "Well, she told me my father was dead. But then I found those letters and that picture, so I got on the internet and…"

Max tried to be gentle, but his patience wore thin. It was obvious the boy had little concrete information on which to base his absurd assumption. He was alternately angry with Anna for putting him in this position and sorry for the boy caught in the middle. Max hated to be the bearer of bad news, but he had no intention of feeding the kid's wild story. He sat back in the booth and tried to think of what to do next. "What exactly did she tell you about me? Me, specifically."

The downcast expression told Max all he needed to know. "You haven't talked with her about this, have you?"

Defensive, he sat up straight, hands fisted on the table. "She won't tell me shit. And your name was all over the place."

Max shook his head, emotions in turmoil. "And you assumed that meant something without having all the facts."

The kid's face got redder, and his jaw clamped tight. But he didn't lower his gaze.

"Where's your mother, Logan? Does she know where you are?"

This time his gaze dropped to the table, and he shifted in the seat. "Home…I'm supposed to be hunting with friends."

A tense silence ensued. *Well shit. What now? Best not to give him any false hope.* "For the record, Logan," said Max firmly, "I'm not your father." He pushed back in the seat and took a breath. "Where are you staying?"

One shoulder rose then fell. "My truck."

Shaken, Max pulled out his cell phone and passed it over. "Call her," he snapped. "When she gets here, we'll talk."

"I deserve to know the truth!" His exclamation had customers looking their way.

"Keep your voice down," said Max firmly. "Call your mother."

He stood and stalked toward the counter where Maddie sat with a mug of hot chocolate. Sky stood behind the counter, expression guarded.

Cade made no effort to hide the fact that he had listened in on their conversation.

"Something's come up," said Max. "I'll have to pass on the parade."

Maddie looked past him to where Logan sat talking on the phone. "Who's that?"

"A friend." He looked at Sky. "I'll come over later."

Sky nodded. "Not sure what time we'll get home," she said softly. "Maddie wants to talk to Santa, and I'm sure the line will be long."

"Who's the kid, Logan?"

Max ignored Cade's question. "No problem." He looked at Maddie. "I'm sorry I can't watch the parade with you guys or take you to see Santa tonight. I might can make it over there later. I'm not sure."

Maddie heaved a sigh. "That's okay, Max." She looked over his shoulder. "Maybe your friend could go with us."

"Another time, Tink."

Logan walked up and handed the phone to Max. "She's pi—uh, mad, and can't be here till Sunday afternoon."

"Hi. My name's Maddie. What's yours?"

Caught in the middle of a bad dream, Max waited.

"Logan," the kid said at last.

"Logan, huh?" quipped Cade. "Interesting."

Max took the boy by the elbow. "Come on."

Logan had just exited the diner when Max overheard Cade's vindictive declaration. "Well, looks like all those rumors about him knocking up the Watkins girl are true."

Sky's hands shook as she gathered her things from the back, Cade's statement ringing in her ears. Worst of all, Maddie heard what he said. There was no doubt in her mind that questions would abound. Too bad she'd have no answers.

"Y'all have fun at the parade," said Ruby when Sky walked back out front. "Eat a candy cane for me, Maddie."

"I will, Miss Ruby." She looked at Sky. "I wish Max was going with us."

"Yeah. Me, too."

"He was gonna take me to see Santa."

Before Sky could reply, Cade broke in. "I'd be happy to take you to see Santa, kiddo." He looked at Sky and winked. "I have a few things I want to ask him for, too."

"Thank you, Cade but I think we can manage."

"Nonsense." He got up and dropped some money on the counter. "Parades are more fun when they are shared."

Maddie's expression was dour when she looked at Sky, but thankfully, she didn't say anything.

He helped Sky with her coat. "Nice coat. That color looks good on you."

"Max gave it to her," said Maddie firmly. "He's her—"

"Put your coat on Maddie, or we'll be late."

The child's questioning glance brought a rush of heat to Sky's face.

It wasn't easy evading Cade's attempts to join them, but she did and selected a spot on the corner near the drug store to watch. Maddie's excitement was contagious, and she soon found herself enjoying the festive atmosphere as they laughed and grabbed for candy canes being tossed from those riding floats. Several folks asked about Max, and she answered with a simple 'something came up.'

"Hey, kid," said Cade, "I'll take you to see Santa when this shindig is over."

Sky jumped. She didn't know he was behind her.

Maddie ignored him.

"Thank you for the offer, Cade," snapped Sky. "But I've got it covered."

"Aw come on, Skylar," he said a little too loud, "I'm just trying to help." He tapped Maddie on the shoulder as the parade came to an end. "What do you say, kid? Want me to take you to see the big guy?"

Maddie turned, and Sky suppressed a groan. *Oh, dear. I know that look.*

Hands planted on tiny hips, Maddie glared at Cade. "My name is not kid. If you can't call me by my name, then don't talk to me at all." She blew out a long breath and looked at Sky. "Can we go now?"

Face scarlet, Cade straightened. "You need to teach her some manners," he barked. "Kids shouldn't talk like that to adults."

Patience exhausted, Sky took a step toward him, nostrils flared in anger. The man had some nerve. "And adults should know when their company isn't wanted." She grabbed Maddie's hand. "And her manners are just fine."

Still seething, she joined the throng of people headed toward the community center where the festival continued. The room was filled with booths selling everything from soaps to toys to clothes and all kinds of artsy-craftsy things. The room was filled with the mouthwatering aroma of popcorn and caramel apples mixed with a multitude of other smells designed to tempt the room full of shoppers. Christmas music blared over the din of folks anxious to embrace the holiday atmosphere.

Maddie's best friend, Bonnie, met them at the door. "Come on, Maddie! We have to get in line now before it gets too long."

"Can I go, Mama?"

"Okay. I'll be right there." She looked around the room, trying to decide which aisle to explore first.

"Guess now you see I was right."

Cade's statement made her jerk around. She didn't know he was back there. *Oh, for heaven's sake. He's worse than a pesky mosquito.*

"Loser Logan is just that." He hitched up his pants and looked around the room. "How 'bout we find a quiet spot to talk."

The last person she wanted any kind of conversation with was Cade Jackson. "I don't think so, Cade. I need to keep an eye on Maddie." She turned to follow her daughter, but he grabbed her arm.

"Come on now, Skylar. Don't be like that. I just want us to be friends." His smile bordered on a leer. "Good friends."

It was like he never heard a word she said. She pulled her arm free and didn't answer as she turned to walk away.

"The kid even looks like him, don't you think?"

Initial thoughts of how the young man looked familiar slowed her steps.

Cade sneered. "He tell you about Anna Sue? His high school sweetheart? How he left town after graduation to keep from manning up?"

"I don't believe you."

He leaned in closer, his heavy cologne pervaded her senses to the point she wanted to hold her breath to shut it out. Or maybe it was his hurtful words she wanted to avoid.

"The proof walked in the diner tonight." He paused, smug face radiating superiority. "You can't deny what you saw."

She whirled and looked at him, anger, hurt, and resentment rolling into one huge knot in her stomach. She had no way of knowing how much was truth and how much was Cade's version of it, but she didn't think for a minute Max would have deserted someone like that.

"You're right. I can't deny what I saw. A young man with brown hair and hazel eyes." She brought one finger up to her chin as though in thought. "Come to think of it, you have brownish hair and hazel eyes, too."

Cade stiffened and jerked back. His face turned dark red, thin lips pulled into a tight line.

He opened his mouth, and Sky held up her hand, palm out.

"Not another word," she hissed. "Not one." Body tense with anger, she stalked off. The crowded walkway disguised her faltering steps as she headed to the back of the hall. Her lungs constricted, and each labored breath became a chore.

"Ms. Ward," came a familiar voice, "are you all right?"

Sky blinked rapidly and focused on the face of her landlord. "Mr. Jenkins. Um, yes...I...think I'm too warm is all."

"Frankly, I think they could turn down the heat a bit with all these folks in here." His kindly face showed concern. "Maybe you should take off your coat?"

"What? Oh. Yes. Of course."

He held out his hand for her bag as she removed the coat.

Folding it over her arm, she took her bag and smiled. "That's better. Thank you."

"My pleasure." Keen eyes focused on her face. "Are you sure you're okay? Perhaps I could get you some punch or something?"

"Oh no, thank you. I'm fine. Just got a little too warm I think." She hugged the coat against her body, still tense with anger. "I best go find Maddie. Thank you again for your concern, Mr. Jenkins."

She hurried off before he could say anything else.

The rest of the evening passed in a blur of mixed emotions. The atmosphere was festive, the throng of people excited and happy, but the sense of being alone in a crowd rolled over her in waves. Ever since Max had come into her life, those feelings had subsided, and she could handle watching happy couples and families doing what families did.

Not tonight.

Without Max at her side, all the old feelings of isolation came rushing back, and she struggled to keep the melancholy at bay as family groups surged around her, their laughter and lively conversations like a dagger in her heart, reinforcing the fact that she was alone. Always alone.

The clincher came when she caught a brief glimpse of unbridled sadness in Maddie's eyes as she watched a man place his child on Santa's knee, face beaming with pride, while the smiling woman beside him snapped pictures.

It took a monumental effort to swallow the lump in her throat. *I will not cry. Not now. Not tonight.*

As much as Maddie might want to be that family, Sky wanted it more. She longed for someone to come home to. Someone to be there for her when nights like this came along. Someone to hold her close in the darkness, whisper words of love in her ear, kiss away the sadness that ate away at her soul.

Someone to make love to her.

She wanted Max.

But was that even possible now? The young man who showed up tonight gave her a glimpse of the part of him she knew nothing about. A past that obviously included the possibility of him being involved with someone and maybe even producing a child. She didn't readily see a family resemblance, but she knew that didn't necessarily mean anything.

Doubts and questions bounced around her head like BBs in a bathtub. The bottom line, though, was one question. Did she believe Max's assertion that he was not the boy's father? The answer was a simple yes, but the complications presented by the situation were anything but.

She forced a smile and engaged in conversations with townspeople as Maddie pulled her from one vendor to another, her mood decidedly upbeat after a short visit with Santa. When Sky asked what she wished for, Maddie smiled and said, "I can't tell you or it won't come true."

Dinner consisted of chili dogs from the local VFW booth and chocolate pie from the Kiwanis.

By nine o'clock, Sky was physically and emotionally exhausted. The food she'd eaten earlier sat like a stone in the pit of her stomach.

"Do we have to go now?" groused Maddie, "I don't have school tomorrow."

"It's late, and I'm tired." The statement came out shorter than intended, and Sky sighed. "It's been a long day, Munchkin. The festival goes all weekend. Maybe we can come back on Sunday since I don't have to work."

"Maybe Max can bring me back tomorrow."

"He has to work."

"Oh yeah. I forgot."

Maddie grew silent, mouth moving from side to side, a sure sign she had something on her mind. They were almost home when she found out what.

"What does knocked up mean?"

Oh crap.

CHAPTER
Eighteen

ike a moth to a flame, the welcoming light from Sky's
kitchen window pulled Max forward. As crappy nights go,
this one pretty much topped the heap. Max had no experience in dealing with kids in general and certainly not resentful
teenagers. It took a lengthy call to Dr. Bellamy to come up with
a plan, which took almost three hours to work through. In the
end, Logan more or less accepted Max was not his father, but
nothing diminished the truckload of anger the kid harbored
toward him and his mother.

Max certainly understood the resentment. He suppressed
a bit himself, but he'd deal with it when the time came.

Right now, he needed to talk to Sky.

He drew in a lungful of cold air, ignoring the gooseflesh
on his bare arms. He should have donned a jacket before step-
ping outside, but his need to see her overshadowed common
sense.

Knots of anxiety filled his belly as he stood outside the
door. Would she understand? Would she believe him? Would
she send him away?

And what about Maddie? He hated disappointing her almost as much he hated the questions he now had to answer.

He thought the past would stay buried in time. Obviously, that was just wishful thinking.

Embrace the suck, Marine. Persevere. Adapt. Overcome.

He rapped lightly on the door, then stuffed both hands in his pockets as a blast of cold air blew through the drive.

"Hey," she said softly as she opened the door.

"I'm sorry. I know it's late, but…"

She motioned him inside. "Come in. It's freezing out there."

Suddenly, anxiety threatened to overwhelm him, and he stopped in front of the stove. His breath came in short pants, and he forced himself to breathe deeply. *Persevere. Adapt. Overcome.* He silently repeated the mantra he had learned in the Corps. *Persevere. Adapt. Overcome.*

He flinched at the light touch of her hand on his arm.

"It's all right, Max. I'm here. You're okay."

The calmness in her voice and the gentleness of her touch soothed him. He closed his eyes and straightened. A deep breath brought with it the lemony smell of her shampoo and a light, floral scent uniquely hers. *Please, God. Let her understand.*

"Are we…" he mumbled. "Are we okay?"

She rubbed one hand over his forearm, the other rested against his lower back. "Yes. We are."

The soft utterance of three little words filled him with a sense of relief so intense, his thoughts scrambled, and he couldn't formulate a single word in response. He swallowed twice before he could turn and face her, hands still in his pockets. "I'm not Logan's father."

"I know," she offered. "You would never sluff off that kind of responsibility."

He could barely breathe. "I heard what Cade said when I walked out."

She gave a dismissive shrug. "Yeah, well, he's a jerk, and I don't believe anything he says."

He wanted to touch her, let her goodness and warmth take away the pall that went to his soul, but he didn't move. "I was afraid…"

"You thought I'd take that creep's word for something like this?"

He flinched at the hurt registering loud and clear in her voice.

"Without talking to you first?"

"I'm sorry." He stepped back and raked both hands through his hair as he paced in front of the stove. "I'm just not used to anyone…"

She walked over and placed both hands on his chest, her eyes clear and bright, filled with compassion and understanding…and something else that made his pulse jump.

He wondered if she knew the power she held over him.

"You're a good man, Max. I believe in *you*."

This time, he groaned and gave in to the urge to pull her tight against him, unable to speak the words filling his heart.

She stepped into his embrace without hesitation and slid her arms around his waist. Her uneven breath against his chest accelerated his already racing heart to the point he thought it might burst from the exertion. Her soft curves molded to the contours of his body as her arms tightened around his waist.

This was right. This was real.

I'm whole again.

Sky held Max tighter, her breath coming in rapid puffs. A few minutes ago, she had stood at the sink, coffee pot in one hand, tea kettle in the other, the sense of being alone in the world suffocating in its intensity. Now, in his arms, all the sadness fell away, and she felt complete, like putting the last piece of a complicated puzzle in its place.

She was whole.

Sky luxuriated in the tightly controlled passion she sensed in him. The tenderness of his embrace was so male, so bracing; breath lodged in her lungs, and her senses spun. Blood coursed through her veins like a raging river.

She heard the drumming of his heart against her ear as it raced, then matched her own erratic rhythm.

Ever so slowly, beat for beat, two hearts soon beat as one as they remained locked in a tender embrace.

It was amazingly sensual.

Max backed away slightly, the smoldering flame in his eyes unmistakable.

His mouth lowered.

A tingle of anticipation made her breath hitch.

Soft as a whisper, his lips brushed across hers. Once…twice… then covered her mouth.

Slow and surprisingly gentle, the kiss solidified the fragile bond between them before his lips seared a path along her jaw, down her neck to her shoulders, and back up again. He recaptured her lips, more demanding this time.

His tongue explored the recesses of her mouth, parried with hers until desire, hot and potent, flooded her veins with liquid fire.

She matched his passion with her own, moaning softly when his lips left hers to deliver a series of slow, shivery kisses that left her weak and clinging to him for support.

His arousal pressed against her middle adding fuel to an already blazing fire.

He pulled back, eyes locked with hers, their breath coming in ragged gasps.

"God, Sky. I need you," he whispered. "I want you."

"Me, too, but…" She meant to say Maddie might hear, but speech failed her.

"…I know."

He pulled her against him again, pressing a soft kiss on her forehead as they swayed to an internal melody of contentment.

"You complete me, Sky," murmured Max.

His warm breath drifted over her ear, and her heart sang with delight.

"You make me feel whole again."

A delicious shiver raced through her. "You complete me, too."

Never had she felt more cherished. More alive. More wanted. And she gloried in the moment.

A soft moan escaped as he pulled her snugly against him.

The clock on the wall ticked away time, yet neither moved.

Max evidently felt someone needed to be the voice of reason. "One of us needs to step back." His assertion lacked any degree of finality.

She rubbed her cheek against his chest, inhaling the scent of freshly laundered cotton mixed with cardamom and spice. "I like it here just fine."

He sighed. "So do I, but it's late."

Before she could protest further, he continued. "And I still need to tell you about Logan."

As mood busters go, that was a pretty good one, and Sky took a slow step back. Immediately, his stiff posture and closed expression told her how anxious he was about the impending conversation. "How about we sit on the couch. It's more comfortable than kitchen chairs."

She pulled two mugs from the cabinet. "Coffee's done. Go sit. I'll bring it with some cookies I bought tonight."

A few minutes later, they sat side by side on the couch, coffee and cookies untouched on the end table.

Max cleared his throat. "Maddie asleep?"

"Yeah. She was beat."

"I'm sorry I messed up our plans for the evening."

She shrugged. "Things worked out. We missed you, of course, but it worked out."

He fidgeted beside her, a light flush on his cheeks. "Um, did Cade say anything else?"

Sky scoffed. "Tried to worm his way into our parade watching and offered to take Maddie to see Santa." She couldn't help but smile at the memory. "She basically told him to buzz off and not talk to her again."

For the first time all evening, he smiled. "That's my girl." The smile disappeared when he continued. "Um, I, uh, called Dr. Bellamy earlier." One hand rubbed his knee. "I'm so out of my element here. I needed some advice on how to talk to him. Logan, I mean. And to you."

"And?"

This time, he rubbed his thighs with both hands, a sure sign he was nervous.

She covered one hand with both of hers. "Whatever it is, Max, just say it. Nothing's going to change how I feel about you."

He shifted on the couch, darting a quick glance her way. "His mother is Anna Sue Watkins. We were friends in high school. Not like boyfriend and girlfriend, though. Just friends."

She nodded and waited for him to continue.

He turned his hand over and laced their fingers together. "We met our junior year and just kinda clicked. We were both on the outside, trying to find a way to fit in. It wasn't the best of times, but we survived. She helped me pass science. I helped her with math."

He took a deep breath as though steeling himself for the next words.

"She came to me the week before graduation." Muscles in his jaw worked as he ground his teeth. "I've never seen anyone so upset…she was pregnant. Couldn't face her parents."

His other hand clenched into a tight fist as he spit out words like rotten fruit. "The father denied it was his."

She squeezed his hand tighter, silently offering encouragement.

Max leaned back on the couch and closed his eyes. "I asked her to marry me."

"What happened?" she asked, careful to keep her tone neutral despite her surprise at his statement. But then, that's exactly what she would expect of an honorable man like him.

He cut his eyes toward her. "She refused. Didn't want me to suffer along with her."

A heavy silence ensued as she waited for him to continue when he was ready.

"She missed graduation. Her folks said she was sick, wouldn't let me see her. I was afraid she, well, had an abortion, though I should have known better. Anyway, things happened, and I'd had enough, so I became a Marine. We wrote for three or four months. She wanted to move to Dallas before her condition became too obvious, so I sent her what money I could." He paused. "I never heard from her again."

"Why did he come here?"

He leaned forward, elbows on his knees, hands clasped together. "Evidently, she'd told him his dad was dead. Last week, they were moving some stuff from the attic, and he found one of my letters and some pictures." He paused, then reached in his back pocket and handed her the wrinkled photograph before resuming his previous position. "A little internet search, some assumptions on his part…"

She looked at the smiling young couple in the picture, then turned it over and read the inscription. *I will always love my knight in shining armor.*

"She called me that because I looked out for her. A pretty girl from the wrong side of the tracks was an easy target for some kids. I tried to protect her, but…."

If possible, her love for him grew by the minute. Maddie was right. Max *was* a hero. Her hero. Even at an early age, he stood up for those he cared about. For what was right.

"I'm guessing she thought he loved her?"

"Yeah."

She looked at the back of the photo again, wondering why she named the boy Logan.

As though he read her mind, he spoke up. "I don't know why she named him that. Like I said, haven't talked with her in years."

When he remained silent, she asked "Do you know who his father is? Is he still alive?"

He paused, then fixed her with a steady gaze. "Please understand. It's not my story to tell."

She placed a hand on his forearm. "I do understand, Max.

I do." She hesitated, knowing what she had to say would add to his burden. But he needed to know Maddie heard Cade's crass remark and wasn't satisfied with the old you're-too-young-to-understand answer. "Max…I hate to add to your troubles, but Maddie heard what Cade said. Asked me what it meant."

He jerked his head toward her. "Dammit. This just keeps getting better." Eyes closed, he shook his head. "What did you tell her?"

"That we'd talk about it when she was older."

A sliver of a grin appeared, then vanished. "I bet she didn't like that answer."

"No, she didn't. In fact, she claimed she was smarter than some adults she could name, and I may as well tell her now."

He cleared his throat. "How do you want to handle it?"

Sky met his troubled gaze with one of her own and sighed. "I know my daughter. She has an extremely inquisitive mind and doesn't like not knowing things." She turned sideways on the sofa, curled her feet up under her, one arm on the back and faced him. "Cade is so vile, I wouldn't put it past him to spread it around town."

"You can bet on it."

The hard note in his voice told her Max fully expected it to happen.

If it hadn't already.

"I'll handle it however you want me to. If you want me to talk to Maddie, I will."

"Talk to me about what?"

CHAPTER
Nineteen

Max jumped like the boogeyman had just popped out in front of him.

"Madeline Adele!"

The child flinched.

"What have I told you about eavesdropping?"

Maddie shuffled into the room and stood at the end of the couch by Max. "I had a bad dream, and you weren't in your room."

Sky motioned the child over and pushed disheveled curls behind her ear. Max said nothing as Maddie squeezed in between them.

"Maddie," Sky began, then looked at Max. "What did you hear?"

"Not much." She turned those mesmerizing blue eyes to Max. "Are you not gonna be Mama's male companion anymore? Is that what you want to tell me?"

The pain in her words tore at him. "No. It's nothing like that." He glanced up at Sky, hoping she'd offer some clue as to how he should proceed.

"Then what is it?" She looked at her mother. "Am I in trouble about what I told Mr. Jackson?"

"No, sweetie." Sky chewed her lower lip, looked at Max. "It's...complicated."

Raw hurt glittered in soulful blue eyes as Maddie looked at him. "You're not gonna leave us, are you?"

His heart gave a painful jump. The knot in his stomach tightened, and his lungs constricted. His tongue suddenly seemed too big for his mouth, making his voice thick. Unsettled, he took a deep breath. "No, Tink. I'm not going anywhere." He paused, picking the words with great care. "Your mom told me you overheard something Mr. Jackson said."

She sniffed. "I don't like him. He's a big poopie head."

"Maddie."

At Sky's soft rebuke, the child cut her eyes toward her mother, then back to Max. "Well he is."

Max bit back a grin. *I love this kid. But time to be the adult.* "Remember our talk about people calling other people names?"

She ducked her head. "Yes, sir. I won't do it again."

"Good. Now. What did you hear that you don't understand?"

"He said you hit a woman named Anna, but I know that's not true."

"You do?"

"Of course. You would never hurt a woman."

It took a moment to realize the child thought he had hit Anna Sue. "You're right, Tink. I'd never intentionally hurt anyone. Especially a woman." He racked his brain for a simple explanation to an extremely complicated topic. "Remember our talk about bad words and how sometimes people call other people names?"

She nodded. "The bullies."

"That's right. The bullies. They call other people names and like to say things about them that aren't true."

"'Cause it makes them feel big."

"Right."

"And Mr. Jackson doesn't like you, so he said you hit that woman."

Once again, her intuitiveness surprised him. "Something like that." He faced Maddie and took her small hands in his. "I know this is hard for you to understand, but you might hear some things about me soon, about stuff I've done. Some of it may upset you. But, please, know this. Not everything you hear will be true."

One dainty brow shot upward, and she gave a mild snort. "I know that."

"I know you do, but I wanted you to hear me say it."

Maddie scooted up on the couch where she could lean against his side, and he instinctively draped his arm over the back of the couch.

"Heroes don't hurt people," Maddie said softly.

Max flinched and jerked his gaze to Sky, who silently watched the exchange, her features softened by a tender smile.

"Hero?"

Maddie yawned and snuggled against him, earnest blue eyes radiating unconditional love as she looked up at him. "Miss Gail said you got a purple medal for being a soldier. That makes you a hero."

"Tink…" *Hero? She thinks I'm a hero?* What should he say? How could he explain to a child what it meant to receive a Purple Heart? What it meant to be a soldier on a bloody battlefield? Way out of his comfort zone, he didn't immediately reply.

"I think being a soldier is really hard," said Maddie, her voice soft and gentle. "And sometimes it makes you sad when you think about it." She glanced at her mother, then nestled closer to him, completely at ease. "So, anytime you feel sad, just let us know, and we'll make it all better again." After another long yawn, she continued. "'Cause we love you just the way you are."

Sky watched in loving fascination as Maddie effortlessly curled Max around her little finger. What surprised her even more, though, was the seamless way Max slipped into father-figure mode and wondered if he even realized he did so.

He visibly relaxed when he gazed down at the child burrowed against him. The tightness in his face was replaced by the sweetest smile she'd ever seen. Hazelnut eyes glistened brightly as he looked toward Sky.

"Just the way you are," she murmured. "No matter what anyone says."

He sucked in a long breath. "Thank you." He looked down at Maddie, who snored softly beside him. "Now what?"

"Would you mind carrying her back to bed?"

His eyes widened briefly before he said, "Um, yeah. Sure." He shifted on the couch until he could lift the sleeping child without waking her. "Which way?"

Sky led the way to Maddie's room and watched as Max gently placed her on the bed and pulled the quilt up to her chin. Her heart melted when he hesitated then placed a soft kiss on her forehead.

"Sleep tight, Tinkerbell," he whispered. "Only pleasant dreams tonight."

The softly spoken words held such tenderness, Sky bit her lip for control.

When Max turned and faced her, she smiled and reached for his hand. "We never finished that coffee."

Ensconced on the couch, she passed him his cup of luke-warm brew with a couple of napkin-wrapped cookies. "I can nuke it if you like."

She noted the slight shake in his hands as he took the proffered items. "This is good. Half the time it gets cold before I can drink it anyway."

"I appreciate how you handled things with Maddie."

He stuffed one whole cookie in his mouth and followed it with a deep gulp of coffee. "I had no idea what I was doing."

"Couldn't prove it by me." She nibbled on a cookie. "Kids can be tricky, but you handled it like a pro."

"She's a swell kid, Sky." He stared into his cup and swirled the liquid around. "What about her dad?" He straightened. "I'm sorry. You don't have to answer that."

She placed a hand on his thigh and waited for him to look up. "If we're going to move forward in whatever this relation-ship is, you have a right to ask."

A slight tilt of his head encouraged her to continue.

"My mother was severely injured in a car wreck when I was sixteen. There wasn't any other family, so I basically took care of her and me, too." She leaned back on the couch and looked at the ceiling. "I was in my second year of nursing school when she died. Even though I knew it was coming, I was still devastated. Nearly flunked out before I got myself to-gether." She drew in a deep breath. "Then there was a house fire, and I basically lost everything but a few trinkets and the linens we used for Thanksgiving."

He laced their fingers together and squeezed. "Damn. I'm sorry, Sky."

She shrugged. "I got through it. Buried myself in my studies and graduated at the top of my class." She turned her head toward him. "I got a job at this hospital in Dallas. Work was great, but I was still lost. That's when I met Brett. He was related to one of my patients."

Max said nothing as she gathered her thoughts. "He was charming, had a good job. I was so lost and lonely, he pretty much swept me off my feet. A whirlwind courtship, then married on a beach at sunset. The whole nine yards."

"What happened?"

Memories of those years still threatened to crush her a times. "Maddie." She sat up straight and turned toward him, hands still laced together. "I told you she was born early. What I didn't tell you was all the health problems that come from a premature birth. She barely weighed two pounds and spent months in a NICU, a neonatal intensive care unit. I brought her home with a monitor to wake me if she stopped breathing." She couldn't control the quiver in her voice. "She required constant supervision. Her resistance was so low, any infection was potentially life threatening."

"I can't even imagine how awful that must have been for you."

"I was terrified something would happen. I quit my job to care for her." Eyes closed, she inhaled deeply. "Brett tried, but…."

"But?"

She shook her head slightly. "It was more than he could

handle seeing her in that place. Monitors, tubes, and wires everywhere, knowing any minute she could die. Then, he got this promotion at work and had to travel a lot." She shrugged. "We needed the money and the insurance, so…"

"How long did she stay there?"

"Five months, three weeks, and four days." She looked at him and smiled. "Not that I counted or anything."

He squeezed her hand again.

"I spent so much time caring for Maddie, I didn't realize how far apart we'd drifted until it was too late." She looked down at their hands, then back up. "She was two and a half when we divorced. By then, her health was better, but…"

"Does he see her?"

She swallowed hard, bit her lower lip to stop the tremble. "No. He tried at first, but then he remarried and moved to Austin." She ducked her head, squeezed his hand for support. "When she was four, she got pneumonia." Her voice dropped to a hoarse whisper. "I almost lost her."

She didn't resist when he pulled her in his arms and hugged tightly.

Neither spoke for several moments.

"How is she now?" asked Max at last.

She didn't raise from her spot against his chest. "Good. Thank God. She has bouts of asthma, but Doc has her on an inhaler if it flares up."

"And he still doesn't see her?"

"No. He did a few times at first, but that stopped along with child support. The only thing I stipulated in the divorce was that he keep her on his health insurance because I had no idea what the future held. I can't bear to think about what might have happened if he hadn't agreed to that." Mimicking Maddie, she shifted to a more comfortable position at his side. "That ended two years ago when he lost his job. He was unemployed for six months. When he finally found work, it was at a lower salary, and he couldn't put her on his insurance."

"Can't you take him back to court or something? Get some of the back child support at least?"

"I thought about it, but that takes money." She sensed his preparation to speak and pressed a hand to his chest. "No. I won't take money from you, so don't offer. Besides, I found out I can get a lawyer through one of those legal aid groups for free."

"Are you going to do it?"

"I honestly don't know. He sends me money occasionally, but he has a wife and two kids to support, too, so I haven't pushed it. She hadn't asked about him in a long time until this week. Not sure what sparked it." She sighed. "But we're making it okay for now. Maddie's prognosis is great, and her general health is good, too."

"That still doesn't erase his obligation to her."

"No. It doesn't."

Muscles tensed beneath his shirt, and he sucked in a breath. She knew he was angry for her, for Maddie, and that made her happy. How crazy was that? She eased back and touched his cheek with her finger. "Let's talk about something else, shall we? Did I tell you I got the info from Doc about getting back into nursing?"

His jaw muscles worked up and down as he clenched his teeth. "No, you didn't mention it."

"It's not going to be as hard as I thought. She gave me the paperwork a few days ago, and I just got through all of it last night. She wants me to give my notice to Ruby soon so we can start on it right away."

"That's great news, Sky. I'm happy for you. And for Doc. She seems like a really nice person."

"She is. She offered me a job in her office, sorta like a work-study program, and she'll help me jump through all those hoops." She sighed and snuggled against him, enjoying the heat emanating from his body, the rightness of being here with him, knowing he cared for her. That he wanted her. Years of waiting, of dreaming of this moment finally came to fruition, and she savored it like fine wine as she drank in the comfort of his nearness. She took a deep breath, dropped her hand to his chest, and rubbed lightly. "I'd like you to kiss me right now, if you don't mind."

His heartbeat thumped under her palm as the smoldering anger in his eyes softened to a passion-sparked mocha.

"If you insist."

"I do."

The kiss was slow and surprisingly gentle as his lips skimmed hers with tantalizing persuasion. The tender massage sent the pit of her stomach in a wild swirl as the kiss went on. And on.

"Sky..." he murmured as his lips left a moist trail down to the pulsing hollow at the base of her throat then up to the sensitive skin under her earlobe.

She buried her face in his neck and breathed a kiss there, enjoying the sharp intake of breath that said he liked it.

His mouth reclaimed hers, more demanding this time, and she gloried in the delicious sensation of his touch. A touch that pooled heat in her middle and ratcheted up her pulse.

The man was a kissing ninja.

Slowly, he pulled back, and the look in his eyes made her insides jangle with excitement and her heart pound out an erratic rhythm as he traced one finger along her jawline, over her lips, and down her neck.

"You are so beautiful," he whispered hoarsely. "So beautiful." He pulled in a ragged breath and tucked her against his side, her head resting on his shoulder.

His uneven breath on her cheek as he held her close was oddly comforting as they waited for normalcy to return.

Her whole being seemed to be waiting for this moment. This man.

Her instinctive, passionate response to him was so powerful, it gave her a moment's pause. A part of her reveled in his open admiration, but a cautious voice asked if all her loneliness and confusion had welded together in one upsurge of untamed yearning.

An undeniable attraction existed between them from the very beginning. But was it too soon? Was she letting her emotions rule her decisions again?

The hard thump of his heart against her ear said he felt something for her. But what?

It was difficult to think straight this close to him, when everything about him saturated her senses and robbed her of rational thought. But one thing she could not deny was that she loved him. Crazy as it may sound to some, she loved this man.

She relaxed against him, enjoying the tenderness of his embrace, conscious of every spot his flesh touched hers, and letting her thoughts drift where they willed.

She loved the way he was with Maddie and Big John. She loved his innate goodness that dictated he propose marriage to a girl in trouble with no plan other than to save her from disgrace.

Thoughts of Anna threatened to put a damper on her fledgling emotions, and she thrust them aside. There'd be time for that later.

"Any chance you could get Gail to watch Tink tomorrow night?"

Max's quiet question brought her back to the moment.

"As a matter of fact, she's having a sleepover at Bonnie's." She shifted to look up at him. "Why?"

He cleared his throat. "I thought maybe we could go out. You know…on a date."

Beneath her palm, his heart gave several hard *thumps*.

"I'd love to. But I won't get off until seven, maybe a little earlier if things are slow."

"How about I come by about eight? Will that give you enough time?"

"Eight is good." Her smile grew. "What did you have in mind?"

"I thought we'd grab a bite at that steakhouse near the interstate. Maybe check out the dance at the VFW. If that's okay with you."

"I don't care where we go or what we do…as long as we do it together."

An infrequent smile tugged up the corners of his mouth. "Same here."

She sighed and snuggled against him again.

Long minutes passed in silence before he spoke up. "I hate to leave, but…I left Logan asleep on the couch."

Hand in hand, they walked to the back door. Max reached for the knob and stopped. "You know I'll do anything I can for you and Maddie, right?"

She smiled. "I know."

"No strings attached."

She lowered her eyes, then glanced up at him. "What if… what if I wanted some strings attached?"

Nostrils flared as he sucked in a breath. "Then I'd say we should discuss those strings."

She ran one hand up his chest. "I look forward to our date." She smiled and kissed him softly on the lips. "Don't be late."

CHAPTER
Twenty

"Out with it," said Ruby as Sky placed a ticket on the cook's order holder. "You've been grinning like a jackass eating briars all day. What gives?"

Still smiling, she looked at her boss. "I have a date. Tonight. An honest-to-goodness date for the first time in… years, with the sweetest, most thoughtful, and handsomest man ever."

Ruby placed a hand over her heart and sighed. "Well, in that case, girlfriend, smile away." She glanced at her watch. "What time is this momentous event taking place?"

"He's coming by the house about eight."

"Things have been slow all day. Why don't you go ahead and take off? Louise and I can handle things."

Sky hesitated. She could use the extra time for an important errand but hated to leave in case things got busy. "Are you sure? It's just after five. I'd hate to leave y'all in a lurch."

"Go. We got this."

She quickly untied her apron. "Okay. You talked me into it." Tossing the apron on a nail by the employee lockers, she grabbed her things and headed for the back door. Suddenly, she remembered Ruby hadn't posted the schedule for next week, nor did Sky mention her impending departure, so she turned and went back out front. As she waited for Ruby to finish with a customer, a woman walked in the front door.

It took all of ten seconds for Sky to recognize the now grown up and beautiful Anna Watkins.

The years had been kind to her. She was tall, slender and moved with an easy grace. The long chestnut hair of the girl in the prom photo was now worn in a short, wavy bob. Her face was well modeled and feminine, radiating both delicacy and strength. She shrugged out of her coat and threw it over one side of a booth, then slid into the other seat.

In a moment of insanity, Sky placed her things on the counter and walked toward the newcomer. "Hi. I was just getting off, but since the others are busy, can I get you something to drink and a menu?"

Liquid brown eyes darted around the room, then settled on Sky. "Just coffee, please."

When Sky placed the requested drink and a menu on the table, the woman looked up.

"Are you from around here?"

Before Sky could answer, she continued. "I'm looking for someone who lives on Pin Oak Lane. Four-thirty-two. Can you give me directions? My GPS doesn't have a clue."

It took monumental effort to keep her voice light and her expression neutral. "Of course. I live on that street." She gave the woman directions and turned to go.

"You said you live on that street. Do you know Max Logan?"

She paused. "We're…friends. He lives next door to me."

Color drained from the woman's face before it returned

with a vengeance, staining it a bright red. "Thank you for your help."

Sky didn't miss the tremble in Anna's hands as she picked up the menu. "You're welcome. Someone will be by to take your order in a minute."

She turned around and walked to where Ruby prepared a fresh pot of coffee. "I gave the woman in six some coffee. Left her a menu but not sure she wants to eat. And I forgot to ask about the schedule for next week."

Sky left with a heavy heart. Anna's sudden appearance didn't bode well for her date tonight.

She pushed the encounter from her mind and headed across the street to *The Sassy Sash*. The owner was one of Sky's friends and a regular customer at the diner. Jeannie had excellent taste, and Sky always enjoyed browsing the selections while they visited.

But today, for the first time in forever, she intended to indulge herself a bit. She had a date. A real date. With a handsome man. The prospect of a better job soon was icing on the cake. And that called for a celebration of sorts. She couldn't remember the last time she did something so utterly selfish and maybe even extravagant. Obviously, the sexy young girl was long since gone, but tonight, she wanted to be her again, if only in her mind, and racy new undergarments would help.

Thirty minutes later, she exited the store with a pink, lacy bra and panty set…and three condoms courtesy of the store's owner.

When Jeannie asked if she was prepared, Sky thought she meant prepared to go out. After her friend stopped laughing and said, "I mean *prepared*," Sky nearly died of embarrassment.

Jeannie just smiled and pulled the foil packs from her purse. "A woman should always be prepared."

Sky didn't bother with the heater all the way home. The heat from her face was enough to melt an iceberg.

Max's truck wasn't in his spot when Sky arrived home with Maddie, though Logan's remained parked out front. As she pulled to a stop, she saw the teen sitting on the back step, elbows on his knees, head down.

He looked up as they exited the car but didn't speak.

Something about his dejection touched her mother's heart. "Maddie…go on inside and get your things so we can go to Bonnie's."

"Okay." She looked toward Logan and smiled. "Hi, Logan." She turned to her mother. "Mama, can Logan come over for some cookies while I get my stuff ready? He's Max's friend, and it wouldn't be nice not to."

To refuse at this point wasn't an option. "I have some cookies I bought at the Christmas festival. Would you like some?"

At first, she thought he would refuse, but he sat up a little straighter. "What kind?"

"Chocolate chip."

He hesitated, then glanced around. "Sure. I guess so."

"Does Max have any milk to go with them?"

He ducked his head. "I drank it this morning."

"Would you like me to bring them over or would you rather come inside?" *First his mother, now him. I'm just a glutton for punishment.*

159

He rubbed his hands on his knees and stood. "I guess it'd be okay to come over there since you and Max are together."

Maddie skipped over and took his hand. "Come on, Logan. These cookies are really good. Not as good as what Mama makes for Max, but they're still good."

Thankfully, the house was warm since she'd lit the heaters before she picked Maddie up from Gail's.

"You can sit here at the table, Logan," instructed Maddie. "I have to go get my stuff. I get to have a sleepover at Bonnie's tonight so Mama and Max can have a date."

Sky closed her eyes as heat crept into her cheeks. She needed to have another talk with Maddie about filters. "Scoot, Munchkin."

Maddie skipped off down the hall.

Sky plucked a glass from the drainer by the sink. "Won't take but a minute." She pulled milk from the fridge and placed both items on the table. The plastic container of cookies was next, along with a paper towel she yanked off from the roll on the counter. "Help yourself."

Hands in his lap, head lowered, he didn't move.

"Is something wrong?" The moment the words were out, she wished she could take them back. When his head jerked up, she tried to smooth it over. "Besides the obvious, I mean?"

Jaws tight, cheeks tinged bright red, he didn't immediately reply. "Why are you being nice to me?" he hissed. "I'm not his kid."

The bitterness in his voice didn't conceal the hurt underneath.

She sat down across from him, surprised when his troubled eyes locked with hers. Something about the look he gave her caused a sense of déjà vu, but she shrugged it off.

"I won't insult you by saying I know how you feel, because I don't."

His stiff posture marginally relaxed.

"But I do know hurt when I see it."

"She lied to me." His voice cracked, and the redness in his face spread to his ears. "All my life…she lied to me."

Oh crap. What do I say to that?

"…I know this is none of my business, but I can tell you from a mother's perspective, we sometimes do things we think are right for our child, only to find out in hindsight we should have done it differently."

Jaw tight, he glared at her. "Did you ever lie to Maddie?"

She sighed, tore off a piece of the paper towel-slash-napkin, then rolled and unrolled it between trembling fingers. "No, but I have let my own fears keep me from even considering another relationship, which has deprived Maddie of any male influence in her life."

Widened eyes and a slack mouth said her answer surprised him.

"But I thought you and Max…"

She risked a timid smile. "Only recently. It's all still new to us."

"My mother will be here tomorrow. The shit's gonna really hit the fan then." Immediately, he sucked in a breath, and his face glowed scarlet. "I'm sorry, ma'am."

"It's okay. This time."

"I'm ready, Mama," chirped Maddie as she bounced back into the kitchen. "You didn't eat your cookies, Logan."

The teen stood and headed for the door. "I better go. Y'all have stuff to do."

Sky pressed the plastic dish in his hand. "Take this with you. If nothing else, you'll have a snack for later."

"Thanks."

"You're welcome."

Maddie looked at her mother as the door closed behind him. "Why is Logan so sad?"

"I…it's complicated."

"I don't like to see people sad," whispered Maddie. "It makes my heart hurt."

Sky choked back a sob. How could one seven-year-old child have so much wisdom and compassion? "I know, sweetie. Mine, too." She straightened her shoulders. "So, we'll just do what we can to make him not sad."

"Like giving him the cookies?"

"Yeah. Like that."

"I'm ready to go to Bonnie's so you can get ready for your date with Max." Maddie was practically jumping up and down. "Aren't you excited?"

Sky laughed. "Yes. I'm excited. Let's go."

A few minutes later, they rang the doorbell on Janet Orm's front porch.

Maddie wasted no time spreading the news. "Mama has a date with Max tonight."

"How wonderful," said Bonnie's mother. "I'm so glad for you both."

"I have to be at work by eleven tomorrow, so I'll be by to pick her up about nine if that's okay," said Sky.

"Don't worry about it. She can stay till you get off. Around two, right?"

"Yes. But are you sure? I don't want to impose on you."

"Of course. They'll be up half the night anyway and sleep late in the morning." She ushered Maddie inside. "Bonnie's waiting upstairs for you." When the child scampered off, Janet turned back to Sky. "I'm glad to see you and Max together. He needs someone like you in his life."

Sky chewed her bottom lip. Dare she ask questions? "Um, have you known him long?"

"He was a year ahead of me in school. He and my Johnny were in several classes together. Kinda quiet. Mostly kept to himself. About his only friend was Anna Watkins."

"Anna Watkins?" Sky ignored the jump in her heart rate.

Janet quickly placed a hand on Sky's shoulder. "Oh, not like a couple or anything. Just friends. She was head over heels for Cade Jackson."

"Cade?"

A gust of cold air swirled around them, and both ladies folded arms across their midriffs.

"You think he's arrogant and self-centered now, you should have known him in high school."

Before Sky could comment, Bonnie called from upstairs. "Mom…I can't get the player to work."

"Sorry. Better get up there. Thanks for letting Maddie spend the night. Bonnie has been pestering me about it for a week. Have fun tonight."

Sky was almost back to her car when a sudden realization blindsided her.

She knew who Logan's father was.

CHAPTER
Twenty-One

Max glanced at the caller ID before he answered his cell. "Hey, John. What's up?"

"You still at work?"

"Yeah. Waiting for Jason to get back from late deliveries."

"You gonna be home later?"

"Yes and no. Sky and I are going out." He couldn't keep from smiling. "Our first official date. You need something?"

There was a short pause before he replied. "I don't like doing this on the phone."

Something put Max on full alert. "What's wrong? Are you all right?"

There was an audible sigh before Big John spoke again. "Okay. Fine. We'll do it on the phone. What are your intentions?'

"Intentions? Intentions about what?"

"About Sky. And Maddie. What are your intentions?"

Friend or no friend, Big John was putting his nose where it didn't belong. "I intend to take Sky to dinner and maybe a dance. What business is it of yours?"

"That girl is like a daughter to me, boy. I don't want to see her get hurt."

"And you think I'd do that?" Pain slithered to the surface and put an edge to his voice. "That I'm no good for her?"

"Hell, no!"

"Then what is it?"

A muffled curse preceded another long sigh. "I knew I'd mess this up on the phone. Look, son, you and Sky and Maddie are as close to family as I got in this world. I heard about that boy being in town and what he claims."

Anger spiked, and Max fought to remain calm. "I'm not his father."

"I believe you. I'm just saying there's talk already, and it's bound to get back to her."

"I talked to her. She knows I'm not his father."

A heavy silence lingered.

"Spit it out, John. Whatever you got stuck in your craw, just spit it out."

"Maddie's awfully fond of you."

"The feeling is mutual."

"And Sky. How do you feel about her?"

His first impulse was to scream back off, but he bit his tongue. From their first meeting, he and John hit it off. Two battle-hardened combat veterans with more scars inside than out. John listened when he needed to talk, sat quietly when he needed companionship, and understood better than anyone the hell he'd gone through.

John protected those he cared about, and he cared about Sky and her daughter. And Max.

"I'm crazy about her, old man. And Maddie, too." He took a deep breath. "I tried not to. God knows she could do a damn sight better than me, but…I want to be with her. With them."

After a slight pause, John spoke again, a noticeable smile in his voice. "Good. That's great. Y'all have fun tonight."

Before Max could form a reply, John hung up. *What the hell brought that on?* He slid the phone back in his pocket and looked at the clock. Five-thirty. Jason would be back any minute, and then he could leave. And do what? Kill time for three hours while he waited for eight o'clock to arrive? Face his taciturn houseguest who hadn't said two words to him this morning? He pushed Logan from his mind and thought about his date with Sky.

He couldn't remember ever being so nervous. *It's just a date, not brain surgery. We're going out to dinner then maybe to a dance.*

But what about the strings Sky mentioned? Where did they fit into the program? And better yet, what the hell were they? Of course, he had his own ideas, but he'd learned a long time ago not to hope for anything special.

His revelry was interrupted when his boss scurried in the front door.

"Sorry the deliveries took so long this time," said Jason as he rounded the counter. "Everywhere I went people wanted to talk."

"No problem, sir." Max resisted the urge to salute. Old habits were hard to break. "All ready to lock up for the night."

"There is no rank here, Max. It's just us."

"Yes, sir—I mean, right Jason."

"So, ready for the big date tonight?"

Max didn't bother to hide his shock. "How'd you know about that?"

Jason laughed and clapped him on the shoulder. "You forget how things are in a small town, son. You can't do anything that somebody doesn't see or know about. With nothing better to do, they talk." His steady gaze met and held Max's. "They talk a lot."

He didn't need him to elaborate. John's call told him the gossipmongers were already having a field day at his expense. He was sure he had Cade to thank for that. "Unfortunately, they don't always have the facts, or they choose to spread lies for shits and grins."

"Well, personally, I've never put much stock in rumors and gossip."

Max nodded, unsure how he should respond.

"So, where are you taking her?"

Jason's easy change in the conversation helped lift the pall settling around him. "Steakhouse out by the interstate. Maybe take in the dance at the VFW."

"Well, you deserve some fun. Take off. I'll finish up here."

Max didn't need to be told twice. He rushed around the counter and headed for the door. "Thank you, sir. See you on Monday."

His good humor lasted until he pulled into his drive and saw a strange vehicle parked behind Logan's truck. *Shit. Anna. Has to be.*

He parked in his usual spot and sat inside for several deep breaths. As soon as he opened the door to get out, he saw Sky at the kitchen window. Her sad expression said it all. She knew he had more company.

The door opened before he knocked.

"Hey." She motioned him in. "It's cold out there."

He shuffled into the kitchen and stopped at the stove, engulfed in old fears and the dull ache of foreboding. A whiff of her floral perfume said she stood behind him.

"She arrived a few minutes ago."

Max turned around. "I didn't expect her until tomorrow." To his dismay, his voice wavered slightly.

Arms folded, she shrugged. "Well, speaking as a mother, if my child took off like that, I'd be here sooner rather than later, too."

"I don't know what's going to go down tonight, but it shouldn't interfere with our date."

"I hope not," she said softly, then looked away, teeth biting her lower lip.

He scrubbed his face with both hands. "Dammit. I wanted tonight to be special."

After a brief hesitation, she took his hands and wound them about her waist, sliding her arms around his neck. "I know. Me, too. But stuff happens, Max. We both know that." Biting her lip again, she looked down, then reached up and kissed him lightly on the lips. "I won't lie to you. I'll be really disappointed if things don't work out."

She lowered her eyes, then glanced up, a sensuous flame shimmering in their hazel depths. The look was so innocently seductive, his libido headed for the stratosphere.

"Do what you have to. I'm going to take a long, hot bubble bath." She rubbed her hands up his chest again. "And get ready for our date."

He pulled her to him, rougher than he should have, and covered her mouth with his, devouring its softness. She tasted so damn good. Felt so damn good pressed against him. He couldn't be gentle. He wanted her with an intensity unlike anything he'd ever experienced. Needed her goodness and warmth to fill the empty spot in his soul. Only she had the power to ease the hurt inside. He loved her.

With all his heart and soul, he loved her.

Tremors racked her body as she returned his kiss, opening her mouth to his probing tongue, matching his intensity with her own.

The sharp ring of the telephone made its way through the mush in his brain, and he pulled back.

Emotions whirled and skidded as he rested his forehead on hers, breath coming in rapid puffs through parted lips. "Damn."

"I better get that." She pulled away and answered the phone. "Hello? Is she all right? Are you sure? Okay. No, I'll bring it by now."

She turned back to him, her face a mask of worry and concern. "Maddie forgot her inhaler. I need to take it to her."

The thought of Maddie being ill made Max queasy. "Is she all right? Does she need a doctor?"

"She's just a little winded. They went outside to feed Bonnie's dog and got to playing. Sometimes the cold affects her that way. The inhaler will take care of it."

A shadow of unease crossed her face, and he gathered her against him. She hesitated only a moment before she wrapped her arms around his waist.

He relished how right being with her was and debated if now was the time to tell her how he felt. There was so much unsettled. PTSD was one thing, but now this mess with Logan and Anna.

And Cade.

Her grip tightened, and she muttered against his chest. "This is more than just a—an itch for me, Max."

Her words were muffled, but he got the message and pushed back a little. One finger under her chin, he raised her face to look at him. "It is for me, too, Sky. I've never felt this way about anyone. Ever. You smile at me, and my heart skips a beat. I'd do anything, anything for you and Maddie." He swallowed, determined to get the words out. "You make me forget all the bad shit that's happened in my life and look forward to tomorrow." His voice dropped to a rough whisper. "For the first time in a very long time, I'm glad to be alive."

Her chin trembled, and moisture glistened at the corners of her eyes. "Oh, Max—"

"I don't know what the future holds, but as long as we're in it together, I don't care."

"Me, too."

He brushed a gentle kiss across her forehead. "I best go see what new and exciting adventure awaits me next door."

"I'll see you later."

He kissed the tip of her nose. "Count on it."

He stepped out into the chilly air, determined not to let anything spoil this night with Sky.

Logan's raised voice greeted him as he opened the kitchen door.

"You lied to me!"

Daniel to the lion's den, door number one.

CHAPTER
Twenty-Two

Anna stood in the middle of the kitchen, her back to him, while Logan stood near the table, hands fisted at his sides as he glared at his mother.

She spun around when Max entered, and for a moment, he was struck speechless. Time had been kind to her. He always liked her long, wavy hair, but this short cut suited her even better. It framed an oval face unlined by time, but nonetheless etched with concern, and sparkling green eyes that glistened like polished jade. The skinny girl with crooked teeth was now a beautiful woman.

And the last person in the world he wanted in his kitchen.

"I want to know why you lied to me," snapped Logan. "I have a right to know."

"Baby, please," began Anna, "I—I did what I thought was best for you."

"By letting me believe my father was dead?" He hissed. "Or maybe you don't even know who he was."

Max took a step toward him, remaining calm yet firm. "I understand you're angry, boy, but you will not disrespect your mother. Not in my house."

Logan's breath hissed in and out as he glared at Anna, his

face a mottled red, a vein in his temple visibly throbbing. "And what about him?" He pointed to Max. "Why did you keep all those pictures and stuff if it wasn't him?"

Max quashed the urge to speak up again. What a mess. Would he ever get rid of Cade's interference in his life?

"I told you. Max was—is—my friend." She wrung her hands and turned haunted eyes to Max. "And he always will be." She faced her son. "But he is not your father."

"Then who is, dammit! I have a right to know."

Anna sighed, arms laced together across her chest.

"Does he even know about me?"

Max pointed to a chair at the table. "Why don't we all sit down?"

"You can't tell me what to do," Logan snapped.

In full-on Marine mode, Max turned toward the belligerent young man, eyes locked with his as he towered over him. "This is my house. You do what I say, when I say. Now. Sit. Down."

Logan hesitated only a moment before he dropped into a chair, his face a mask of undisguised hostility and pain.

Max and Anna joined him at the table.

Anna finally broke the prolonged silence. "I did what I thought was right."

"For who? You?"

"Logan—"

"Did he know about me?"

"What good—"

"Or did you lie to him, too?"

"…We were young, barely out of high school—"

Logan slammed his fist down on the table. "Did he know about me?" Each word was clipped and hard.

172

Anna sighed deeply and looked down at her folded hands. "Yes and no."

"What the hell does that mean?" His volume rose a notch. "Did he, or didn't he?"

"Easy, son," said Max calmly. "Yelling won't get your message across any clearer."

"Don't call me that. I'm not your son."

"No, you aren't," said Anna. "But you are mine. So, please. Lower your voice."

A surge of pity filled Max as he watched the scene unfold. It was a no-win situation, and yet, he was compelled to try to mediate the damage. "Annie—the fuse is lit. There's no way to blow it out now."

She swallowed hard and clinched her eyes shut. "He knew I was pregnant."

"And?"

Silence.

"Mom? What happened when you told him?"

"He did you both a favor by being an ass about responsibility." The words were out before Max could stop them, and he choked back a groan. *So much for keeping my mouth shut.*

Logan fixed pain-filled eyes on Max. "So, you knew him?"

"…Yes."

"And you didn't like him?"

"No."

Logan looked at his mother, then back at Max. "Because she went with him and not you?"

"No. Because he—" Max stopped himself before he said what he really thought. "It's like your mom said. They were young. Too young for things to have worked out between them."

Logan ducked his head, hands fisted on the table. "Is he dead or not?"

Max remained silent this time, determined to try and stay out of this mess.

Logan rapped the knuckles of one hand on the table and repeated the question. "Is he dead or not?"

Anna closed her eyes and took a deep breath. "No."

He sat up straight. "Does he still live here? Have a family?"

She glanced at Max, one brow raised in a silent question.

In a futile attempt to delay the inevitable, Max tried to be the voice of reason. "What do you hope to gain from this, Logan?"

His eyes bored a hole in Max. "Does he?"

"Trust me on this. Having the man who fathered you in your life is no guarantee of a happy home." Max kept his expression neutral, despite the pain his statement wrought.

"But I never got the chance to find out for myself, now did I?" Logan pushed his chair back and stood. "I need some air."

Before anyone could react, Logan stormed out the back door.

Anna rose, uncertainty creasing her brow, and her lower lip trembled. "I've made such a mess of things." A sob escaped, and she covered her mouth. "He hates me."

Suddenly, Max was eighteen again, watching someone he cared for fall apart in front of him. "He doesn't hate you. He just doesn't understand."

"What am I going to do?" Her eyes clouded with tears. "He's going to find out."

Just as he did all those years ago, he opened his arms, and she fell into his embrace, slender body shaking with uncontrolled sobs.

He held her against him as he had that night so long ago, whispering words of encouragement he didn't really believe. "It'll be okay, Annie. We'll figure this out."

He caught movement from the corner of his eye and looked up in time to see Sky standing beside her car, eyes wide.

Watching.

Sky froze, mind and body numb, her heart all but stopping as she watched Max embrace Anna. A thousand logical explanations raced through her mind as she fumbled with the door handle and finally got inside Blue.

Her exit from the house coincided with Logan's dash out Max's back door, his expression dark when he glanced her way and headed for his truck. All of which led her to believe the meeting had not gone well, and Max was just trying to comfort Anna.

A very natural thing for friends to do, right? The hug meant nothing. So what if her face was buried in the hollow of his neck, and his arms held her close? It meant nothing. Or did it?

Rational thought evaporated as the image replayed in her head. It took a great deal of effort not to look back toward the kitchen window as she backed out of the drive, intent on getting Maddie's inhaler to her.

Thankfully, Maddie was fine when she arrived and had no desire to visit with her mother, so ten minutes later, Sky sat behind the wheel of her car wondering what to do. The demise of her first date in years was bad enough, but the prospect of her relationship with Max ending before it really began broke her heart.

"You're overreacting," she chided herself. "They're friends. She's upset. He's just trying to comfort her."

All that sounded logical, even probable. But it didn't take away the pain.

Nor did it stop the tsunami of questions and doubts that swamped her. Is there more to their friendship than he implied? What happens now? How could I have let myself fall so quickly for someone I barely knew? Again. And Maddie. Oh God. Maddie.

She made a U-turn and drove away with no destination in mind. After a circle around the town square and a pass through the parking lot of the local chain store, she found herself parked in the alley behind the diner.

"This is ridiculous," she muttered, "I'm wasting time and gas I can't spare. I just need to go home, take a hot bath, and go to bed." *Alone* was the unspoken end to that thought, followed by a long sigh of defeat. Eyes closed, she leaned her head back. *I will not cry. I will not cry.* Despite that admonition, a painful tightness gripped her throat, and she drew in a shaky breath.

A light tapping on her window jerked her away from a meltdown. Heart racing, she blinked several times before Big John's face came into view.

He was bent nearly double to look in the window. "Miss Sky? Are you all right?"

She lowered the window and struggled to keep her voice even. "Evening John."

"Ever' thing, okay?"

"I'm fine. Really. Just…" *Just sitting here, all alone in the dark feeling sorry for myself when I don't even know if I have anything to feel sorry about even though the man I'm crazy about is this moment holding another woman in his arms. Yep. That 'bout sums it up.*

He grunted as he squatted down beside the car door, one hand resting on the bottom of the window. "I'm a good listener."

Intense blue eyes locked with hers. He would understand. How she knew that, she couldn't explain, but she knew he would. Still, she fought the instinctive urge to unload her troubles. "Thank you, John. I appreciate it. I do. But, well, I just have some stuff to work out."

He looked around the darkened alley. "This ain't a good place to do that, ma'am."

"You're right, of course. I should get home."

Neither made a move to go.

John ducked his head, then looked up, his eyes once more fixed on hers. "I know I got no right to say this, Miss Sky, but you and that little girl of yours are like family to me." He paused, then continued. "So is Max. And regardless of what you may think right now, that boy cares about y'all."

"I—"

"He's been through hell and lived to tell about it." He shook his head slightly. "I never thought I'd see him smile again. Not till you and Maddie come along."

"There's stuff —"

"Cade's making sure ever 'one knows about the boy."

She shouldn't have been surprised by this, but she was. "He didn't waste any time."

He nodded. "Saw him at the store earlier. Told me the boy's mama is coming tomorrow."

"She's already here." Even she heard the desperation in her words. "She's at his house right now."

"Well, guess that explains why you're out here."

"Yeah." What else was there to say? She rubbed cold hands over the steering wheel, then clasped them in her lap. "I had to take Maddie's inhaler to her at Janet's. I saw Logan storm out as I was leaving." *And saw Max embrace her like a long-lost lover.* She shook her head to dispel that line of thought.

"He came in here a while ago," offered John. "Didn't stay long."

Despite all the ramifications his presence meant to her, she couldn't help but feel sorry for Logan. "Poor kid."

"Yeah."

"Max isn't his father." Immediately, she regretted her words. She had no right to discuss that with anyone, but the need to defend him was strong.

"I know. Max wouldn't shirk that kind of responsibility." He paused, then looked up at her. "I'd be glad to buy you a cup of coffee, Miss Sky."

Her first instinct was to refuse, but she bit it back. "I'd like that."

A few minutes later, they sat opposite each other in a booth, nursing steaming mugs of hot coffee and chatting with various people in the diner.

"Hey, John," called a patron across the room, "Got a minute? I need to ask you about some work I'd like done."

He looked at Sky.

"Go ahead."

As soon as he got up, Billy Ray Thomas left his seat at the counter and took John's place. "Now I see why you would never go out with me," he teased. "You had eyes for that old coot."

"What can I say?" she quipped. "I like beards."

"I thought you and Max had a date tonight?"

The smile faltered. "Something came up."

Hazel eyes, gleaming with interest, clearly assessed her. "Must've been pretty important. He's been looking forward to it all day."

"How do you know that?"

"You forget how small towns operate." He chuckled and held up one hand, ticking off fingers as he talked. "Maddie told Gail Brown." He touched another finger. "She told her sister Mavis who works at the bank, and she told Edith at Jenson realty."

She smothered a smile. "Biggest gossip in the county."

"Yep." He dusted his hands together, then clasped them in front of him. "And the rest is history." He paused. "Plus, I saw him at the auto parts store earlier. He sure looked happy to me. Wanna talk about it?"

"Not really."

He ducked his head, then glanced back up at her. "I saw Edith at the gas station. Cade told her about Max's visitor, too."

She huffed out a breath and sat back in the booth.

"Which I guess explains why you're sitting here with John looking like someone just kicked your dog."

Before she could reply, he continued. "I'd be happy to fill in, you know."

There was no mistaking the open invitation in those smoldering depths, and for a moment, she was stunned into silence. "Bill, I—"

In the blink of an eye, the come-on persona was replaced

by the flirty affectation she was comfortable with. "I might have to put you on a waiting list, though." He winked and smiled. "But I will move you to the top."

His throaty laugh was contagious, and she found herself joining in the gaiety. It had been a while since she really laughed, and she found it cathartic.

They were still laughing when the bell above the front door jangled announcing a new arrival.

The smile froze on Bill's face, and his eyes widened. "Things are about to get interesting."

She started to twist around to see what sparked that comment, but he stopped her by putting both his hands on one of hers.

"Max just walked in. I'm guessing the woman with him is the reason you're here."

CHAPTER
Twenty-Three

Dammit!

Max struggled to keep his emotions in check as he watched Sky back out of the drive. The look on her face when she glanced up and saw Anna in his arms was forever burned in his brain. Just when he thought he'd escaped the cesspool that defined his world, he found himself neck deep in the muck again.

The first inkling of the approaching panic attack surprised him. It had been a while since the last one. A tingling in his left hand, quickly spreading to his right, then up both arms. Sweat broke out on his brow and upper lip, and his heart rate jumped. Oh God. Not now.

Embrace the suck, Marine. Persevere. Adapt. Overcome. He closed his eyes and slowly sucked in a deep breath. *Breathe in, count to four, breathe out.* He repeated his mantra again. *Embrace the suck. Persevere. Adapt. Overcome. Breathe in, count to four, breathe out.*

More of Doctor Bellamy's instructions made their way through the fog. "Focus on something else. Some other emotion. Anything other than the panic or anxiety."

Out of the blue, Maddie's face came to mind as she looked

at him and said, "anytime you are sad, just tell us, and we'll make it all better again because we love you."

He focused on her sweet smile, the absolute trust in her all-too-seeing azure orbs and took another breath, letting it out slowly. Then another. And another. Gradually, the panic subsided enough for him to regain a measure of control. Thanks to my seven-year-old guardian angel, he thought.

If Anna had any suspicion of his discomfort, she gave no indication as she pulled away slightly and flicked away tears with her index fingers. "I'm—I'm so sorry." She waved one hand in a circle. "About all this."

Still shaky from the near panic attack, he didn't know what to say, so he opted for a non-committal shrug and a dash of truth. "It was bound to happen sooner or later, Annie."

She took a step back and braced one hand on the chair she recently vacated, a feeble attempt at a smile edged up one corner of her mouth. "You're the only one who ever called me Annie." She pulled in a ragged breath. "It's good to see you again, Max. It's been a long time."

He nodded toward the table and chairs. "Let's sit."

Max took a chair across from her and folded his hands on top of the table, grateful they were now steady.

She ducked her head, slender fingers laced together so tightly her knuckles were white. "I'm so sorry he got you involved in our problems." She laced and unlaced her fingers, then met his gaze. "Did you tell him anything?"

"Not my place."

She nodded but remained silent.

"He's still in town," said Max.

"I know."

"He knows Logan is here."

Her head jerked up, and fear flashed in the depths of her eyes.

"He's taking great relish in feeding the rumor mill." He clenched his jaw, anger making his voice harsh, but she had to know the facts. "His version is that I'm the father and left town to avoid manning up."

She sunk down in her chair like a balloon with a slow leak. "Oh no." Unnerved eyes connected with his. "It's all my fault. I'm so sorry, Max."

He wanted to agree but knew that wasn't true. Takes two to tango. "Cade shares responsibility in this, too."

"I thought he'd grow out of his dislike for you. Or at least grow up."

"Guys like him rarely do."

"I never thanked you for what you did." One red-tipped nail made circles on the table. "Trying to talk to Cade, I mean."

He gave a non-committal shrug. "No big deal."

"It was to me." This time the smile was genuine and reached her eyes. "My knight in shining armor to the rescue again."

"For all the good it did."

"Well, he did get the ass kicking he deserved."

Max grunted. Ancient history.

"He called me the day before you left town."

This was news to him, and he jerked upright.

"He said if I knew what was good for me, I'd keep my allegations to myself."

"He threatened you?" It took tremendous effort not to shout. "And you didn't tell me?"

She pulled at a thread on the hem of the coat in front of her. "I knew he was bluffing. Besides, I had no intention of staying around at that point and told him so." She sighed and looked at him again, her gaze open and assessing. "I often wondered what might have happened had I taken you up on the marriage thing."

He shook his head slowly. "We both know that would have been a mistake."

"Why?"

"Aside from the fact that we were kids ourselves," he said firmly, "we didn't love each other. Not in that way."

"Well, with the hindsight of adulthood," she said softly, "I can't help but think it might have worked." She paused. "You'd make a great father."

Uncomfortable with her train of thought, he changed the subject. "Have you lived in Dallas since you left here?"

She watched his face closely, then nodded. "Yeah." She leaned back in the chair. "The money you sent helped me get set up in a small apartment."

"Your folks?"

"Logan is their only grandchild. They helped out until I was able to go to work." She straightened, then tugged on that thread again. "They moved to Frisco when he was four."

"You never married." It was more statement than question.

"No."

"Why not?"

Both shoulders rose as she sighed. "I dated some, but most weren't interested in a ready-made family." She looked up, emerald eyes probing his. "What about you?"

He shook his head and changed topics. "What do you do? I mean, your job?"

"I work at a bank in North Dallas." She gave a timid smile. "Made vice president two weeks ago."

"Congratulations."

"Thanks."

Max broke the extended silence. "Why Logan?"

She rested her chin on her palm. "It reminded me of you." Her voice grew soft and reflective. "The only good thing that ever happened to me here."

Another uneasy silence ensued.

"Did they think it was me? Is that why they wouldn't let me see you back then?"

"Maybe. I don't know. I told them it wasn't you all along, but I don't think they believed me. When you left so abruptly…I finally told Mom several years ago. I don't know if she told Dad or not. As far as they're concerned, his father is dead."

"Why didn't you push it? Make him take a test or something? The Jacksons had the money to support him."

"Cade knew, Max. He knew and denied it." Her face turned scarlet. "He told me I wasn't the first piece of tail to try and tie him down."

All the old anger and resentment came boiling back to the surface in a heartbeat. "I'll kill him."

She reached across the table and took his clenched fist between her hands. "No. You won't because he's not worth it. It took me a long time to realize that, but I did. Now I don't want him anywhere near my son."

Max took a couple of deep breaths before he could speak. "Cade is already deflecting this away from himself, just like always, putting his own spin on things."

She sat back in the chair and picked at that damn loose thread again.

He wondered if the hem would survive after all this was done.

She glanced around the kitchen. "It's getting late. I need to find a place to stay." She stood and gathered her things. "I'm sorry you got caught in the middle of this. I truly am."

"There's a couple of motels in town." He rattled off the names. "It's the weekend, so better call and see if they have any vacancies."

She pulled out her phone and looked up the numbers. "Thanks."

Max hurried to the bathroom while she placed the call, just to put some distance between them. The thought occurred to him she might want to pick things up where they left off, maybe take it further this time. Maybe he read too much into her actions just now. He hoped so. He still cared about her, of course. As a friend. Nothing more. His heart belonged to Sky.

He shut the door and splashed his face with cold water, then canvassed his reflection with candor. Fear, stark and vivid, glittered in the eyes staring back at him. Fear? Of what? Losing something he never had in the first place? Or fear Sky would turn her back on him like everyone else in his life he cared about?

"Embrace the suck." His mind a crazy mixture of hope, fear, and resignation, he pulled out his phone and dialed Sky's number. After five rings, her answering machine picked up. Several seconds passed as a cold knot of anxiety formed in his stomach. He hadn't checked to see if her car was back. What if she knew it was him and didn't answer? What if something was wrong with Maddie? What if that scene in the kitchen killed any chance he had?

Mouth bone dry, it took two attempts to get past the tightness in his throat and find his voice. Uncertainty rang in every drawn-out word. "Hey… It's me…Max. I'm helping her find a place to —" The machine cut off before he finished. "Great. Just effing great." He ended the call and crammed the phone back in his pocket. He knew she had a cell phone but had not asked for the number. And she hadn't volunteered it, so had no other way to contact her.

His mood see-sawed back and forth from cliff-jumping despair to blazing anger as mumbled curses filled the small room. He wanted to hit something. Hard. Anything to release the tension building inside him like a volcano on the verge of eruption.

"No," he whispered to the tortured man in the mirror. "I won't let it in. I am stronger than the anger. I won't let it in."

Two deep breaths later, followed by another splash of cold water, and he was himself again. He walked back to the kitchen to find Anna sitting at the table.

"The one near the interstate was full. The other one only had one room with a single bed. Told him I'd be there shortly." She didn't look at him as she continued. "I called his cell, but it went to voicemail."

"Give me his number. I'll call and tell him he can stay here tonight."

Her head jerked up.

"You said there's only one bed. He can sleep on the couch again." He casually glanced out the window and saw Sky's car wasn't there. Concern for Maddie made his voice sharp. "He needs to cool off."

She flinched but said nothing.

He shoved his hands in his pockets. "Have you eaten anything?"

She stared a moment, then shook her head. "I got some

coffee from your friend at the diner. Planned to take Logan out for dinner later, but…"

"My friend?"

"The pretty girl at the diner. She said y'all were friends and that she lived next door." She nodded toward Sky's house.

"We had a date tonight." Why the hell did he tell her that?

Her face turned a brilliant shade of red. "Oh, no. I ruined it, didn't I?" She rose and stood in front of him. "Max…" She reached out and touched his arm. "Once again, all I can say is I'm sorry."

He stepped away, effectively brushing off the hand on his arm. "Why don't you follow me to the diner. You can get something to eat, and I'll give you directions to the motel. It's nothing fancy but will do for tonight."

She hesitated only briefly before nodding in agreement, then turned in silence and grabbed her things from the table.

Neither spoke as they walked outside.

Ten minutes later, they walked into the diner.

His heart gave a painful jerk when he spotted Billy Ray.

Holding hands with Sky.

CHAPTER
Twenty-Four

Max glanced around the conspicuously silent diner.

The collective group cast furtive glances between him, Anna, and Sky and waited for the other shoe to drop.

Sonofabitch.

His jaw tightened, and he ushered Anna toward the booth where Sky sat with Billy Ray. Her expression revealed nothing, which scared the hell out of him. She should be angry at least, hurt even, yet her countenance showed none of that.

Before he could take two steps, Big John clamped a huge paw on his shoulder. "Y'all are late," he boomed loud enough to be heard in the kitchen. "We were going to order without you."

Confused, Max simply stared at his friend.

And then Sky was in front of him, a smile on her face as she patted his chest and turned to Anna. "I hope he didn't rush you too much." She looked at him again, and her smile grew. "He can be a bit bossy."

Anna frowned and blinked. "No. Well, maybe a little."

Billy Ray stood and held out a hand to Max. "I tried to talk her into ditching you and going out with me."

He grinned as Max numbly shook his hand, confusion increasing by the second.

"But she'd have none of it." He turned toward Anna. "Hey, Anna Sue. You probably don't remember me. I graduated before you." His grin widened. "But I remember you from the Dairy Barn."

"Um, I …your face is familiar."

"Billy Ray Thomas. Friends call me Bill." He gave her an appreciative glance. "You're even prettier than you were then."

"Save the sweet talk, Bill," groused John. "I'm hungry."

Max stared at the group in turn, unable to form a coherent thought, much less a sentence.

John didn't appear to notice anything askew as he lowered his voice. "You and Sky need to sort your stuff out and get on with the program." He turned and extended his hand to Anna. "I'm John Andrews, Miss Anna. How about we grab us a booth over here and order a bite."

"Mind if I join you?" asked Bill.

"You already ate," said John.

"But I haven't had dessert."

The two men moved away, with John guiding a silent Anna along.

Sky hooked her arm through his and pulled him into the booth beside her.

"What's going on?" he whispered. "What did I miss?"

"I'll explain in a minute."

He met her earnest gaze and fought to stay focused. "I don't understand."

She touched his face with her fingertips. "I admit, I was a little behind the curve myself at first. But when John said what he did, I knew immediately what I should do."

"Which was?"

She lowered her voice. "There's not a person in this room who hasn't heard the talk." Sky placed her arm through his again and laced their fingers together. "They wanted to see a show. So we gave them one. Just not what they were expecting."

His whole body tensed, and he tried to pull his hand free. "So, this is all just a put-on? A show?"

She tightened her grip, refusing to release him. "No. Of course not." She glanced around, then back to him, cheeks a lovely shade of pink, her eyes glistening. "I admit I was taken aback earlier."

Further explanation wasn't necessary.

She looked down, one hand rubbing the tight muscles of his forearm. "The ugly head of jealousy will rob a perfectly normal and sane person of all rational thought."

"Jealousy?"

"I've never been jealous before, so it took me a while to figure it out." She inhaled deeply and met his gaze. "Common sense should have told me all I needed to know. But, well…I was jealous and a little hurt, too, and…overreacted."

He immediately sobered. "She's an old friend, Sky, who had a meltdown. I didn't know what else to do."

When she smiled this time, the lead weight around his heart disappeared.

She reached up and touched his lower lip with her index finger. "I know I've said this before but it bears saying again. You're a good man, Max, with a good heart." She reached up and kissed him lightly on the lips. Right there in the diner. In front of God and everybody.

"And I'm crazy about you."

The kiss was spontaneous and not something she would normally do. But this was not a normal situation. One look at Max's face when he saw her with Bill, and she knew. He experienced the same hurt and confusion she'd suffered earlier.

Because he cared. He may not love her as she did him, but he cared. And that was a start.

Sky didn't regret her actions. It was her way of telling Max, the town, Anna, and anyone who watched—*he's mine. I'm his.*

His jaw muscles tightened and released. "God, I'm crazy about you, too." He sealed his vow with a tender kiss. "I don't ever want to go through that kind of hell again."

"Me neither."

"Ahem."

They jerked apart and saw Ruby standing there, hands on her hips, face boasting a huge smile. "Y'all need a room, or you gonna order something?"

Heat rushed to Sky's face, and she couldn't meet her boss's teasing gaze.

Max looked at Ruby. "No offense, Miss Ruby, but I promised her dinner at the steakhouse. I'm just a little late on following through."

"I can't go like this," said Sky as she motioned to the jeans and sweater she had donned after her bath. "I don't even have makeup on."

He tucked a wayward lock of hair behind her ear, then lightly touched her cheek with his knuckle. "You look beautiful to me."

Deep and sensual, his voice sent a surge of awareness through her, and her heart did a little flip.

"No worry," said Ruby. "You look just fine." She turned toward the booth where Bill appeared to be holding court. "I reckon they can fend for themselves. Let me know if y'all need something." She walked back to the kitchen without a backward glance.

About that time, Bill jumped up and walked over to them. "Hey, Anna said she was going to stay at that motel off forty-three." He shook his head. "Bad idea. Lot of shi-uh, stuff goes on out there. Not a good place for a woman alone."

"What about the one out by the interstate?" asked Sky.

"Full up."

She looked at Max. He shook his head. "Logan's sleeping on my couch. And no way in hell can she be there, too."

"Well," offered Bill, "you could bunk at my place. Then she could stay there."

"I don't know," said Max. "They aren't really speaking right now."

"She can stay at my place." Even Sky was surprised by the offer, but she quickly covered it up. "Maddie has twin beds in her room, and she's spending the night at Bonnie's."

"Sky," said Max, "You don't have to do this."

"I want to." *Liar, liar, pants on fire.*

"Good," said Bill as he clapped his hands together. "I'll let her know."

When he was gone, Max looked at Sky. "That's really nice of you, considering all the crap you've had to deal with because of them."

Face flaming, she ducked her head. *Dammit. What was I thinking? I just invited HER to spend the night when it's HIM I want. I'm such a sucker.*

He placed a finger under her chin and tilted her face up.

His voice held an odd yet gentle tone. "You have a kind and loving heart. One that gives without question." He brushed a kiss across her lips. "It's one of the things I love about you."

CHAPTER
Twenty-Five

Max pulled Sky tight against him, enjoying these few moments of alone time on her couch. "I had a great time tonight," he said softly.

"Me, too," said Sky as she snuggled against him, one hand resting on his thigh.

"I can't remember the last time I drove around looking at Christmas lights," said Max. "That was nice, too."

"Maddie will be upset she missed it. She's already asking when we can put the tree up."

"Maybe we could take her one day next week?"

"Okay."

The evening may have started out rocky, but it would end pleasant enough, all things considered. The steak was good, the company better. Afterwards, they skipped the dance and drove around admiring all the Christmas lights. No destination in mind, they simply appreciated being together, talking about whatever came up. In a typical East Texas weather move, temps were in the upper fifties, so being out at night wasn't bad. Next week would be a different story, though, so they enjoyed it while they could.

"You know," she said wistfully, "I haven't been on a real date since before we moved here."

"You're kidding."

"Nope."

"Are the men in this town blind?" Immediately, his mind conjured up the image of Billy Ray sitting across from her, obviously liking her company. "Except for Bill, of course."

"Jealous, Mr. Logan?"

"Damn straight." He tightened his arm around her shoulders and kissed the top of her head.

She twisted around and brushed her lips across his cheek, then looked into his eyes. "Don't be. He knows my heart is taken."

He took a deep breath. "So is mine."

A comfortable silence followed as they enjoyed the normalcy of just being together.

Max glanced at his watch. "Any idea what time Anna will come back? I haven't heard Logan's truck yet."

Sky shifted beside him. "Ready to go home so soon?"

"Not on your life. Just asking."

"Well, when we spoke earlier, she said she really wanted to talk to him tonight and planned to wait at your place so she wouldn't miss him."

A cramp chose that moment to tighten up his leg, and he stretched it out.

Immediately, Sky sat up. "I noticed you favor that leg some."

"Souvenir from my last tour." He rubbed the knot in his thigh where shrapnel from the IED had torn through him. "Cramps up sometimes."

She looked at his leg. "I'm a nurse. We're good at fixing cramps."

Before he could refuse, she pushed his hands out of the way and massaged the knotted muscle. "How's that?"

The cramp slowly disappeared beneath her skillful hands, and he relaxed. "Better. Thanks."

She skated her hands along his thigh, and he grit his teeth. The resulting discomfort had nothing to do with cramps and everything to do with her hands on his body.

He jumped when his cell phone rang, for once grateful for an interruption. He was surprised to hear Anna's voice. "Hello? What? Um, well. Yeah. Um, Okay. I'll let her know."

He hung up and looked at Sky. "That was Anna. She didn't have your number. Logan's on his way home now. She hopes they can talk things out tonight." Heat burned his cheeks, and he looked away. "She didn't think I'd want to be on hand for it." No way in hell would he tell her what Anna actually said. "Sky's good people, Max, and it's obvious y'all need some time alone. Maybe he'll talk to me, maybe he won't. Either way, I'll stay out of your hair for a couple of hours."

Her eyes connected with his, one brow arched up in question. "So…does this mean you have no place to go right now?"

"…It would appear so."

"Ten's too early to call it a night."

"Yeah." His heart was beating so fast, he thought for sure he'd pass out. It was worse than his first PFT (physical fitness test) in boot camp.

"We could have a nightcap."

Desire sizzled through his body. It was always like that with her. One word, a gesture, a smile, and he was off to the races. It took a lot of effort to tamp it down. "Sure. Whatever."

The air around them sparked with excessive energy.

Sky broke the electrified silence. "We can expect what? An hour, more or less?"

He could speak, or he could breathe, but he couldn't do both. He nodded.

She got up and reached for his hand to pull him up. "Then I don't think we need to waste any more time talking." She raised up on her toes and kissed him lightly on the lips. "Do you?"

Before he could answer, she disappeared down the hall.

Sky's brain raced with warnings and comparisons. Sexy underwear won't cover up my big butt and that little stomach pooch. My boobs are okay, but I bet Anna doesn't have an ounce of fat anywhere. I'm crazy for doing this.

She swallowed hard and pushed open her bedroom door, Max's footsteps close behind. She ignored the negative side of her brain and focused on what she wanted. This time with him. Needed it with an intensity that was almost frightening. Everything up to now had been a prelude, building and growing stronger as her love for him blossomed.

She didn't turn on the lights, opting for the soft glow of her bedside lamp. The discreet click of the door as it closed sent a delicious quiver to the pit of her stomach.

"Are you sure about this, Sky?"

Husky and deep on a good day, this new gravelly rasp made her senses spin. She turned the covers back with trembling hands and faced him. "I've never been surer of anything in my life."

He roughly cleared his throat. "This is a hell of a time to bring this up, but," primal and raw, his raspy voice faltered. "I haven't been with anyone in a long time."

"Me neither."

The muscles in his throat moved up and down when he swallowed. "I didn't expect…I didn't bring anything."

Heat rose up her neck and covered her face. "Um, well, I…didn't…damn." She forced herself to meet his burning gaze and gestured toward the nightstand. "In there. I got them from Jeannie today."

"Jeannie? At *the Sash*?"

"If she hadn't mentioned it…"

A flash of humor crossed his face before he gave her body a raking gaze, his eyes eliciting pinpricks of heat everywhere they touched. Calloused hands cupped her face with the utmost tenderness. "I never thought I'd ever say this to anyone." He swallowed hard. "I love you, Skylar Ward."

"I love you, Max Logan. With all my heart."

One step, and she was in his arms. He lowered his head and sought her lips in the semi-darkness, the anticipation almost unbearable.

His mouth devoured hers as his hands explored the hollows of her back.

She wrapped her arms around his neck and returned his kiss with all the suppressed hunger coursing through her. This was what she craved. This connection. This passion.

This man.

His demeanor roughened as he tightened his hold on her body.

She moaned softly when his lips left hers to spin a trail of fire from her earlobe, down her neck and across her shoulder. Shivers racked her body when his hot breath warmed her skin, and she clutched his arms to keep upright.

He slid one hand underneath the sweater to cup her breast.

She gasped when a thumbnail scraped across the sensitive nub before he covered it with his hand and squeezed. Her head lolled back as his lips continued their sensual assault. Her senses reeled, and she panted through slightly parted lips.

Consumed with the desire to have his skin against hers, she yanked at his shirt, pulling it roughly up his torso. He stepped back and stripped it off and tossed it aside.

She raked her hands over his chest, delighting in the quivering muscles under her fingertips.

And then she saw the scars.

One on his shoulder, another on his left side. Still another across his chest.

She touched the one on his chest, and he covered her hand with his. "I'm sorry. It's not a pretty sight."

"Shhh," she whispered as she leaned in to kiss the welt on his side. He shuddered when she traced the line across his chest with her tongue. "We all have scars, Max," she said softly and moved to the one on his shoulder. "Some are visible." The one on his cheek came next. "Some are not." She took his face in her hands. "I want to know everything about you…scars and all…when you're ready to tell me."

He pulled her roughly against him and rocked gently back and forth. "I don't deserve you," he whispered into her hair. "I don't."

"We deserve each other." She skated her hands up and down his back, fingered yet another wound, smaller than the others, then pulled back far enough to run her tongue around first one taut nipple then the other, the sharp hiss of his breath saying he liked it. When she scraped her teeth over it, he groaned and stepped back.

He pulled the edge of her sweater up and over her head,

trapping her arms in the sleeves as he brushed kisses down her neck and across her chest.

Breath lodged in her throat when his tongue delved down the valley between her breasts and nipped at the nipple through the lacy fabric of her bra.

"Pink is my new favorite color," he groaned.

Blood surged from her toes to her fingertips, followed by tremors of delight. She gulped air through constricted lungs, face half hidden in the folds of her sweater. "Max…"

He pulled the top all the way off and tossed it over his shoulder.

Her whole body shivered like a leaf in the wind when he pulled one bra strap down her shoulder, then the other.

He rubbed his chin over the soft mounds, the scruff of his beard making her overly sensitive skin tingle.

She gasped when bare chest met bare chest as her bra vanished.

Her jeans soon landed atop the growing pile, leaving her with nothing but the matching lace panties.

She suffered a moment of insecurity, resisting the urge to cover herself. Did he notice the flaws? Would he be disappointed?

The smoldering flame in his eyes as he stepped closer de-railed that train of thought.

He ran both hands over her shoulders, down her arms, and around her waist to cup her bottom, pressing her firmly against him. His uneven breath was warm against her cheek as they held the pose.

The coarse hair on his chest rubbing against her nipples stimulated a moan of pleasure, so she did it again. And again.

Her trembling fingers fumbled with the buttons on his

jeans and managed to get them down past his hips before he kicked them off, followed by his boxers.

Her own breath sputtered as hunger and need blazed in the whiskey-colored eyes watching her. She closed the distance between them and placed her hands on his chest, enjoying the hard thumps of his heart beneath her palms that said she wasn't the only one on fire.

He made a guttural noise low in his throat and lifted her into the cradle of his arms. "My beautiful Sky," he whispered as he gently placed her on the bed and lay down beside her, claiming her lips once more.

She squirmed under the hand that glided across her midriff all the way to her thigh, while his mouth nibbled her earlobe and down her neck. Fingers fisted, she sucked in a breath as his tongue scorched a path down her ribs to her stomach and back up again, his ardor surprisingly, touchingly restrained.

Her breasts surged at the intimacy of his touch, the way he shaped and molded each one before his lips touched a hardened tip with tantalizing possessiveness.

She moaned and pressed his head down with one hand, while the other ran up and down his back, her nails digging into the taut flesh.

He suckled first one dusky tip and then the other as his hand slipped lower, gliding over her waist to her thighs. He suckled harder as his fingers slid under the edge of the scrap of lace covering her core to explore the hidden softness.

She arched upward as his fingers rolled over the sensitive flesh sending shockwaves through her and bringing her perilously close to the abyss.

She cried out and angled to grip him in her hand, exploring his length in quick, even strokes.

His tormented groan was a heady invitation, and she increased the pressure.

"Wait," he grated as he got on his knees beside her. Ten seconds later, the lace disappeared. He grabbed the foil pack and sheathed himself.

She lifted her arms in silent invitation.

Anchoring her with one searing kiss, he joined them together in the primordial act of possession. He was hers. She was his.

Her body melted against him, the pleasure pure and explosive. The earth careened on its axis, and she gasped in sweet agony. "Max…" Her hands raked up and down his back. Waves of ecstasy throbbed through her, and the world was filled with him. Only him.

Their bodies moved in exquisite harmony, the tempo changing as the flames of passion soared. Slow and steady became fast and furious as she matched his urgency with her own unsated needs.

She wrapped her legs around his waist as he propelled himself forward, withdrew, and pushed again. Each move brought new sensations, taking her higher and higher.

Sweat-coated bodies slithered against each other, adding to the sensory overload that pushed her closer and closer to the chasm.

Frantic hands raked up and down his back as Sky sucked in air, her body thrumming with incredible sensations. Her fingers gripped the bulging muscles in his back as his thrusts came harder and faster. She sensed it building, growing stronger, as she teetered on the edge of the precipice.

She couldn't get close enough, move fast enough to soothe the aching need that ballooned inside and begged for release.

Max smothered her cry with a kiss as they crested the peak together, their bodies convulsing as one in a shattering explosion of pleasure.

Heavy breathing was the only sound in the room as they waited for equilibrium to return.

Braced on his elbows, Max bowed his head until his forehead touched hers. He'd never had such an experience before. It went way beyond sex. Beyond the physical. She touched his soul, melded his heart to hers forever.

It was exhilarating. And scared the hell out of him at the same time. If he lost her…he wouldn't let himself complete the thought.

He couldn't.

When their breathing regained some semblance of normal, he rolled to the side and rose to dispose of the condom. "Be right back."

A few minutes later, he slid under the covers next to her. The beauty of her naked body, still moist from their lovemaking, called to him like a siren, and he tucked her against him.

Her head on his shoulder, she snuggled close, one leg thrown over his, her knee near his groin, one hand splayed over his heart.

"I wish I had the words to say what you mean to me, Sky," His throat tightened to the point he feared choking. "I wish I did."

She raised up on her elbow and fixed those rustic honey-gold eyes on his. "Oh, Max," she whispered.

"You're my heart. My soul. Without you, I'd be nothing more than a speck of dust on the ground."

Tears gathered in the corners of her eyes, yet she smiled. "Those words are perfect." She bent down and kissed him.

A slow, drugging kiss that sang through his veins like hundred-proof whiskey, unleashing a sudden tremor of arousal.

She pulled back and flashed a sexy smile that sent another burst of blood southward.

"Already? I'm impressed."

He rolled her onto her back and straddled her knees. "You think that's something, lady, just wait."

CHAPTER
Twenty-Six

Sky woke when Max slowly slipped his arm from under her head, depriving her of the heat radiating from him. "What? Is something wrong? What time is it?"

He grinned and tapped her nose. "Nothing's wrong, and it's after two."

She flinched and looked around. "In the morning?" She couldn't get rid of the cobwebs of exhaustion caused by a night of lovemaking with Max.

His husky laugh raised gooseflesh on her arms. Damn. Even his laugh was sexy.

"Yes. In the morning. I'm sorry I woke you. You need some rest."

She stretched like a cat and smiled when his hooded eyes got *the* look. "Whose fault is that?" She patted the space beside her. "Just a few more minutes. I'm cold. You're hot."

He resumed his spot and took her in his arms.

I could get used to waking up like this, she thought but didn't voice it, unwilling to put a damper on what was definitely the best day of her life. Well, except for when Maddie was born, but that was different.

"I can almost hear the wheels in your head turning," he mused. "What gives?"

"I was just thinking about how my life has changed in such a short period of time."

"Good change, I hope."

She rubbed her hand across his chest, fingering the tight curls there. "Definitely good."

The soft rumble of his laugh vibrated in his chest. "You had me worried there for a minute."

She rubbed her knee against his leg, up to the jagged scar, stopping when he flinched. "I'm sorry. Does it hurt?"

"No…it's…ugly." He paused. "You're the only one besides the medical staff who's seen it."

She raised up on her elbow so that they were eye to eye. "I know there's a lot we haven't talked about, stuff we may never talk about. But know this, Max. There is nothing—nothing about you that will ever be ugly to me. If you want to talk, I'll listen. I won't judge, and I won't preach. And I will always be here for you."

His heart beat steady and strong beneath her hand as he gazed at her with eyes so full of tenderness, her own heart skipped a beat.

She lay back down and sighed, soft curves molding to the contours of his lean body.

It was Max who broke the prolonged silence. "War is nothing like the movies," he said softly. "People die for real. It's…it's ugly."

He covered the hand on his chest and squeezed. "I don't want tonight to be spoiled by bringing that up right now. But I will tell you. All of it. Or as much as you want to hear." His hand tightened. "But not tonight. Okay?"

She nodded and tried to think of something to bring back the blissful mood. "I can tie a cherry stem in a knot with my tongue."

"…Oh yeah?"

"Uh-huh." She raised her head slightly and looked at him. "One of my many talents."

"That a fact?" He pulled her on top of him and ran his hands down her back and over her hips, cupping her bottom.

"Play your cards right, and I'll show you."

He groaned. "You're killing me."

"You complaining?"

"Not on your life." His last words were smothered against her lips.

Sweet and tender, it was a kiss to remember for all time.

Max pushed back gently. "But I really should leave. Anna came in a long time ago."

She jerked back. "She did? I never heard her."

His charming, self-satisfied grin was sexy as hell.

"You were—busy."

"Well, if I was busy, so were you." She tapped his chest with her finger. "How did you hear? Was I boring you?"

His chuckle made her bounce on his chest, and she found that mildly erotic.

"Hardly. I'm trained to multitask." He rubbed his hands on her backside and gently squeezed. "You have a great ass."

She stared a moment, finding his remark oddly endearing. "Is that supposed to be an example of multitasking?"

"Maybe."

She stretched out along the length of him, marveling at how well they fit together. "Now that I think about it, you are able to do several things at one time."

In one smooth move, she was on her back looking up at him.

"Keep that up, and I'll never get out of here."

"Like I'd complain."

"You have to work tomorrow. And you have company."

Heat rushed to her face as she recalled her rather active life the last few hours. "Oh dear. Do you think she heard us?"

He snickered. "Probably."

She gasped.

He kissed the tip of her nose. "Relax. I'm sure she was exhausted from dealing with Logan and slept through it all." He looked around the room. "Maybe. Where are my clothes?"

She donned her robe and helped gather his things, then sat on the edge of the bed. The intimacy of watching him watch her as he dressed was one thing. The sense of fulfillment she experienced was another and totally astounded her.

When he was done, he pulled her up and kissed her again. "Go back to bed. I'll see myself out."

"Will you be over for coffee in the morning as usual?"

"Better see how the natives are first."

"Oh. Yeah. Right."

One more extended embrace, and he left, closing the door softly behind him.

Sleep was a long time coming, but when it did, it was the deep, pleasurable slumber of a very satisfied lover.

Sky woke to sunlight streaming in the bedroom window. She yawned and stretched, then pulled Max's pillow to her chest, inhaling the tangy aroma that lingered. The smile of contentment vanished in a heartbeat when she saw the time. Seven o'clock. She hadn't slept that late in forever. And she had a guest in the house.

She rolled out of bed and took the fastest shower on record. She left her hair wet as she hurriedly dressed and headed for the kitchen.

Anna sat at the table, a cup of coffee in front of her.

She cleared her throat and sat up straight. "I, um, hope you don't mind. The pot was ready, so I turned it on."

Sky couldn't look at her as she grabbed a cup. "Good. Now I don't have to wait for it."

She filled her cup and faced her guest, unsure of what to say.

"I have to thank you. Again," said Anna. "I don't know that I could be as gracious under the circumstances."

She shrugged. "No big deal, but you're welcome."

Anna gave a light scoff. "I'm a total stranger who put you in the middle of an unmitigated mess. Not to mention causing problems for your date."

Sky grinned, tried to make light of the situation. "Well, when you put it that way…"

Anna twirled the cup in front of her, and Sky noted the dark circles under her eyes, the strain in her face. "Did you sleep all right?" Immediately, heat crept up her neck as she contemplated one of the possible reasons for her sleepless night. "Was the bed comfortable?"

Anna nodded but didn't look up. "Max is a great guy and a good friend. That's all. We knew each other in high school and haven't been in touch in years."

"I know." Sky stopped herself from asking questions she might not want to know the answers to.

Anna continued to stare at her cup. "I will say, though, when I found out where Logan was and that he'd talked to Max…" She looked up and watched Sky closely as she continued. "I wondered what would happen."

Before Sky could speak, her houseguest continued. "He was my knight in shining armor back then, my best friend." She nibbled her lower lip. "I wasn't sure how it would be to see him again. I mean, we're not kids anymore, and I shouldn't have to depend on him to drag my butt out of the fire again. But he's nothing if not loyal to his friends." She paused. "When I saw y'all at the diner, I knew right away."

Sky gulped her coffee, flinching when the hot liquid burned her tongue.

"A blind person could see he's crazy about you."

Embarrassed, Sky could only nod. "The feeling is mutual."

For the first time since Sky walked in the room, Anna smiled. "I gathered that last night."

Coffee sloshed all over the table, and Sky's face burned like fire.

"I'm so sorry," offered Anna as she yanked a paper towel off the roll on the table. "I didn't mean that the way it sounded. I—I said it before I thought."

It took a moment, but Sky managed a reply. "Yeah, well, that's the elephant in the room."

"You've been beyond kind to me," said Anna sincerely. "And I repay that by embarrassing you. I'm so sorry."

"It's fine. Really." Sky tossed the wet towels in the trash and refilled her cup. "Refill?"

"I'm good. Thanks." Anna cleared her throat. "So, about the other elephant in the room."

Sky looked at her.

"Max is not Logan's father."

That was unexpected. She returned the pot to the coffee maker, trying to keep the surprise from showing in her voice. "I know. He told me."

There was a slight pause before Anna spoke again. "Did he…did he tell you who is?"

Sky resumed her seat at the table. "No. Said it wasn't his story to tell." Sky debated saying more. *What the hell.* "I have my suspicions, though."

Silent, Anna looked up, eyes probing.

Sky blurted out, "Cade."

Anna's face lost all color, and she squeezed her eyes shut. "How…what?"

"I just put some bits and pieces together." She left it at that for now.

"Max said they met at the diner. Cade and Logan."

"Briefly. Cade overheard Logan ask about his father but barely even glanced his way. He was more interested in implying it was Max."

Deflated, Anna sank back in her chair.

Curiosity got the best of Sky. "Why does Cade dislike him so? Max claims he doesn't need a reason to hate, but it has to be more than that."

"You mean more than me?"

"I'm sorry, I didn't—" Sky fumbled for words.

"With the clarity of adulthood, Cade was jealous of Max from day one."

Dumbfounded, Sky sat back in her chair. "Jealous?"

She nodded. "Max was smarter, better looking if a bit skinny. He had this air about him, even back then."

"What kind of air?"

She shoved hair away from her face. "Part rebel, part peacemaker. He didn't make friends easily, but when he did, he was as loyal as they come. Girls were drawn to him. Maybe it was the I-don't-need-anyone attitude. I don't know, but they sought him out." She sipped her coffee. "If Cade thought he was interested in someone, he stepped in and ruined it. Made a big deal about him being a foster kid, and a bad one at that. Had no qualms about making stuff up to reinforce his point. Went out of his way to humiliate him, provoke him."

Sky simply couldn't understand that. "Why?"

She lifted her shoulder in a half shrug. "Cade could buy anything he wanted except respect. Max had it in spades. Cade hated him for it."

"Then why— I'm sorry, that's none—"

"Why did I fall for him?" She inspected her fingernails.

"…Yes."

Anna rubbed her forehead and expelled a long breath. "My folks were your basic working-class people. I was pretty enough, I guess, but shy and naïve." She tore off a corner of a paper towel and put it in front of her. "Cade was the local heartthrob. Family had money, prestige. When he first started coming around, I was thrilled. *The* Cade Jackson actually spoke to *me*." She pinched off another piece of the towel. "Then he started eating lunch with me, walked me to second period, hung around my locker." She made a pile of the towel pieces, then moved it around with her finger. "Max tried to tell me, but I wouldn't listen." She cleared her throat again. "I accused him of being jealous, of not wanting me to have a life."

She raised her head. "What's the one thing women do when they fall for someone everyone says is no good for them?"

Sky leaned back in her chair. "Believes she's the one who can change them," she said softly.

"Bingo." She smoothed down her slacks and rolled her shoulders. "I believed every lie he told me. When I discovered

I was pregnant, I was ecstatic. I envisioned this whole scenario of how I'd tell him, and he'd be overjoyed. We'd be married and live happily ever after."

Pity for Anna's plight came unbidden. "I can't imagine how horrid that was for you. And scary, too."

"I don't know what I would have done if not for Max. He even tried to talk to Cade, get him to do the right thing."

"I can't see that going well."

She snorted. "It didn't. Max ended up beating the crap out of him. Took three people to pull him off." She lowered her head and toyed with the paper shreds. "I don't know what he said to push Max that far."

Silently, Sky waited for Anna to continue.

"Anyway, Cade's family had money, his father was president of the school board, so Max was the bad guy. Got kicked out of school right before graduation. Thankfully, that didn't keep him from getting his diploma, though Mr. Jackson did try and stop that, too. Max joined the Marines, and here we are, almost eighteen years later, dealing with the same crap all over again."

"What are you going to do?"

"I don't know."

"This is a small town. Most of the people who were there then are still here." She let Anna draw her own conclusions.

They both knew it was just a matter of time.

Anna's voice cracked. "I know." She tore up more paper. "All his life, I've preached about responsibility, respect, even abstinence." Emerald eyes glistened with unshed tears. "He already thinks I'm a liar. Now, he'll think I'm a hypocrite, too."

Sky didn't know what to say. She understood the difficulty of being a single parent, could even sympathize with

Anna's plight. But in the end, only Anna could decide what to do.

Sky took a breath. "Being a parent, especially a single one, is the hardest job in the world. We have to be perfect, always know the right answer, do the right thing. We aren't allowed to make mistakes. We can't be human."

"Bill said you have a daughter?"

"Maddie. She'll be eight on Christmas Eve."

Anna chewed her bottom lip. "Her dad?"

"We divorced when Maddie was two and a half." Sky read the unspoken question in Anna's eyes. "He hasn't been a part of her life since."

"Does she…"

"Ask about him? She did recently, but it was the first time in a long time." In an effort to bring some levity to the conversation, she continued. "She's the reason Max and I are together." By the time Sky finished the story, Anna was laughing.

"I'd like to meet her."

"She'll be here this afternoon and thrilled to have a roommate. She'll talk your head off, though."

Anna shook her head. "I called the hotel this morning, and they should have a room available later today. I won't impose on your hospitality any longer."

Further conversation ended with a knock on the door.

Sky opened it to find Logan standing there, his face tight and drawn.

He walked in without preamble and tossed a cell phone on the table. "You left your phone last night. That guy Cade Jackson has called twice. Said it's important that you call him right away." He shoved his hands in his front pockets. "It's him, isn't it? He's my father."

CHAPTER
Twenty-Seven

Max couldn't remember the last time he woke so refreshed. No troubling dreams, no waking up a gazillion times, no tossing and turning waiting for sleep to come. Just wonderful, restful sleep. Evidently, a round of lovemaking with the most beautiful woman in the world was the secret.

A quick glance at the bedside clock said he had time to grab a cup of coffee with Sky before she left for work. If his houseguest was still asleep.

He peeked in the living room as he walked by, curbing his disappointment when he saw the empty couch.

Logan wasn't in the kitchen either. He debated the advisability of going next door anyway when he saw Logan enter Sky's house. Unsure of what his presence might mean, he walked across the drive.

Before he could knock, Sky opened the door.

"Come on in and join the party."

He noted she didn't smile, and her voice was strained.

Anna sat at the table, one hand at the base of her throat, twin lines of worry creasing her brow. "You talked to Cade? What did he say?"

"He sounded pissed," snapped Logan. "Said you better not be starting that same shit again."

He held up a hand and looked at Max. "His words, not mine." He turned back to his mother. "It's him, isn't it?"

The rhythmic tick-tock of the big clock on the wall and steady drip-drip from the sink faucet were the only sounds in the room. Max did a double take at Sky when he noted no surprise at all in her expression. Only sympathy and understanding emanated from her concerned gaze as she looked between mother and son. How did she know? Did Anna tell her?

Logan took an unsteady step toward the table and drug out a chair. Without a word or even a glance around, he sat down.

Tick-tock.

Drip-drip.

Max didn't realize he held his breath until Sky crossed his vision with a glass of water, which she placed in front of the boy.

She walked back to her spot by the sink, placing a hand on Max's bicep and squeezing lightly as she passed.

Tick-tock.

Drip-drip.

Tension buzzed and crackled in the air like electric sparks. The ominous silence continued, as though everyone was unable or maybe afraid to break it for fear the room would explode from the immense pressure inside.

Logan picked up the glass and downed half of it before putting it back on the table.

Tick-tock.

Drip-drip.

Max glanced at Sky, who watched Anna closely.

The women gazed at each other as though communicating on some secret level, like those whistles only dogs could hear.

If he hadn't been watching so closely himself, he might have missed the almost imperceptible nod from Sky.

He jerked his gaze back to Anna, who inhaled deeply and turned to Logan.

All color drained from her face, and her eyes clenched tightly shut as she whispered, "Yes. Cade Jackson is your father."

Logan's body tensed, and he drew in an audible breath as the impact of Anna's words hit him.

Tick-tock.

Drip-drip.

"Now what?" she asked.

Logan's face paled, and he stared mutely at his mother.

Max's heart ached for the pain reflected in those two words. He tensed at Sky's light touch on his arm, understanding eyes silently offering support.

Logan cleared his throat, and Max turned his attention in that direction.

"Now what?" he stammered, his croaky voice gaining an octave at the end. "That's all you have to say?"

Anna wrung her hands together, then placed them in her lap, eyes focused on her son. "What do you want me to say?"

His previously ashen complexion suddenly bloomed with color. Body tense, he lurched upright in his chair and sucked in a lungful of air. "I want to know why. Why you lied to me my whole life. Why you kept me from him."

Anna's shoulders slumped. Her jaw worked as she ground her teeth together. Arms crossed over her chest, she sighed. "I did what I thought was best for you, son. That's all I ever cared about."

"Why. Did. You. Lie. To. Me." Logan's clipped enunciation

of each word, accompanied by a light tap of one finger on the tabletop, emphasized his grief.

"Nothing good will come of this, Logan," said Max. "That bullshit about the truth setting you free is just that. Bullshit."

He jumped from his chair and whirled on Max. "You know, don't you? You're part of this…this lie."

"I know that your mother did the right thing—"

"For who?" he shouted. "For who?"

"He didn't want you," said Anna softly.

Logan turned to his mother, chest heaving with each labored breath.

"He didn't want either of us."

She swayed when she stood, and both Max and Sky took a step toward her.

"I didn't want you to know." She extended one hand out, then let it drop. "I wanted to protect you from…from that."

A tormented silence once again engulfed the room.

Max put his arm around Sky and pulled her to him, needing the comfort of her nearness.

Logan shook his head. "How could he not want his own kid?"

Tears trailed down Anna's cheeks as she hugged herself tightly and shook her head. "I don't know."

"Because he's an asshole," snapped Max, "who never thinks about anything or anyone except himself." He pulled away from Sky and stepped over to Logan, who didn't resist as Max urged him back in his chair.

This is crazy. I can't do this. I don't want to do this. Even as denial screamed through his brain, he pulled a chair close to Logan and sat down.

"I wish my mother would have been as strong as Annie and told her old man to go to hell."

CHAPTER
Twenty-Eight

Max clutched his hands together in front of him, gaze locked on Logan. "Believe me, kid, we would have all been better off." He paused. "Being forced into something against your will doesn't bode well for happily ever after."

Logan's stiff posture didn't change as Max continued.

"When her old man found out my mother was pregnant, he insisted they get married right away. So they did."

"What happened?"

Logan's hesitant question opened the door to a past he never wanted to remember much less reveal to anyone.

"They made life miserable for all of us." Max took a steadying breath and marginally relaxed at Sky's gentle touch on his shoulders. "I was too young to remember a lot of it, but I do remember the fights, the yelling, the name calling." Painful memories, long buried out of self-preservation, were exhumed one by one.

"He blamed her for ruining his chance to be a big-time football star. She blamed him for drinking away what little money he made." He had to swallow hard before unearthing the next one. "And they both blamed me for being born in the first place."

Sky's grip on his shoulders tightened, but he didn't react. The floodgates opened, and words poured out. Words he'd never spoken to a single human being before.

"I never understood what I did wrong. Tried to be good, do as I was told." Chest so tight he feared something would break, he forced a painful breath. "But…I was nothing more than excess baggage forced on them…and they hated me for it."

Perspiration dotted his forehead and edged its way into his left eye. The sting was nothing compared to the pain of knowing your own parents wished you were never born.

"I was eight when she dropped me off at school one day." He couldn't keep the shake from his voice now or stop the muscle spasms in his chest as the memory washed over him. "I never saw either of them again. I sat outside on the steps till almost dark before the cops came and got me."

Sky listened with rapt attention, her heart breaking with each new revelation. She could not imagine doing something so heinous to Maddie. Or Logan. Or any child.

Torn by what to do, she settled for keeping her hands on his shoulders. When he reached up and grabbed them, holding them against his chest, she knew it was the right thing to do.

"I spent the next ten years going from one foster home to another."

He squeezed her hands so tight, she gritted her teeth against the pain. His chest rose and fell on a long, measured breath, as his head tipped back against her chest, and he closed his eyes.

"Because young boys with anger issues are not considered

adoptable." The words came out in a hoarse whisper, filled with pain, bitterness, and resignation.

A flash of grief so intense it took her breath away swept through Sky. Grief for the small boy who didn't understand what he did wrong. And grief for the man who still carried the pain of that rejection.

But fast on the heels of that came a rush of love for the man he'd become, a man willing to sacrifice himself for his friends, to lay bare his deepest hurt in order to help someone else.

No one spoke as each digested what he had said.

"Oh, Max," said Anna at last. "I didn't know."

He focused on Logan. "You see what she did as lying to you."

Sky glanced at the boy whose dazed, open-mouthed stare remained fixed on Max.

"But I see it as putting your welfare above all else." He paused. "She made sure you had a stable home, food on the table, and never once doubted that you were loved. Because that's what a mother who loves her child does." His voice cracked. "…I wish mine had done the same."

She heard Anna's light gasp but didn't glance her way. Instead, she hugged Max closer. How that revelation must have hurt him.

"She made a mistake by falling for the wrong guy," said Max. "Marrying him would have made bad matters worse."

Defiant, Logan sat up in his chair. "You don't know that."

"Yes. I do," said Max firmly.

"He's right, son." Anna spoke up louder. "It took a while for me to realize that, but I finally did."

"You never gave him a chance!"

"I stopped giving him chances when he…"

"He what, Mom?"

"I did what I thought was best for you."

"What did he do, Mom?" Logan's somber tone implied he didn't really want to know the answer but asked anyway.

"Son, please—"

"Tell me."

"He…wouldn't admit to being your father, even though he knew he was." She paused, then continued in a sinking tone. "He wanted me to get an abortion, but I refused." She stood up straight. "You are the light of my life." She took a step toward him and stopped. "I thought I was doing the right thing. Thought I was protecting you from getting hurt."

Logan stood so quickly, the chair toppled behind him. "I need some air."

Before anyone could react, he was out the back door.

Tick-tock.

Drip-drip.

A suffocating silence filled the room as Sky processed the sequence of events and wondered what on earth would transpire next.

Anna finally broke the protracted quiet. "I'll get my things and get out of your hair," she said softly. "The hotel should have a room available soon."

"Wait," said Sky. "Maybe—maybe you should stay here."

Anna opened her mouth, but Sky interrupted. "I'll be gone till two-thirty or so. You can have some time to yourself." She glanced at the back door. "And you'll be close if y'all need to talk or something."

"I've already imposed on your hospitality enough."

"It's no imposition since I won't be here." She looked at the clock. "Speaking of which, I need to get to work. Ruby wanted me in by ten, and I still have to get dressed."

Anna nodded and left the kitchen.

Sky remained behind Max, arms draped over his shoulders. She wanted to comfort him, say something to ease his pain, but words failed her. She bent down and kissed the top of his head.

He pulled her around until she sat in his lap, her arms around his neck. He buried his face in her chest as he pulled her tightly against him. "I can still remember that day," he said at last, his voice muffled against her shirt. "I kept thinking she's just late again. She'll be here soon."

Sadness tore at her heart as he continued.

"The cops came with social services."

Sorrow closed her throat when he pulled back and looked at her. Had he worn a neon sign, it could not be more clearly discerned. Pain, loneliness, loss, rejection.

"I found out later she'd made the call herself and told them where to find me."

She waited.

"Never heard from either of them again."

"What about her parents? His parents?"

His half-hearted shrug broke her heart.

"Don't remember them. Not even their names." He inhaled, rested his head on her chest again. "They gave me up, and that was the end of it."

She pulled him closer. *No wonder he's so loyal to his friends. He suffered the ultimate rejection.*

"My last foster home, the one that brought me here, was the best I guess, though I was such an ass by then I didn't realize it." One hand made small circles on her thigh. "Guess that's why I ended up back here. Only place I ever stayed more than a few months." He sighed. "I sent them a card maybe five years ago. Wasn't sure what to say except thank you and I'm sorry. No idea if they got it or not."

"Are they still around?"

"…He died two years ago. Heart attack. She moved away. Houston, I think." He expelled a noisy breath. "Told you I was messed up."

"Nobody's perfect."

"You are."

She scoffed and shifted on his lap. "You're biased."

He pulled back to look at her. "You're perfect to me…for me."

She smiled. "And you're perfect for me."

He cupped her chin with one hand, and his thumb caressed her lower lip. His lips slowly captured hers, and she drank in the sweetness of it.

After years of dreaming impossible dreams, hope fluttered in her chest.

CHAPTER
Twenty-Nine

Sky made it to work with ten minutes to spare. "Is Ruby in her office?" she asked the cook on duty this morning.

"Yeah. Said tell you to go on back when you got here."

A million thoughts ran through her mind as she made her way to the back room that served as an office. The door was open, so she cleared her throat to announce her arrival.

"Hey," said Ruby with a big smile. "Come on in. Shut the door."

Uh-oh. A closed-door meeting. What did I do? Crap. I bet she's already heard about Doc's offer.

"Have a seat."

Nothing in Ruby's manner suggested bad news, so Sky tried to relax.

"I'm guessing the date night went well after all?"

Sky sputtered and ignored the rush of heat to her face. "Um, yes. It did."

"I must say, it was really nice of you to offer Anna Sue a place to stay last night." Ruby chuckled. "I'm not sure I'd have been so noble."

"It's no big deal. She and Max are friends, and she was in a bind."

"And that doesn't bother you?" Ruby shuffled papers on her desk. "The friends part, I mean."

"No. Why should it?"

Ruby sighed and crossed her hands on top of the desk. "I'm not one to beat around the bush, so I'm just gonna say it." She paused as though gathering her thoughts. "I like Max. Have from the beginning."

"But?"

"But he's carrying around a lot of baggage."

"Aren't we all?"

"And now that baggage contains a woman and a boy."

"Your point?" It was difficult not to take exception to her remarks, but Sky kept her voice calm.

Ruby sat back in the chair and ran one hand through copper-colored curls. "I'm handling this all wrong. I'm sorry." She sat forward, hands folded together on the desk. "I want you to be happy. You deserve to be happy. If Max is the ticket to achieving that, great. But right now, all I see is you caught in the middle of a hot mess. I'm worried about you."

Explained that way, Sky understood her friend's unease. Nonetheless, she resented the interference but chose her words carefully. "I appreciate your concern, Ruby. I do. But I can handle things."

"Cade is feeding the damn rumor mill fast as he can. He's saying—"

"I know what he's saying. So does Max. Nothing of what that—that SOB says is true."

"I know that." She paused. "We're a small town. The majority of folks are decent, God-fearing individuals. And then you have people like Edith Huffman who loves gossip like a cat loves cream." She held Sky's gaze. "Her favorite adage is where there's smoke—"

Patience limited, Sky spoke up. "I don't care what Edith or anyone else says. People who matter know the truth. The rest are irrelevant."

"I like Max, honey. I do. He's a good man and has helped a lot of people around town. Including me." She shook her head sadly. "When those gossipmongers get their teeth in something, they won't let it go. I just don't want you to be hurt by something they might say."

"Words are just words. A few days from now they'll have someone else to rake over the coals." She straightened in her chair. "If there's nothing else, I have something I meant to talk to you about yesterday."

Ruby hesitated. "You mean Doc's offer?"

Disappointed, Sky sank back in her chair. "I'm sorry you had to hear that from the rumor mill and not from me."

Ruby waved a dismissive hand. "Not to worry. I know how much you want to get back into nursing. So, what's the plan?"

"Well, evidently it's not going to be as difficult as I thought to get my license reactivated since it's been less than four years, but I need to start the process soon."

The next few minutes passed quickly as Sky outlined the details Doc provided in the package Coop had dropped off the other day.

"So, basically, I'd work for her in the office until I complete all the steps needed to get reactivated." She couldn't keep from smiling as she added, "Then I'll be a nurse again."

Ruby nodded. "That's terrific, Sky." She rubbed her hands together. "There's no need for you to wait to accept the offer. You can start whenever you want." She pulled an envelope from a drawer and slid it across the desk. "A little early Christmas present for you."

It took a couple of heartbeats for her words to sink in. "You're firing me?"

Ruby regarded her with frank amusement. "Of course not. Doc is ready for you anytime, and while we'll certainly miss you around here, you're going to be much better off working there."

Sky looked at the envelope like it was a snake.

Ruby chuckled. "It won't bite, you know."

She took the packet and slowly opened it. The cash inside shocked her. "I don't understand."

"I told you. An early Christmas present."

When Sky opened her mouth to protest, Ruby put up a hand to stop her. "You're not only a good employee, Sky, you're a great friend. You have a way with people, and that's a gift not to be wasted. This is just my way of saying how much I appreciate all you have done for me the last couple of years."

Sky stood when her boss rose and came around the desk.

"Christmas is around the corner," said Ruby. "I know things have been tight for you. Maybe this will help."

Tears slowly found their way down Sky's cheeks. She swallowed with great difficulty and finally found her voice. "Oh, Ruby. How can I ever thank you?"

"Invite me to the wedding." She placed an arm around Sky's waist. "And let me bake the cake."

Sky walked around on cloud nine all day. She called Doc right after her conversation with Ruby and said she could start anytime. They agreed Sky would begin work a week from

Monday, which would allow her time to get things in order. Thanks to the gift from Ruby, Sky not only had the option of working or not the next week, she could give Maddie the Christmas she deserved. And pay the rent on time.

But first, she would splurge on a Christmas tree.

A quick call to Max, and they were set to go that afternoon. She then took the time to call Janet Orm's and let her know they would pick Maddie up as soon as Sky got off work. Just thinking about how delighted her young daughter would be made Sky smile even more.

"That must have been some date," teased Bill from his usual spot at the counter. "You've been grinning like a jackass eating briars all day."

She ignored the rush of heat to her face. Bill was Bill. He'd rather tease—and flirt—than eat. "I was just thinking how thrilled Maddie will be when I tell her we're getting a Christmas tree today."

"Cool. Kids love Christmas. Y'all going to the tree farm off ten-oh-two?"

She nodded. "Yes. Mr. Jenkins told me about it this morning. They have wagon rides and hot cider, and you get to cut down your own tree."

"You've never been out there?"

"No. We usually get one at the store." After they went on sale, was the unspoken end to that sentence.

"It's a neat place. Love the smell."

"More coffee?"

"No, thanks. Time to get back to work."

"Must be hard watching TV all day."

Bill shrugged. "Being a jailer is the most boring job in the county. Except for the weekends. We got a lively crowd in there right now."

"I heard there was a fracas after the dance last night."

He snorted coffee when he laughed. "Some of them old codgers still got fire in 'em." He stood and placed some bills on the counter. "Have a good one." He turned around, then stopped. "Say, is, uh, Anna gonna be around a while?"

"I think she has to be back on Wednesday."

"She plan on coming back anytime soon?"

Bill was interested in Anna. That was good to know. "I guess that would depend on whether or not she had something—or someone, to entice her back, now wouldn't it?"

He winked. "I'll have to work on that."

Sunday lunch was usually a busy time, and today was no exception. Sky had just finished ringing up a customer when Logan walked in.

He looked around the crowded diner and turned for the door.

"Hi," she said quickly. "There's an empty booth back in the corner." She shut the cash drawer. "Just give me a minute to clean it."

She hurried off without giving him a chance to reply.

He slid into the booth without looking at her. "Thank you."

"Need a menu?"

He shook his head. "Just coffee. With cream."

"Sure you don't want something to eat? Today's special is Chicken Fried Steak."

The tips of his ears turned bright red when his stomach issued a soft grumble. "I'm good."

She placed the cup on the table, then went to the kitchen and turned in an order for the daily special.

He looked down at the plate when she placed it in front of him a short time later. "I didn't order this."

She smiled. "My treat. Max is a great guy, but I know for a fact he has the least stocked kitchen in the county. A mouse would starve at his place."

When he stared at the steaming plate, she thought for a moment he might refuse it.

"Thank you," he said at last.

"You're welcome." She glanced at a table to the left. "Ready for that dessert, Jason?"

"Yes, ma'am," replied the burley gentleman. "And a warmup on the coffee."

"You got it."

Half an hour later, only a couple of tables were occupied, and Logan remained in the corner booth. When he'd finished the special in record time, Sky added a slice of pecan pie to his meal. He didn't object, merely thanked her and made quick work of devouring it as well. At the moment, he was staring into his cup as though the answer to his woes lay hidden in the heady brew.

How I wish life were that simple, she thought as she took a breath and headed over to clear the empty plate.

"Can I get you anything else, Logan? More coffee?"

He shook his head. "No, ma'am. Thank you." He glanced around the diner. "Is—is my mom still at your house?"

"Yes."

He looked up, and Sky ached for him. Sad eyes radiated so much hurt and confusion, she wished there was something she could do to help.

"I don't know what to do," he said softly. "Or where to go."

Maternal instinct kicked into high gear as the look of

despair washed over his face. She glanced around the near-empty diner and slid into the seat opposite him. She hesitated, then reached across the table and lightly placed her hand over his.

"I can't imagine how difficult this is for you, Logan. And I can't tell you what to do. But I know this. Your mother loves you very much. Everything—everything she did was for that reason."

"How can you say that?" His voice edged up. "You don't know her. Us."

She shrugged. "I'm not sure. Instinct. One mother to another. Call it what you like. The bottom line is, she loves you. And everything she did was with your best interest at heart."

"Would you do it?" His voice contained no animosity, only curiosity.

"None of us can say exactly what we'll do in a given situation. We know what we think we would, but until you're actually faced with it, you don't know." She pulled her hand back and moved the empty pie plate closer and spun it on the table. "Being a parent, especially a single parent, is the hardest job in the world."

"How—I mean, where…" Face bright red, he looked away. "I'm sorry. That's none of my business."

"We divorced before Maddie turned three." She took a deep breath. "He's not been a part of her life since."

"Do you know him? Cade Jackson, I mean?"

"He owns the local hardware store."

He straightened. "I hear it in your voice. You don't like him, either." His statement was flat, resigned. "Why?"

Uncertain, she hesitated. "I don't know him all that well since I've only lived here about three years."

"Why won't anyone give me a straight answer?" This time his voice took on the hard edge of someone about to reach their limit.

Quickly reaching a decision, she took a breath. "What do you want to know?"

CHAPTER
Thirty

Max glanced at his watch. Again. One-thirty. A whole ten minutes had passed since the last time he looked. *Damn. Will two-o'clock ever get here?*

Sky drove herself to work, so there was no need for him to pick her up. But, he rationalized, it would save time if I'm there when she gets off. We can pick Maddie up and go get the tree, then I'll bring her back to get her car.

It sounded like a good plan, but he wondered if she would object to leaving her car. He finally decided to just go when a soft knock on the kitchen door drew his attention.

Maddie stood on the steps, trademark smile in place.

"Hey, Tink." He looked behind her and around the yard. "What are you doing here?"

She hurried inside, her voice bubbling with excitement. "Miss Janet said we're going to go get a Christmas tree. Isn't that terrific!"

Before he could get a word out, she continued in that same breathless kid-like voice that never failed to generate a smile from him.

"I told her I'd just come down here and ride with you. That way, Mama wouldn't have to go pick me up." She clapped her hands together, blue eyes sparkling like sapphires in sunlight. "I can't wait. We've never chopped down a tree before. We always got one at the store. And they have this wagon you get to ride, and they have hot chocolate and stuff."

Evidently, his silence finally penetrated her euphoria because some of the joy in her face gave way to confusion. "Aren't you excited, Max?"

He squatted down in front of her, ignoring the stiff leg muscles that reminded him he'd missed his stretches this morning. Since it meant extra time with Sky, he decided it was a good swap. "Of course I'm excited, Tink." He tapped the tip of her nose. "Just hard to get a word in edgewise."

The smile returned. "We have to get one for you, too, even though you'll probably be with us most of the time."

"I will?"

"Of course. You're Mama's boyfriend, and boyfriends spend holidays with their girlfriends."

Like a caffeine buzz, happiness coursed through him, and his smile widened. "I see."

She cocked her head to one side and studied him closely. "You have a really nice smile, Max. You should use it more often."

Before he could reply, the energetic child on a mission returned.

"Can we go now? Mama might get off early."

She tugged his hand, and he stood.

"Do you have any Christmas decorations?"

"No. I—"

"Don't worry. We'll take care of that, too." She was all smiles and giggles as she pulled him toward the door. "And don't forget your jacket."

Max couldn't stop the chuckle that rumbled in his chest. Maddie would make a good Marine. Determine the objective. Devise a plan. Execute. At the moment, the plan was to get going on the great Christmas Tree hunt. Never once in his whole life had he done such a thing. The prospect of sharing this momentous occasion with the two most important people in his life caused unfamiliar joy to bubble inside him. *I'm going to chop down a Christmas tree. My first Christmas tree.*

Her non-stop chatter all the way to the diner should have perturbed him. Instead, it made his chest tighten. For so long, he had hungered for this...this normalcy. To know he stood on the brink of having the one thing he craved more than anything was far more frightening than any battlefield enemy he had ever faced. He knew how to deal with that. How to fight back, how to win.

But this was different. He had no clue what the rules of engagement were, or if there were even rules to be mindful of. On top of that insecurity, a lifetime of hurts and doubts threatened to worm their way into his head. *I don't deserve this happiness. I'm no good for them. I got more baggage than Amtrak.*

He took a deep breath. *Nothing good comes easy. You gotta fight for what you want.*

Maddie was still talking when he stopped in front of the diner. "This is going to be the best Christmas ever, huh, Max?"

He helped her down from the back seat of the truck, and she took his big hand in her small one. When she looked up at him, her eyes so full of trust and love, a chunk of doubt fell away.

"Absolutely," he said. "The best ever."

Hand in hand, they walked inside. A quick scan of the room showed only a few patrons remained. He stopped when he saw Sky in a back booth talking to Logan. By the expression on their faces, the conversation was serious. He hesitated, unsure if he should interrupt.

Maddie, however, had no such reservations and hurried forward.

"Hi, Mama. Hi, Logan."

Sky looked at Maddie, then Max, her eyes asking a silent question.

"I told Max we could surprise you," offered Maddie. "That way, you don't have to pick me up, and we can go get the tree quicker." She turned to Logan. "We're going to chop down a Christmas tree. Do you want to go with us?"

"Maddie," cautioned Sky.

Before she got another word out, Maddie-on-a-mission took charge.

"He's staying at Max's house so he can come, too." She turned to Max. "Right, Max?"

The last thing Max wanted was to share this afternoon with a virtual stranger. But, on the other hand, maybe the kid needed a break. "You're welcome to come if you want."

"I'd be in the way," said Logan softly. "I'll just head back to your place if you don't mind."

Suddenly, Max was a kid again, being told over and over he was in the way, a mistake, a problem, and unwanted.

No way in hell would he ever be the reason any kid experienced that kind of rejection. He may be pushing eighteen, but Logan was still a kid to Max. "You won't be in the way at all," said Max. "In fact, you can help me cut it down."

Logan's features brightened slightly. "Are you sure?"

"I think that's a splendid idea," said Sky. She slid out of the booth and stood beside Max. She looked around the diner, then kissed him softly on the lips. "I won't be long. Ruby just locked the doors, and it will take a few minutes to finish up."

While Sky finished clean-up duties, Max listened quietly as Logan and Maddie discussed the attributes of the perfect tree. Well, truth be told, Maddie did most of the talking, with Logan barely getting in a word. But judging by the smile on the kids face, he didn't mind. The little pixie had that effect on people.

Logan insisted on driving his truck, despite Maddie's assertion they all ride together. She wanted them to sing Christmas songs on the way and said it would be fun. It certainly didn't sound like fun to Max, but evidently it was important to her, so Max would sing.

And sing they did. A little halfhearted at first, at least on his part, but after some talking-tos from Maddie, he sang "right," and thoroughly enjoyed himself, though he doubted he would ever sing *Jingle Bells* again.

By the time they reached their destination, everyone was in high spirits. They met up with Logan and headed for the wagon they would ride to the actual trees.

The first person they saw was Cade Jackson.

CHAPTER
Thirty-One

Sky's heart dropped like a rock when Cade stepped into view. *Oh, no. Not this. Not now.*

"Hello, Max," he crooned, "Need help finding a family tree?"

Max ignored him and took a step to the side, Maddie in tow.

Cade stepped in front of Logan, and Max turned around, lips compressed into a thin line, eyes suddenly dark and cold. The muscles in his cheeks jerked as his jaw clenched and released. Tension bounced off him like shock waves as he edged Maddie forward. "Go to your mother," he snapped.

Maternal instincts kicked in, and Sky reached for her daughter's hand as she took a step closer to Logan, pushing Maddie behind her.

The boy stared at the man he knew to be his father as though trying to confirm it.

This close, it was easy for Sky to note the resemblance between father and son. Almost the same height, they shared the same tawny-gold hair and athletic build, though the dimple in Logan's left cheek was more pronounced than the one Cade sported. Where Cade's mouth was thin and cynical, Logan's was generous and full.

But there was one glaring difference. The eyes. While the same color, Logan's exuded the wide-open honesty of youth. Cade's showed only contempt.

"You're Anna Sue's kid." Cade's voice was cold and clear as ice water.

Logan nodded. "Yeah."

"I don't know what kind of crap she's feeding you, but I can tell you it's a bunch of lies."

"If you don't know what she said, how do you know it's lies?"

Cade glared at Logan's quick comeback.

Sky mentally gave the kid a high five.

But Cade rallied. "I just know the kind of woman she was then." He paused. "And some things never change."

Logan flinched, and Sky grabbed his arm. "Enough, Cade," she snapped. "Come on, Logan." She tugged again and glanced up to find Max right behind Cade.

If she thought he looked angry before, it was ten times worse now. His fingers flexed at his side, his nostrils flared, and she could almost hear his teeth grinding together. The vein in his temple doubled in size and pulsed with each beat of his heart.

Oh crap.

Cade didn't look at Sky; instead, he focused on Logan. "She claims I'm your daddy." He studied the face that was a younger version of himself and shook his head. "I wonder how she can be so sure."

The weasel had the audacity to wink at Logan.

Sky sucked in a breath. The proverbial shit was about to hit the fan.

Logan lunged at Cade a split second too late.

Max already had him spun around. It took every ounce of restraint not to plant a fist in his face right then and there.

Undaunted, Cade continued to feed the fire. "Ain't that right, Lover Boy? You tell him you and his—"

Hands fisted in his shirt, Max jerked Cade close to his face. "So help me God, Cade. You finish that sentence, and you'll regret it the rest of your life." Flames of rage shot through him, clouding his judgement. He saw each rapid beat of his heart as a dark spot before his eyes. *Control. Don't let him get to you.*

"Hey, I'm just trying to protect my reputation here." He took a step back and pushed Max's hands away. "Anna Sue is spreading lies about me and—"

"The only person spreading lies," barked Max, "is you. And it stops. Now."

"Or what?" Cade looked around at the crowd gathering, obviously enjoying the precarious situation he'd put Max in. "You gonna go all postal on me again like you did in high school? Prove what I been saying about you all this time is right?" He looked at the throng again and smirked. "Ever 'one knows all that killing and shit messed you up. You're nothin' but a ticking time bomb waiting to explode."

Every muscle in his body tensed with anger. He read the taunt in Cade's eyes as clearly as if he had spoken out loud. Max wanted to put the past behind him. Cade wanted to use it to intimidate and humiliate.

The entitled bully from high school was now the entitled adult who still derived pleasure from hurting anyone he considered weak or vulnerable.

Or a threat to the power he craved. Like Max.

He would push until Max pushed back, then he would play the innocent, place all the blame on Max while he walked off scot free.

Not this time.

He took a deep breath and looked at Sky. Her face had lost most of its color, but she managed a weak smile.

Maddie stood beside her, eyes wide, bottom lip trembling.

When Max didn't react to his last remark, Cade sneered. "Loser Logan. You still can't get over the fact that I had her first."

Max heard Sky's quick intake of breath, before he blocked everything except the man in front of him.

He saw Logan lunge for Cade again, but Sky pulled him back.

"And you know what?" He grinned. "All I gotta do is this." He snapped his fingers for emphasis. "And I'd have her again." Cade smiled and looked around. "Cause that's all a woman like her needs."

Logan roared and lunged at Cade. Hampered by Sky's grip on his arm, he only succeeded in driving the man off balance. Surprised by the sudden attack, Cade stumbled and ran into Maddie, knocking her to the ground, where she cried out when her head hit the compact earth.

White-hot anger erupted through Max in a single heartbeat. Hurting Maddie was the last straw. He grabbed Cade's arm and spun him around. Every hurt, every injustice, every slight he had ever endured because of him exploded in the fist that connected with Cade's face. The blow knocked him to the ground, and Max jerked him up and hit him again.

Cade fought back, landing some punches. Max tasted the

blood in his mouth but never felt the blow that put it there. Driven by an anger more intense than anything he'd ever experienced, he hit and hit again.

Shouts from the crowd penetrated the ringing in his ears, but they fought on, rolling around on the ground, punching and kicking, grunting as they flailed about.

Hands tugged at his arms, trying to pull him off Cade, whom he now had pinned to the ground.

"That's enough," shouted someone behind him. "Dammit, Max, that's enough!"

Strong arms jerked him back, and he fell to his knees, muscles quivering as the anger-induced surge of adrenaline raced through his body.

"What the hell is going on here?"

Max turned his head toward the familiar voice.

Sheriff Cooper Delaney stood beside him, hands fisted on his hips, as he glared between the two men.

Someone helped Cade stand, and he pointed an unsteady finger at Max. "I want him arrested for assault," he shouted. "I'm pressing charges."

"Cade started it," said a voice Max didn't recognize.

"He hit me first!"

"You had it coming and then some," said another.

"Max?" asked the Sheriff, "What happened?"

Max remained bent over, hands on his thighs, striving to get his breathing under control, fortifying himself for what was sure to happen next.

It was over.

Sky witnessed the part of him he feared and hated most. Anger. Loss of control. She would never look at him the same way again.

He'd ruined any chance they had of being together. He let Cade goad him into a fight. Again. It didn't matter what provoked it, who said or did what. All that mattered was Loser Logan threw a punch at *the* Cade Jackson.

And this time, there were more than enough witnesses to make the charges stick.

He swallowed hard to quell the hurt burning the back of his throat. He was so close to having it all. So close to realizing the dream that kept him alive through the darkest of days…the hope of a future that included a real home. A wife. A family. Gone in the blink of an eye.

A chilled gust of air washed over him, matching the coldness that coursed through his body. This is what death feels like, he thought numbly, cold and dark and alone.

He vowed not to look at anyone as he struggled to stand, shaking off the arms that attempted to help. He didn't need anyone. Not now. Not ever again. Need brought pain.

And he'd had enough.

"I threw the first punch, Coop," he said hoarsely. "Do what you got to do."

"I told you," blurted Cade, "the crazy bastard assaulted me for no reason. I want him arrested."

Unsteady, Max spread his legs to maintain balance and put his hands behind his back, waiting for the cuffs to seal his fate.

"No need for that," said Coop. "Let's go see if we can straighten this out."

Max dug his keys from his pocket and passed them to Coop. "Give these to Sky so they can get home. Tell her to get the damn tree first."

"Keep the keys," snapped Coop. "Until we get this sorted out."

He staggered over to Coop's Bronco and leaned against the hood. Against his better judgment, he looked toward the crowd around Coop and found Maddie's tear-stained face staring at him as she clung to her mother's hand.

The fear in her eyes broke his heart.

She's afraid. Of me.

CHAPTER
Thirty-Two

Sky poured herself a cup of coffee and sat down at the table with Anna. Strange as it may seem, she enjoyed her company. Maybe it was her connection to Max, or maybe it was just having another woman to talk to; Sky didn't know. Nor did she waste time trying to figure it out. *It is what it is.*

Anna spent the last half hour sitting in Logan's truck while they talked. Judging by the smile when she came in a few minutes ago, things were better between mother and son.

"I can't believe it came to that again," whispered Anna. "All because of me."

"I don't think that was all of it," offered Sky. "Like you said, there's a lot of bad blood between them." She sipped her coffee. "I honestly think Cade accidently knocking Maddie down was the match that started the fire."

Anna sat up straighter. "Is she okay?"

"Yeah. It scared her, of course, but she wasn't hurt."

Anna's voice cracked, and she inhaled deeply. "Seems all I do is apologize, Sky, but I am so very sorry my problems ended up on your doorstep."

Sky shrugged. "It was bound to come to a head. There's

too much history between them. Maybe now they can get past it and move forward."

"Have you talked with him? Max?"

She shook her head. "No. He left without saying anything to me. Or Maddie." She paused. "He asked Logan to bring us home while he stayed and talked with Coop."

"I'm sure the fight was upsetting for him, too."

She considered her earlier conversation with Max about his PTSD. He'd feared he would say or do something that might scare them, even hurt them. Is that why he left? Did he think she blamed him? That she feared him?

"Far as I'm concerned," said Sky, "Cade didn't get near what he deserved."

"Logan told me what he said—"

"Don't pay any attention to what Cade said. He was only trying to get a reaction out of someone. Mainly Max."

Anna hesitated. "Logan and I had a long talk." She heaved a deep, satisfying sigh. "He apologized for coming here. Said he understands now why I didn't want him to know."

Sky nodded. What else was there to say about that?

"At least Max wasn't arrested," offered Anna.

"There is that," said Sky. "Coop insisted Cade sleep on it and come in tomorrow to talk about it." She smiled as she remembered how flustered Cade became when Coop told him. "You should have seen his face when Coop said he had a good mind to arrest him for disturbing the peace."

"Bet he didn't like that."

"No. And when everyone there said Cade instigated the fight with his nasty remarks, he shut up and left."

"I'm sorry you didn't get a tree."

"Wouldn't be the same without Max." She stared into the depths of her cup.

"Max has a good heart," Anna said at last. "Always standing up for the underdog."

"Knight in shining armor rides again, huh?"

"Something like that." Anna shook her head. "The same thing that makes him that, means he's beating himself up over the fact that he fought in front of you and Maddie. And all those other people."

"I know. I want to talk to him, but I'm afraid he won't see me." She shook her head. "Maybe I just need to let things cool down a bit."

"Maybe." Anna pushed her cup aside. "Max is a great guy, Sky. You two belong together. Don't let him push you away."

Sky smiled. "Thank you. I'm not giving in that easy."

"I called Max to say goodbye, but it went to voicemail." She shook her head. "I knocked on his door when I saw him come home earlier, but he didn't answer. I understand why now." She exhaled slowly. "I'll be headed home shortly. My stuff's already in the car." She sat up straighter. "I think Logan wants to talk to Max before he leaves, so he'll come home tomorrow."

Sky shook her head. "Don't be silly. It's too late to drive back tonight."

Anna stood and put her cup in the sink. "You're too kind, Sky. I've been nothing but trouble since I got here. It's time you got your life back."

The two women faced each other in the kitchen.

Anna spoke first. "Once again, I really appreciate all your hospitality. I doubt I'd be so accommodating if the roles were reversed."

Sky ducked her head, then smiled. "Well, I will admit I wasn't all that thrilled with things in the beginning, but I'm glad we met." She paused. "And I hope if you come back to town, we'll have a chance to get better acquainted."

Anna's cheeks turned a lovely shade of pink. "Well, Bill did ask if we might see each other again."

"That's wonderful," said Sky. "He's a great guy."

"He seems like it."

"And you're really not that far away."

Anna paused. "Logan will graduate this spring. I never thought I'd say this, but maybe I'll give some thought to coming back. Cade notwithstanding, this is a nice town with nice people."

The silence continued for several moments, then Sky stepped forward and pulled Anna into a gentle embrace. "You're welcome here anytime. Please be careful going home."

Ten minutes after Anna left, a soft knock on the back door had Sky's heart skipping a beat. Max.

She jerked open the door to find Logan on the step, hands thrust in his front pockets. "May I come in a minute?"

"Of course." She stepped aside, glancing next door to the darkened house. Poor Max. How he must be hurting. "Your mom gone?"

He nodded. "I, um, just wanted to check on Maddie. Is she okay?"

Touched by his concern, she smiled. "Yeah. She's in the living room watching television." Sky shut the door. "I was about to make some hot chocolate and popcorn. Care to join us?"

He nodded. "That would be nice."

"Go on in and say hello. I'll bring the goodies shortly."

Max lay on his bed in the dark and ignored Anna's knock on the door as well as her earlier phone call. He listened to her message without emotion. She was sorry. She hoped he'd forgive her. Logan was staying one more night. She wished him and Sky the best.

Well, thanks, friend, but that ship has sailed.

He heard the boy's truck when he stopped outside but didn't bother to get up. The kid knew where the couch was and could take care of himself.

Besides, he glanced at the bedside clock, he still had ten minutes left in his personal pity-party allotment. He debated giving Dr. Bellamy a call. But in the end, Max was the only one who could pull his ass out of the shithole he found himself sinking into.

He groaned against the injustice of it all and turned on his side. He still wore the same clothes, though he'd cleaned up the worst of the cuts and abrasions.

Damn, he hurt all over. You'd think after sixteen months of rehab he'd be in better shape.

One eye was swollen shut, his bottom lip was split, and his battered body was covered in scrapes and bruises. None of the pain associated with his injuries compared to the pain of losing Sky. And Maddie. The look on her face at the end would haunt him forever.

He'd put it there. He'd put the fear in her eyes. Destroyed her faith in him. Some hero he turned out to be.

It's over. They're gone. Move on.

Even as the dire thoughts materialized, that tiny voice inside his head that refused to admit defeat shouted loud and clear…*never give up hope.*

He wanted to hang on to the idea but couldn't.

He rolled onto his back, arms spread out to the sides, replaying his last conversation with Coop after he'd sent Sky and Maddie home with Logan. He didn't want them to see his injuries, certain they would hate him for his actions.

Coop disagreed and wasted no time telling him so. "How do you know that? Did they say so?"

"Well, no, but—"

"No, they didn't, jackass, because you turned tail and ran without even talking to them."

"They deserve better."

Coop took off his Stetson and slapped it against his knee. "The first time I met Sam I knew I was in deep shit." He slapped his hat against his leg again. "She was everything I never knew I needed. And that scared the hell out of me. By the time I got my head out of my ass and realized I loved her, it was almost too late."

Max knew the story of the crazed killer who nearly succeeded in making Doc his victim and how happy Coop and Sam were now. Was there a message there?

Coop wasn't done preaching. "Hell, everyone who's seen y'all together know Sky and Maddie think you hung the moon. You really believe they're gonna think less of you for standing up to Jackson?"

When Max didn't reply, Coop got in his face. Again.

"You know better than most that there comes a time when a man has to fight to protect what's his. To stand up for those who can't stand for themselves. It ain't pretty, Max, but sometimes it's necessary."

Coop's words had the ability to do what Max couldn't do for himself at the moment. Keep the faintly glowing ember of hope alive.

"What do I do?" he said to the darkness. "What do I do?"

Like whispers on the wind came the answer. You got a choice, Marine. You fight back. Or Cade wins.

"My daddy didn't want me, either."

Sky stopped in the hallway, nearly dropping the tray of hot chocolate and popcorn when she heard Maddie's softly spoken statement.

"No shit? I mean, really?" came Logan's reply.

"Uh-huh. Mama never said so, but I figured it out."

"Figured what out?"

"He didn't want me. If he did, he would have stayed."

There was a short pause, and Sky choked back a sob as she listened to her precious, wise-beyond-her-years daughter try and ease Logan's pain by sharing her own.

"How do you know he didn't want you?"

"I was really sick when I was little. And he had to go away a lot with his work and stuff. One day, he didn't come back."

"I'm sorry, Maddie."

"It's okay. I don't really remember him anymore. Mama said he loved us in his own way, but I think she just says that to make me feel better."

There was another pause.

"Besides, I wouldn't want him anyway if he didn't want me."

"You wouldn't?"

"No. I mean, if somebody doesn't want you, why would you want them?"

"Yeah. I guess so."

"Is Max gonna be your daddy?"

"What? No. I mean, he's a friend and all but no, nothing like that."

There was another short pause before Maddie spoke again.

"I wonder why he didn't say goodbye before he left? We didn't get to pick out our tree or ride the wagon or anything."

"He probably thinks y'all are mad at him."

"Why would he think that?"

"He got into a fight."

Sky heard the indignation in Maddie's voice as she spoke up.

"So what? Max didn't start it. That poopie head Mr. Jackson did! And you were gonna fight him, too. I saw you."

"Yeah, well, he was talking about my mother."

"I bet he don't do that again," said Maddie firmly. "Max will kick his butt."

Logan snickered. "You're a pistol."

Sky decided now was a good time to intervene. "Snack time." She walked in and placed the tray on the coffee table.

"I'll be right back," said Maddie as she left the room.

Assuming she was going to the bathroom, Sky set the goodies down and joined Logan on the couch.

Max winced and pushed himself up from the bed and limped toward the kitchen, grabbing a bottle of alcohol and some gauze from the bathroom on his way. He needed strong coffee, sooner rather than later. The shower could wait.

He placed the meager first aid supplies on the table. As he filled the carafe with water, he spared a quick glance toward Sky's kitchen. She walked through the door toward the hall that led to the living room, a tray in her hands.

He assumed it was hot chocolate and popcorn—Maddie's favorite treat, one they'd enjoyed just last week watching some cartoon movie the child wanted to watch.

He pulled himself away from the window and started the coffee. As he headed toward the bathroom, a light knock pulled him to the back door.

He frowned. *I thought I'd left it unlocked for Logan.*

Only it wasn't Logan on the other side.

It was Maddie.

"Can I come in, please? We need to talk."

She stalked in without waiting for a reply and stood by the table.

Max looked outside, then shut the door. "Does your mom know where you are?"

When he turned around, her blue eyes widened until the whites were visible all the way around. "Oh Max, you're really hurt."

Suddenly self-conscious, he lowered his head. "I'm sorry, Tink. I'm a mess."

She came over and took his hand, pulling him back to a chair at the table. When he sat down, she stood beside him, one hand on his shoulder, one still holding the hand she led him by.

Head down, he opened his mouth to speak, but nothing got past the lump in his throat. Nausea rolled in his stomach, and he clenched his jaw tight, willing the contents to remain where they were. His other hand rolled into a tight fist on his thigh.

The silence didn't last long.

Maddie delicately patted his shoulder. "I'm so sorry you got hurt, Max."

He got hurt? She was worried about *him*?

To keep her from having to look at his bloody and swollen face, he kept his head averted. "I'm so sorry you had to see that, Tink." His voice cracked, and he swallowed hard before he could continue. "And I'm so sorry I scared you and that you got hurt and I—"

"I didn't get hurt. But I was scared. A little. At first anyway, cause Mr. Jackson is a bad man, and I was afraid he might hurt you. But I should have known better cause you're a soldier, and you know about fighting, and he's a dipstick, and I'm glad you beat him up." A quick intake of breath, and she continued. "But don't tell Mama I said I was glad you hit him. Even though I think he deserved it."

What?

He straightened and faced her, only to duck his head again, ashamed of how he looked.

She calmly put a finger under his chin and turned his face to hers.

All four-foot-nothing-Maddie-on-a-mission met his one-eyed gaze. "He said bad things about Logan's mother, and he made me fall down, so you kicked his butt. That's what heroes do."

"H-heroes?"

She gently touched the seepage from his swollen eye. "Heroes don't let bad people hurt other people," she said softly before placing a kiss on his cheek. "You're a hero." She patted his shoulder again. "Where's your first-aid stuff?"

"My what?"

"First-aid stuff. Mama always says you have to clean cuts so they don't get infected."

She stood beside his chair, one brow arched up.

"Oh." He nodded toward the stuff he had picked up in the bathroom.

"Mama's gonna have to get what you need. This isn't much, but will do for now."

She opened a gauze pad, soaked it in alcohol, then gently dabbed it on the abrasions across his face and both hands. "Sometimes Mama will blow on it when she uses alcohol, but it doesn't really stop it from stinging."

Her soft breath warmed more than his skin.

"But I like how it feels."

She said nothing more as she continued to work on his face and then his knuckles. When she was done, she stood back and checked her handiwork.

"Okay. That's all I can do. Mama will take care of the rest."

She took his hand and led him out the back door.

CHAPTER
Thirty-Three

"Where's Maddie?" asked Sky.

"I thought maybe she went to the bathroom," answered Logan.

Sky walked down the hall and checked the bathroom, then Maddie's bedroom. Where could she have gone? In a flash, she knew.

Max.

She hurried back toward the kitchen, stopping as the door opened and Maddie came in, dragging Max behind her.

"I did the best I could, Mama, but you're gonna have to clean his mouth and his eye cause all he had was alcohol, and I don't think you're supposed to use that there." She literally pushed Max into a chair at the table, barely taking a breath. "I told him we'd take care of him."

Sky wanted to laugh, to cry, to...something, but couldn't move.

He was here.

Max must have taken her hesitancy as a bad omen because he tried to stand. "I better go."

She morphed into action. "Move from that chair, Max Logan, and I'll black your other eye. Sit down and let me look at you."

"I'll get the first-aid kit," said Maddie.

A silent Logan lounged against the kitchen counter as she cleaned the cut on Max's lip. "It's not bad," she said softly, "No stitches needed. Might make…some things painful for a few days." Heat infused her face. She wondered if he knew she meant kissing?

When his one good eye narrowed and his breath hitched, she knew he did.

Maddie stood beside Sky, carefully watching her every move. Her daughter had such a kind and loving nature, Sky knew she would make a wonderful nurse. Or doctor.

The fact that she had taken it upon herself to check on Max said volumes about their relationship, which made Sky even prouder.

"You did a good job cleaning his hands, Munchkin," she said softly.

"I remembered how you did my knee when I wrecked my bike." She leaned in for a closer look at his lip. "Does it still hurt, Max?"

He cleared his throat. "No. Not much anyway."

"I would have decked him."

Logan's quiet statement had them all looking his way.

"I know," said Max. "But this was between him and me."

"It was my mother he dissed."

"And my friend."

There was a tense pause before the boy spoke again. "He's really an a—uh, jerk, isn't he?"

Max nodded.

"Thank you," said Logan. "For standing up for us."

Sky saw Max swallow hard before nodding again. It didn't surprise her that praise embarrassed him. He didn't think he was worthy of it. He was wrong.

"Is the sheriff gonna arrest you?"

Logan's question interrupted her musings.

"He better not," snapped Maddie as she stood beside Max. "Mr. Jackson had it coming."

"Maddie…"

"Tink," Max turned to face the child. "Fighting rarely makes a situation better."

"He started it."

"Doesn't matter who started it." He looked at Maddie, then Logan. "I'm not proud of what happened today."

He ducked his head as though gathering his thoughts, and Sky's love for him grew. He was an honorable and decent man. He wanted them to understand that fighting didn't solve the problem.

"I've learned that sometimes you have to fight to protect what's yours. Or to help someone who can't help themselves."

"I know," said Maddie firmly. "That's what heroes do."

He shook his head. "I'm no hero, Tink. I'm just a man. A man who's made mistakes, done things I'm not proud of." He pulled in a deep breath and looked at Sky.

Her heart swelled. Could she possibly love him any more than at this moment?

"I'm just a man who would do anything to protect those he loves."

Max held his breath and waited for Sky to respond. He got the impression she wasn't upset, but at the same time, his own insecurity was at an all-time high, and he prayed Coop's insistence that he talk to her was the right move.

Then, she bent down and took his face in her hands and brushed a tender kiss over his swollen lips. "And that's one of the reasons I love you, Max."

Without thinking, he pulled her into his lap and wrapped his arms around her, his faced buried in her chest. "Oh God, Sky. I love you," he whispered.

"I love you, too."

Maddie clapped her hands and laughed. "Finally!" She looked at Logan, who remained against the counter. "Wanna go watch a movie with me while they talk some more?"

"Is it all right, Miss Sky?"

She didn't get up from Max's lap as she smiled at the boy. "Of course. I'll order us a pizza in a minute."

He looked at Max. "Thanks for letting me stay another night."

"Anytime."

He started for the living room, then stopped. "Maddie's lucky to have you in her life." Face scarlet, he added, "So am I."

Once they were alone, he turned his good eye toward Sky. "I really am sorry things got so out of hand today."

"To be honest, Max, I think it was bound to happen sooner or later. There's just too much history there."

"Doesn't make it right."

"No, but it doesn't make it wrong, either." She sighed. "I don't like fighting. Like you said, it rarely solves a problem. The thing is, I don't believe you should ever start a fight, but when one is thrust on you, you don't walk away."

She shifted on his lap and looped her arms around his neck. "So, just how sore is your mouth?"

CHAPTER
Thirty-Four

"**S**ure you don't mind picking Maddie up after school today?"

Max tucked her against his body, still flushed from their midday tryst. It was difficult to find alone time with Maddie around, but since Sky was off this week, he'd made it a point to come home for lunch every day.

The week was almost over, and he'd yet to have a meal. And couldn't be happier about it.

"I don't mind. I already cleared it with Jason. Thought I'd take her by the Dairy Barn for a soda. Maybe give you enough time to finish your schedule before we head out to the tree farm again."

Sky's hand made little circles on his chest, interrupting his train of thought.

"Maybe they won't run me off." He was only half joking.

"There's not a person in this town who blames you for what happened," she said indignantly. "Ruby told me this morning he came in the diner yesterday acting like nothing happened."

"That's how he rolls."

"She also said people are giving him hell over the incident. Some are even refusing to go to his store if he's there and he's letting his manager handle things." She paused. "Maybe he's learned his lesson."

Max snorted. "I doubt it."

"I talked to Anna today. She's really going to consider moving back after Logan graduates. Her folks are doing the retired and traveling thing and she has no ties there."

"That's nice. I guess. I just hope Cade doesn't ruin things for her."

"Well, according to good ole Edith Huffman, he can either straighten up and fly right or he may as well close up shop and leave town."

Max pulled her tighter against him. *I'll never tire of this feeling.* "We can hope."

"Does Logan still want to join the Marines?"

"Yeah. I suggested he get some college behind him first, maybe go in as an officer."

She turned to face him, a tender smile on her lips. "He really looks up to you."

Embarrassed, he shrugged. "He just needed a male perspective."

"And there is no one who fills that role better than you."

"I'm not—"

She put a finger to his lips. "Enough talk. How long before you have to go back to work?"

He glanced at his watch. "Only have a few more minutes."

"How shall we spend them?"

"I got an idea or two."

At precisely three-fifteen, he waited by the curb with all the other parents, his heart beating a little faster as he considered the plan. As soon as they got home, they would complete the great Christmas tree hunt ruined by Cade on Sunday. Then they would enjoy hot chocolate, popcorn, and Christmas music as they decorated the tree, followed by pizza and more Christmas music.

But there was one thing to be done first.

Maddie came running down the sidewalk toward him, and his chest boomed with pride when she flew into his arms. "Hiya, Tink. How was your day?"

"Great, now that you're here. And only one more day of school until we get out for Christmas."

He buckled her in the back seat. "I thought we'd stop by the Dairy Barn on the way home, if that's all right with you."

"Yes, sir! May I have a root beer float?"

"You certainly may."

A few minutes later, he parked and took a deep breath. "Before we go inside, there's something I need to talk to you about."

"Okay."

"Unbuckle your seat belt so you can sit up here with me."

Once she sat up front, his courage began to fade.

"Is something wrong, Max?"

"What? No. It's just…well, I…I need to discuss something with you."

"Okay."

"I love you and your mother very much. You know that, right?"

"Of course. You tell us that all the time."

"Well, when two people, a man and woman, love each other, they, well, they…"

"Get married?" Her question was so soft he almost didn't hear her.

He nodded. "Yes."

Her expressive face brightened to the point he thought she would jump out of the seat in excitement. "You want to marry us?"

He smiled. "That's exactly what I want to do. But only if it's okay with you."

She clapped her hands together in front of her chest. "Of course it's okay with me!"

He smiled and took one of the velvet boxes from his pocket. "I got this for her. Do you think she'll like it?"

She leaned forward and gaped at the sparkling diamond solitaire he'd picked out this week. "Oh Max, it's beautiful. She's gonna love it."

Then her face drew up in frown. "So, if you marry us, do I still call you Max?"

This was the part he wasn't sure about. He had yet to talk adoption with Sky, wasn't sure how she'd feel about it, but in his heart, Maddie was already his daughter.

"I'm going to leave that up to you. I'm okay with whatever you want to call me. As far as I'm concerned, you're already my little girl."

"Y-you want me to…to be y-your daughter?" Her tender voice shook, and tears crowded the corners of her eyes.

"I do."

Her chest rose and fell quickly. "So…so…I could…I could call you…Daddy?"

He swallowed hard. Hearing the word from her mouth made his heart roll over in his chest. "I'd like that very much. But, know this, Maddie. Whatever you are comfortable with is all right with me."

She launched herself across the seat and threw her arms around his neck. "I want a Daddy more than anything."

So choked up he couldn't speak, he simply hugged her to him. After he composed himself, he pushed her back a little. "Okay. For now, Tink, this has to be our secret, because you see, I haven't asked yet if she wants to marry me. She might say no."

"Oh please, get real." She patted his arm. "She's just waiting for you to ask."

He laughed, something he'd been doing a lot of lately. "Tonight's the night."

"I have never seen a more beautiful tree in my life," said Sky as she stood back and eyed their handiwork.

"Yes, ma'am, Miss Sky," said John, who was a last-minute addition to the party thanks to Maddie. "That is the prettiest tree I've ever seen."

"Turn out the lights, Da—uh, I mean, Max so we can turn on the Christmas tree ones."

Sky looked at Maddie and not for the first time tonight wondered why she was so excited. At first, she passed it off as the sugar high from their stop at the Dairy Barn, but it was more than that. And she and Max kept looking at each other and grinning like they had a secret.

Max turned out the room lights and hit the switch on the tree just as the first notes of *Silent Night* drifted through the television speakers.

The room went silent for several heartbeats as they gazed at the brightly lit tree.

Max came to stand beside her, one arm around her waist,

a sprig of mistletoe in his other hand, which he held over her head.

"I believe I'm due a kiss now."

"I believe you are."

His lips touched hers, and he whispered softly. "Marry me, Sky."

She hesitated, unsure she heard him right. "What?"

He stepped back and reached into his pocket. He opened the velvet box and presented it to her. "I love you, Skylar Ward. Marry me and put me out of my misery."

"Oh, Max." She wrapped her arms around his neck. "Yes. Yes. Yes, I'll marry you."

Maddie jumped up and down, hands clapping furiously. "Finally, Daddy. I didn't think you'd ever do it!"

Max took the beautiful solitaire from the box and slipped it on her trembling finger, then kissed her again.

"There's one more thing," said Max. He turned to Maddie and knelt in front of her. "This is for you." He pulled another box from his pocket and opened it. Inside rested a tiny heart shaped topaz ring. "It's your birthstone. I was going to give it to you for your birthday but decided to do it now."

Maddie squealed with delight as Max put the ring on her finger.

Sky had no idea how he got the size right for it was a perfect fit. Just like hers.

"Look Mama! Daddy gave me a ring, too!"

Max stood up and whispered to Sky. "I told her she could call me whatever she wanted when I asked her permission to marry you."

"You asked her permission?"

"Of course."

"Have I told you lately how much I love you?"

"Maybe you could tell me again. I kinda like hearing it."

John interrupted and pulled Sky into a bear hug. "Congratulations, Miss Sky. You have yourself a good man there." He clamped Max on the shoulder. "Congratulations, son," he said, "I couldn't be happier." He clapped his hands together. "When's the big day?"

Sky looked at Max. "Well, gee, we just now got engaged."

"I was thinking," said Max. "I'd like to get married on New Year's Day…to symbolize our new life together."

"That's the most romantic thing I've ever heard," said Sky. "New Year's Day it is."

John reached for his hot chocolate. "Too bad we don't have any champagne to toast with, but this is just as good."

Everyone grabbed their cups and clinked them together as John said, "Congratulations to a beautiful family."

"I almost forgot," said Maddie. "Just a minute." She ran down the hall to her room, returning with a sheet of paper.

She stood in front of John, the paper behind her. "Mr. John, can I ask you something?"

"Of course you can, Miss Maddie. Ask me anything you want."

"You're not married, right?"

"Unfortunately, that is true."

"And you don't have any kids."

"Also true."

She nodded as though confirming what she already knew. "Well, I found out the other day that Bobby Franklin is adopted, so I asked Max, I mean, Daddy, how that works."

John's face scrunched up in confusion. "Okay…"

Sky looked at Max, who simply smiled and nodded at Maddie.

"And he said people can adopt other people to be their family whether they are really family or not. And it's all legal and stuff."

John looked at Max and then Sky, frowning slightly. "Yeah, that's basically how it works."

"Well, since you don't have any kids, and I don't have a grandpa, I'd like to adopt you." With a flourish, she handed him the sheet of paper filled with hearts and Maddie's precise print. "Max helped me with it." Before he had a chance to read it, she pulled it back and said, "Here, I'll read it to you." She stood up straight and tall. "I, Madeline Adele Ward Logan, hereby adopt you, Johnathan Woodrow Andrews, to be my grandfather for now and evermore. Signed, Maddie Logan."

Sky's heart skipped a beat as she watched the exchange between her daughter and the gentle giant standing in front of the Christmas tree, his face beet red, his eyes glistening in the twinkling lights.

Maddie handed the sheet back to John, her smile fading as the silence lingered, and Sky worried he might be offended or refuse.

Then John ducked his head, swiped his face with both hands and got down on his knees in front of her daughter, smiling from ear to ear as he clutched the paper to his heart. "My dear, sweet child, it would give me the utmost pleasure to be your adopted grandfather." His voice broke, and he swiped his face again. "I've always wanted to be a grandfather."

She threw her arms around his neck. "Isn't it wonderful, Grandpa? We both got our Christmas wish! And it's not even Christmas yet!"

"Yes, it is, child," said John as he hugged her to him. "Yes, it is."

Maddie pulled away and looked at Max. "Come on, Daddy. Grandpa can help us string popcorn to put on the tree."

Sky didn't bother to stem the tears flowing down her cheeks as she watched Maddie with her adopted grandfather and soon-to-be father.

And that's when she made a startling discovery.

Blood doesn't make a family.

Love does.

The End

Dear Readers:

When my characters cook a particular dish in my books, I like to include the recipes since the recipes they prepare are my own, so here are Hot Stuff and Chicken Spaghetti. Enjoy!

Hot Stuff

(**Tip:** Wear gloves when peeling onions and chopping peppers! If you don't want it all that hot, you can seed some or all of the peppers first)

About 40 jalapeno peppers, stems removed
4# yellow onions, peeled
2 cups sugar
3 Tbsp Salt
3 cups distilled white vinegar

Process onions and peppers in food processor until well minced. Put sugar, salt and vinegar in large pot and bring to a boil. Add pepper mixture and bring back to boil, cooking 3-4 minutes. Fill hot, sterile jars with mixture and seal. Makes about 6 pints.

Chicken Spaghetti

12 oz pack spaghetti (I prefer Angel hair pasta but spaghetti is fine)
4-5 chicken breasts (or any pre-cooked chicken like Tyson's Southwest grilled fajita chicken)
1 can Rotel Tomatoes with green chilies
1 can cream of chicken soup—undiluted
1 can cream of mushroom soup—undiluted
1 onion chopped
1 bell pepper chopped (optional)
2 cloves garlic, chopped
1 bag shredded Velveeta cheese (2 cups)
Italian Seasoning
Salt and pepper
Butter and olive oil
1 Qt of Chicken broth

If using uncooked chicken: Cut chicken into bite sized pieces. In large pan, put about 2 TBSP butter and 2 TBSP of olive oil. Add chicken and cook till almost done. Add onions, garlic and bell peppers and sauté about 10 minutes over medium heat. Add soups and cheese, stir well and set aside. In large pot, bring broth to a boil and add Italian seasoning to taste. Add spaghetti and cook till desired doneness. Drain. Add to chicken/soup mixture (add a little of the broth if mixture too thick) Pour into a 13x9x2 pan sprayed with non-stick cooking spray. Bake uncovered at 350 degrees for about 30 minutes.

If using precooked chicken: In large pot, put about 2 TBSP butter and 2 TBSP of olive oil. Add chicken, onions, garlic and bell peppers and sauté about 10 minutes over medium heat. Add soups and cheese, set aside. Cook spaghetti in broth seasoned with Italian seasoning to desired doneness then add to soup/chicken mixture. If too thick, add a little of the broth before putting in pan.

ABOUT THE
author

Multi-awarding winning author Dana Wayne is a sixth generation Texan and resides in the Piney Woods with her husband, a Calico cat, three children and four grandchildren.

She routinely speaks at book clubs, writers groups and other organizations and is frequent guest on numerous writing blogs.

A die-hard romantic, her stories are filled with strong women, second changes, and happily ever after.

"I've always wanted to write and knew that one day, I would. I retired in late 2013 and published my first book, a contemporary romance, the summer of 2016. I was over the moon when it was awarded first place by Texas Association of Authors, and I never looked back. All of my books have been nominated for and/or received various awards. To have my work validated in such a manner is very gratifying and humbling. Because I am all about the romance, my stories are heartwarming, have a splash of suspense and humor, and are a little steamy. I believe romance is more about emotion than sex, and the journey is more important than the destination."

Affiliations include Romance Writers of America, Texas Association of Authors, Writers League of Texas, East Texas Writers Guild, Northeast Texas Writers Organization, and East Texas Writers Association.

Want to be in the know about new releases and get a sneak peek at teasers and contests? Join my newsletter team www.danawayne.com/email.

www.danawayne.com

www.Facebook.com/danawayne423

www.Twitter.com/danawayne423

www.instagram.com/danawayne423

Preview of

WHISPERS
ON THE
WIND

CHAPTER ONE

You let him kill her.

The angry female voice in the pre-dawn hour jolted Cooper Delaney from a restless sleep.

Adrenalin pumping, he rolled to the right and automatically grabbed his pistol from the nightstand, fully expecting to see a stranger beside the bed.

Nothing but moonlit shadows. He swiveled his head to the left.

The room was empty.

He blinked and drew in a deep breath, trying to dispel remnants of the dream making sleep all but impossible for over a month. Always the same dream; a shadowy figure begging Coop to find her. That was it…*find me, please.* Two weeks ago, the voice changed and insisted Coop had to stop him.

Stop who? From what?

Tonight, the dream exploded into a full-blown nightmare.

He put the gun back on the table and lay down, right arm over his eyes. "Shit," he whispered as the vision replayed through his mind. *Powerful hands gripped her throat, the eerie silence punctuated by ragged gasps as she struggled for air.*

Blood trickled from her nose and the corner of her mouth. Dark hair wedged into a jagged cut across her forehead. Terror-filled eyes stared at the figure bent over her.

All the while, the voice reproached…you didn't stop him.

At forty-three, Coop considered himself a straight-forward, no nonsense lawman, well known and respected as the Sheriff of Baker County, Texas. He looked at the facts, the evidence, and made logical, rational decisions. And yet, the dream was so real, he smelled the metallic odor of blood, felt the dampness of the earth around her.

"Dammit." He lowered his arm and punched the bed. *I'm losing my fricking mind.*

It was bad enough when the voice invaded his sleep, but two days ago, he heard it at the kitchen table where he sat eating breakfast. Wide awake. This time, she warned he—whoever *he* was—would kill again.

He tossed the sheet aside and sat on the edge of the bed. Heart pounding, his breath hissed as he gulped in air. Elbows on his knees, he cradled his head in his hands. "Just a dream," he murmured, "a bad dream."

He stumbled to the window and shoved it open with an angry thrust, gasping when the rush of cool night air caused gooseflesh to prickle his sweat-coated body. "A dream," he whispered, willing himself to believe. "Nobody died." He pulled down the sash and pressed his forehead against the glass pane. "Nobody died."

When his racing heart finally slowed, he pushed away and headed for the bathroom, stopping at the foot of the bed as he tried to remember if Miss Eva had guests tonight. A curse escaped parched lips as he grabbed his jeans from a chair. *Why in the world did she want to go into the B&B business anyway?*

Even as the thought flitted through his mind, he knew the answer. She decided he needed a wife and used the lovely Antebellum home to lure prospects. Hence, the majority of her guests were single women looking for a good time, or to change their marital status. He lost track of the propositions, both subtle and otherwise, thrown his way in the last six months. *When had women become so forward?*

He opened the door and padded on bare feet to the bathroom he shared with his son, Jason, when he was home from college. Guests used the one across the hall.

Since sleep was out of the question at this point, he threw on a shirt and headed downstairs for coffee.

Light showing under the kitchen door stopped him cold. "Crap. Company."

Today is the first step of starting over.

Samantha Fowler gazed out the kitchen window, transfixed by the beauty of daybreak, convinced the magnificent sunrise was a good omen. The sky, once dark and gloomy, now showcased varying degrees of orange, blue and purple. Giant oaks, pecans and pine trees, previously hidden by darkness, sprang to life, as did the beautifully landscaped yard of the bed and breakfast she would call home for the next two weeks.

Her best friend, Barbara Walker, who grew up in Bakersville, suggested Pecan Grove B&B for her much-needed sabbatical to contemplate what to do with her life. A quick perusal of their website convinced her to give it a try. Located two hours from Dallas in rural Baker County, it was a beautiful antebellum-style home re-constructed after a fire in 1920.

Everything from the graceful columns on the front, to the upper-level porch running across the back, conveyed old-world-south. The interior was painstakingly decorated and furnished like its predecessor built in 1880. Modern upgrades included air conditioning and wi-fi, but the majority of the house retained the serene elegance and charm of the time.

"Oh, Jack, you should see this." A soft sigh of wonder arose as she took in the panoramic view. "No way could I capture this with a camera."

Her companion, a huge crossbreed dog of indeterminate lineage laying at her feet, merely grunted.

She sipped her coffee, still rooted by the window. "Don't be such a grouch. We've been up a lot earlier than this."

The mutt didn't bother to grunt this time.

"Ms. Benton said breakfast will be ready by the time we get back."

A soft groan followed by the swish of his tail on the worn linoleum floor acknowledged he heard what she said.

"No exercise, no food. Time to rock and roll, old man."

Suddenly, Jack growled low in his throat and stood in front of her, attention fixed on the kitchen door as it slowly opened.

A man, barefoot, shirt half-buttoned, sporting a severe case of bed head, strolled into the kitchen.

Every cell in Sam's body began a happy dance.

As a doctor, she was trained to quickly assess every situation and did so now. He towered over her, at least six-three or four, dark, curly hair in need of a trim touched the collar of a half-buttoned chambray shirt, while streaks of gray edged around the temples. Ruggedly handsome, his dark beard stubble projected an explicit manly aura.

Storm-cloud eyes, sharp and focused, assessed her as well. Feminine radar pinged. Hard.

He liked what he saw.

Her fingers tightened around the cup. She attempted to speak but nothing came out. She settled for what she hoped was a smile of welcome but feared it may look more like a grimace.

Her protector didn't appear happy at the intrusion and bared his teeth in a menacing snarl.

She fumbled for the dog's collar. "Down, Jack."

Man and woman stared at each other in silence as seconds ticked by.

She reminded herself to breathe.

He cleared his throat as he ambled over to the pot on the counter. "I didn't expect company." He glanced her way, then focused on pouring his coffee. "Guests usually aren't up this early."

His voice, deep and sensual, coupled with that just-out-of-bed look sent ripples of awareness through her.

Oh my God. Looks like sin and sounds like Sam Elliott. "Oh, yes, well, we arrived late last night."

He looked around the kitchen. "We?"

His mouth moved so she knew he must have spoken, but it took a moment for her brain to stop fixating on the mat of chest hair peeking out the top of his shirt. She blinked and gestured toward the dog. "Me. And Jack. My dog. We arrived last night."

"Don't think I've ever seen a dog like him. What is he?"

An irresistibly devastating grin accompanied the question, and her stomach lurched.

She gulped in air. "Vet said maybe a cross between Mastiff and Rottweiler but even he was stumped."

The man cleared his throat—again—and looked everywhere but at her.

Warning bells sounded.

Holy crap. He feels it, too.

"Unusual coloring," the man offered at last. "Like someone splattered black and brown paint all over him."

She patted Jack's head. "Yeah. He's so ugly he's cute."

Really? That's the best you can do?

Jack, apparently satisfied the visitor was not a danger to his mistress, lay back down with a heavy sigh.

Silence filled the room.

She set her cup on the counter. "Um, I'm Samantha Fowler. Are you a guest here, too?"

When his laser-sharp gaze fixed on her mouth, a swarm of butterflies invaded her stomach.

A muscle flexed in his jaw. "Cooper—Coop—Delaney. Guess you can say I'm a permanent guest."

Awareness bounced off the walls like a rubber ball, charging the room with explosive energy.

She let out an audible lungful of air and moved away from the counter. "Well, I think it's light enough to explore."

Jack snorted.

The edges of Coop's lips turned up. "He doesn't seem interested."

"Yeah, but he needs the exercise."

"Got a route in mind?"

Every word he spoke rolled over her in a tidal wave of heat. A quick shake of her head sent her ponytail sliding to the side. "Just riding around, checking out the area. Got in too late last night to see much of anything."

"Well," he pushed away from the counter, "enjoy your

ride" He headed for the door, stopping to speak to the dog. "Nice to meet you, Jack."

A soft rumble and a couple of weak tail thumps indicated acceptance.

Cooper grinned and walked out.

Sam closed her eyes and took a deep breath. "No. No. No," she commanded, "Hormones fooled me once. I won't let it happen again."

She nudged Jack with her toe and headed out the back door, her unhappy companion lagging behind.

What the devil is wrong with me? Sam sped down the road, tires kicking up rocks and dust. She looked straight ahead, but her mind's eye recalled the chance meeting in sharp detail. Her body still hummed with the force of his effect on it. Lust at first sight? Is that a real thing?

"Oh my God, Jack. What must he be thinking?"

Her silent companion watched intently, head cocked to one side as though listening while she ranted.

"I ogled like a fricking school girl." She shook her head, cheeks burning as she relived the encounter. "But at least, thank you God, I stopped short of drooling, though I'm sure I would have if he hadn't left when he did."

Jack's head cocked the other way, as though silently urging her to continue.

"Okay, okay, I looked. I admit it. I couldn't help it." She licked her lips. "Oh my. That chest," she murmured. "So much hair." Her fingers arched as she imagined running them through the thick mass of dark curls. "And didn't he sound a little like Sam Elliott to you? Kinda gravelly and raspy, and when he smiled—" She slapped her palm against her temple. "What the blue blazes is wrong with me? Did Paul not teach me anything?" She shook her head, sending her lopsided ponytail lower. "But his eyes, they were so, so, intense. Such an unusual color, too. Not grey, not blue; more, I don't know, like the ashes of a cold campfire or the color of storm clouds rolling in. The minute I looked at them," she paused as a light shiver rolled over her. "I swear it jolted me down to my toes." She wagged a finger at her companion. "And I'm not some sex-starved divorcee who can't control herself, either, though I'm sure he thought so. I stared. Fine. Not a crime. God took a lot of extra pains with him, and it would be extremely rude of me not to notice." She focused on the road. "My *goodness* did I notice. If ever a man was built for seven kinds of sin…"

Sam gave little thought to conversing with Jack as though he understood. In fact, sincerely believed he did. She found him beside a dumpster near the hospital two years ago more dead than alive from two bullet wounds. After he healed, they were constant companions. Paul, her now ex-husband, complained constantly about him being in the house, going everywhere with her, but she ignored his rants. Their marriage was already rocky by then, and she needed the mutt as much as he needed her.

Which no doubt explained why Paul and Jack never liked each other. Or maybe Jack was a better judge of character than her.

She sped down the road, wheel gripped in her left hand, her right waving around as she poured out her thoughts. "What did he expect anyway waltzing in there half-dressed?" She inhaled deeply and rested both hands on the wheel. "I shouldn't be surprised, though. Males in general are self-centered jerks who should be lined up and shot at sunrise." She reached over and patted Jack's head. "Well, except you, of course."

A soft whine and a thump of his tail drew her gaze.

"Again? You just went."

Another whine.

"Okay, okay." She searched ahead for an appropriate exit. Seeing what appeared to be a lane off to the right, she slowed and signaled a turn. It was little more than a well-traveled dirt lane leading to a briskly moving stream surrounded by willows, pines and an assortment of East Texas foliage. The nearest bank held a collage of mementos from past visitors, classifying the area as a primo make-out spot. Her mind's eye marked the location of beer cans, towels and discarded condoms even as she pulled under a towering pine. She rummaged in the glove box for tissues and finding them, opened the door and stepped out.

"Come on you big whiney-butt."

Jack jumped out and headed for the pine tree.

Sam headed in the opposite direction and gave a sharp, "Stay," when he turned to follow. Rounding the lone holly bush, thumbs tugging on the waistband of her pants, she saw the body.

Whispers On the Wind is available now!

CPSIA information can be obtained
at www.ICGtesting.com
Printed in the USA
BVHW082031010719
552393BV00001B/26/P